After the Tsunami

After the Tsunami

A Novel

Annam Manthiram

STEPHEN F. AUSTIN STATE UNIVERSITY
2011

For information, address Stephen F. Austin State University Press, 1936 North Street, LAN 203, Nacogdoches, Texas, 75962.

sfapress.sfasu.edu

Book design: Laura McKinney

LIBRARY OF CONGRESS CATALOGING-IN-PUBLICATION DATA

Manthiram, Annam
After the Tsunami: Novel / Annam Manthiram. 1st ed.
p. cm.
ISBN-13: 978-1-936205-43-1

I. Title

First Edition: September 2011

Dedicated to my sisters, Nirmala and Vimala,
whose childhood inspired this story, and to my husband, Alex,
whose faith helped me to continue on,
even when it was difficult to do so.

Chapter One

My friends ask me why I do not eat fish. I tell them that it is difficult to consume something that once had eyes as big as mine. They laugh, and the joke moves the conversation forward and away.

Sometimes they push and want to know where I come from, why my nose is bent, if I have nightmares. When I think of my past, I imagine a bloody circle. The present is a labyrinth with stretches of promise and an underbelly of sickness. Reconciliation seems at times impossible.

The ones I lost emerge in dreams; my wife calls them terrors. Years cannot erase my memory of them. Their spirits continue to draw me to that place over and over and over again because therein lies salvation. *For whom?* I ask, but they do not say. Instead, they compel me to recall their lives, so as to give meaning to their existence. I need to remember; I need them to come back to me.

Chapter Two

BEFORE THE TSUNAMI struck, the sea had been my home. Every morning, my father and I would wait by the shore until the fishermen would return with their daily catch. We were fish cleaners; that was our trade by caste. My parents said it was a favorable position. As proof, we always had to arrive early to meet the fishermen because there were many like us, scrambling at the first light of dawn to wash scores of fish for only a few rupees a day.

My sister, Smita, was four then. She liked sticking her fingers into the fish's eyes, until my mother yelled at her. They were commodities. *We mustn't destroy them*, she said.

Even though I knew that the sea provided the means for us to live, I didn't like the work. The fish were constantly twitching, and my tiny hands could barely hold them in place. When one would slip out of my hand and onto the sand, my father would scream. I was responsible for sorting the fish by size and type. It took me many days to learn. Since, I have blocked out the smell of the anchovy, the feel of the catfish, the texture of a grey mullet.

Working on the hot sand was the only thing we did together as a family. After the fish were clean, my mother and Smita would carry them delicately in their skirts, holding them close to their bodies as though they were still alive. They would keep the fish warm until they were dropped into a large bucket to be transported to the public market. After they were deposited, we never saw them again. Sometimes, if we were lucky, the fishermen would take pity on us – especially on Smita who was still young enough to not understand why we had less than everyone else – and give us a small catfish without whiskers or a diseased eel that had accidentally been captured in a net. But that was rare, and there were so many of us, the fishermen couldn't play favorites.

On those fortunate days, in the small makeshift hut that we shared as a family, we would huddle around my mother while she brewed the stew and boiled the rice. Smita would pull on our mother's sari, begging for just a taste. My father would munch on the bones that she would pick out of the curry. When the food was ready, my mother waited until we finished first. She would only have the fragments of what was left – her narrow hips and thin face a testament to her sacrifice. I would try to slow down my chewing and swallowing, in order to savor every bite, but I couldn't. I was just a boy, but it didn't matter. Whether our bellies were full or our appetites satiated, we were happy. Those were the only moments we ever really were, and I wished that God would've given me more of those days before he took my family away from me.

WHEN I CAME to the orphanage, I was nine years old. I called it the "House" because though I had never lived in one, and they were not common near the ocean, the orphanage looked exactly like the image I'd had in my head of a real house. It had the tile roof, the concrete siding, the front and back yard. It even had a regular outhouse. On the outside, the House looked warm and inviting. On the inside, the Mothers who ran the House were cold and abusive. The floors were hard and the walls were empty. I thought of a prison.

Our lives were handled in much the same way. The House had a small cafeteria, which was where we took our meals. Our rations were based on what the government provided us. Though we saw the white delivery truck every one or two months, we never saw the actual food ourselves. The Mothers would keep us in the backyard while they smuggled the food inside. A few times, I caught glimpses of tan-colored sacks. The amounts seemed plentiful, but we received very little of it.

We were promised one hundred grams of meat (weighed on a scale), and one variety of vegetable or fruit. Usually we received two bananas. That was for our breakfast and lunch. For dinner, if we were lucky, we received rice and rasam, a tomato-soaked curry laden with mustard seeds and salt. There was never enough for all of us. Those who lagged behind or were smaller were left with less than what our rations were supposed to be. Most of the time, the other boys ended up taking our rations. If you were late, you were left with nothing.

Sometimes we received a can of fish – about two hundred grams. I could tell when the fish was rotten. When I tried to argue with the Mothers about the fish, they would slap my face.

"How do you know it is rotten?" one of the upper caste boys had asked me. This was before I had learned everyone's name.

"The fish is smooth, too smooth, and it smells."

"Smells like a woman's you know!" he said, and laughed. "Probably like your amma's, eh?" He smirked. The rest of them laughed too.

The Mothers failed arithmetic because they never had enough of each item to give to each boy. Therefore, those who arrived first were always guaranteed something to eat. These boys were usually bigger, which seemed ironic since they were the ones who needed it the least. I was a small boy, and as a result, often was pushed to the end of the line. When it was my turn to receive my rations, I never received a full share.

Those of us who finished last were responsible for cleaning up after everyone else. Naturally, these chores always seemed to fall to the lower caste boys like me. The Mothers thought we were lazy, and therefore should be forced to do extra chores.

Shortly after I arrived at the House, the Mothers had already made their judgments about me. Even though I had been one of the first to finish my bowl of rice that day, they made me sweep the cafeteria. One of them forced the wood handle into my miniature hands. I remembered that my fingers could barely wrap around the pole, but I held on tightly, the way I remembered Smita holding onto our mother before the sea had taken her life.

That day, in a small corner, I had found a white substance gathering near the wall. Unsure of what it was, I stuck my tongue into it, hoping it was goat's milk. It tasted very sweet, and I kept licking until the entire floor was clean. Mother Jamuna, the matron who ran the House, saw me and hit the back of my head with her hand. Then she laughed.

"There is no future for people like you," she said. I hadn't understood what she meant, and later, when Headmistress Chitra Veli told me that it was ice cream, spilled over from Mother Jamuna's careless hands, I didn't care that she had laughed at me. I had never tasted ice cream before, and a little ridicule had been worth the reward.

Chapter Three

THOUGH SHE WAS not my real mother, I called her Amma. She had come to India and found me, in the way that I had imagined my own mother would. I don't know why she chose me; by the time I left, there were hundreds. When I have asked her, *why? Why an older boy with an ugly face?*

"I saw strength in you," she said.

Chapter Four

FROM THE MOMENT any of us walked into the doors of the House, we were oppressed by the Mothers. They called it tough love, but we called it something profane. By confining us throughout the day – whether we were asleep or bathing – they were successful in taking away our sense of freedom and individuality. We ate what the others ate, slept when the others did, and played games when they told us to. We were their children now, but bad children. We needed to be punished and loved in the hardest way possible.

But they prided themselves on having reasonably educated children. They wanted us all to learn how to read – or at least try. I knew they were afraid we would invent things on our own. Better to read what already existed than to form new ideas, which could lead to arguments, revolts. The opposite was true here than in most places – by educating us, they *controlled* us. They gave the power of knowledge and could take it away as well. We owed them for our enlightenment.

I learned how to read from Headmistress Chitra Veli. Though we all received instruction, I was honored with private lessons because I was exceptionally gifted – more so than the others (which was what she said, although I didn't really believe it). My father had a very mediocre grasp of language, and my mother didn't know how to read, but I wasn't entirely sure. As every day passed in the House, my memories of them were fading.

"Where is there a bright wall?" I asked her. Chitra Veli meant "Bright Wall." If her name meant such, then that should exist, yes? That was how a young boy's mind worked. Or perhaps any young mind – whether a boy's or a girl's.

"In my village, where I am from. It was painted a very deep shade of green. When my mother was younger, she used to climb over the fence and into the neighbor's yard. He had a son who was her age. They thought they were in love, and she got pregnant. The neighbor moved away with the son right before I was born."

"Your father?" I asked.

"Gone, just like yours." I looked up from my book and into her eyes. They were so dark they were almost black.

"And your mother?"

"Still peering over the wall, waiting for him." She stared at me for a while, as if to say something more, but stopped. "You ask too many questions, Siddhartha," she said.

Since I learned how to read better and more quickly than the others, the boys were after me with comic books, newspapers, and even pornography. I didn't ask how they acquired such lewd materials; part of me knew it was the Mothers', but I didn't want to think of them in that way. They were the ones who were taking care of us. As far as I was concerned, they were asexual.

After most of the boys learned how to read fairly well on their own, they stopped pestering me. However, Jagadesh was an exception. His mind struggled with the words, and instead of trying to learn, he would come to me, demanding and expecting that I read to him whenever he needed. I did what he asked because though he was small, he was fierce. We called him "Jaga-Nai," which literally translated into "Jaga-Dog" because he had teeth as sharp as fangs and was about as predictable as a rabid dog. Though most of the boys in the House despised the various nicknames that were given to them, Jaga-Nai welcomed his.

"Sid, what's this say? Eh? Come!" He threw a piece of paper at me, and I saw that it was a letter in Tamil. I still wasn't as good at reading as everyone thought, so I skipped over the parts I couldn't read, afraid that he'd beat me or tie my arms to a tree when the Mothers weren't looking.

The letter was from his mother. She wrote that they were waiting for a woman with a large dowry before they could send for him. She asked that he stop writing to her, asking for money. The rest of the letter scolded him, his mother's angry tone clear in the words she had chosen.

You are lazy. Your father blames me. Stop sending letters. Please, be a good boy. Stop sending letters. Be happy where you are.

"Stop," he said. He grabbed the letter from me and ripped it up. He sprinkled the torn pieces of paper on top of my head.

I was too stunned to respond.

"You don't even deserve to read. If I really wanted to read, I would learn. But I don't care. You know why?"

At this point, I really didn't because he had hurt my feelings. Like the rest of us, we felt alone. We had been abandoned by our families, left to fend for ourselves, and the last thing that we wanted was to fight one another when that's all and who we had. Because Jaga-Nai was the most difficult one to befriend, we all tried extra hard for him to like us, and as a result, cared even more when he hurt us.

"My father will someday pick me up in an auto – you'll see – and you will be stuck here cleaning up everybody's feces,"

Then I felt sad.

Even though I was just a boy, I knew when someone wasn't wanted. Jaga-Nai's parents were never going to come back for him. In their mind, he was already donated property. They probably only wrote him letters to assuage themselves of the guilt parents felt when they didn't know how to love their own children – something that was genetically programmed in all of us. I would've happily cleaned up piles of shit for days if it would have made this truth a lie.

And then he kicked me. And I stopped being sad because as children, we didn't know how to sustain our feelings for anybody or anything.

THE NEXT MORNING, we were awakened by the smell of peanuts roasting. When we didn't have enough money to buy meat, my mother would buy nuts instead. She used peanuts regularly as a substitute for meat, and would make a variety of curries and side dishes with them. Sometimes she'd fry them with red chilis and fennel seeds. That was my favorite. With just the right amount of salt, I could eat a whole bowlful and be satisfied for an entire day.

All of us boys scrambled off of the concrete floor and quickly headed to the cafeteria, hoping for a small bag of peanuts and maybe a side dish of onions and cilantro. Once we got there, the Mothers were just finishing their breakfast. Sometimes they all ate together, huddled over steaming cups of coffee and stacks of flat bread. They looked like a pack of cows grazing, their large behinds thrusting out of the tiny wooden chairs they had assembled.

"You're early. Wait," Mother Jamuna said. She held her hand up to her mouth and tilted back. I saw her throw a handful of peanuts into her mouth. She chewed while staring at us. Not wanting to be punished for intruding on their meal, we formed a line outside of the cafeteria, some of us still drowsy that we risked physical injury and leaned against the boy in front of us. I was pushed to the back, again, and waited for my friend, Goli. I knew he'd be pushed back as well, and sure enough, I saw him shoved aside by Ganesh, one of the larger upper caste boys. He was big like his namesake the elephant god, and only our friend when it benefited him. During meals, we were never his buddies, even though he cared for Goli's story-telling. Goli was the creative one of the bunch and was always crafting imaginative stories that had all of us yearning for more. When I mentioned to Goli about my previous run-in with Jaga-Nai, Goli looked around and noticed that he was absent.

"Maybe his father really does come for him in a magic auto that none of us see at night because they sprinkle us with sleep dust," Goli said. We also had a nickname for him, which I had invented. He reminded me of a story my father used to tell about a wooden puppet named Pinocchio. He said that Pinocchio had a large nose and made jerky movements whenever he walked. After observing Goli for some time, I noticed similarities between the character my father described and him. Goli walked as if he were controlled by strings. His head would dart from side to side, and his arms and legs never made fluid motions. So I called him "Golicchio," and the name stuck.

While we waited, Golicchio provided the entertainment. We all sat down, careful to maintain our positions in line, but eager to listen to what Golicchio had to tell us.

"Who are you talking about?" Ganesh asked from the front of the line. He had a large voice, like that of a lion, so we could hear him perfectly.

"Jaga-Nai," I said. I told him about Jaga-Nai's letter, and his insistence that his parents were going to come for him. Knowing something about Jaga-Nai sometimes earned extra favors with the others – whether it was just protection from the bigger boys or just having the feeling of being included.

Ganesh motioned for me to join him in the front of the line. He wanted to know more about what I had learned, and I gave him little bits, hoping the Mothers would send us into the cafeteria before Ganesh changed his mind about letting me share his space. As I began to tell him about Jaga-Nai's reaction to the letter, I saw Ganesh look to the left of my face. I turned, and I saw the Mothers leaving the cafeteria, peanut skins draping their bodies like skin on a snake.

"Go eat," they said. We rushed into the cafeteria and Mother Kalpana, who looked like Mother Jamuna's twin, stood at the front, serving us our portions. We each received two bananas and a small bowl of mango pickle.

"Where are the peanuts?" someone cried.

"You don't get peanuts," Mother Kalpana said.

"Where are the chairs?" Ganesh asked. Because he was so big, sometimes he had a hard time getting comfortable on the floor. I believed it also had to do with the fact that he was upper caste and not used to sitting on concrete.

"You don't get chairs," Mother Kalpana said.

After the last of us was served, we sat on the ground, our legs crossed underneath us. I looked around the room at everyone's leaf. Some of the boys had three bananas. Golicchio had only received one banana and half a bowl of mango pickle. He sat with me, and I gave him half of mine.

We ate until Jaga-Nai disrupted our silence.

Chapter Five

AMMA PASSED AWAY several years ago. I am thankful that she died in a manner that I could accept – not quickly, like I was so used to.

I didn't speak for a year after she brought me to the States. The psychiatrist said I suffered from Post Traumatic Stress Syndrome, but that didn't mean anything to me. My English comprehension was basic, and Amma knew only conversational Tamil.

The first time I spoke to her was the day I found her despondent, crying over a letter. We didn't have the vocabulary then to express how we felt. She used several words that I didn't understand; I gathered the letter had been written by her husband, who had died a year before she had adopted me. I offered her my consolation out of habit – a reflex – but I don't believe my words penetrated her sadness.

Our attempt at a meaningful exchange stirred me. Until then, I had not permitted her to kiss or even touch me. Her hands were like acid, and my heart was cold. But at that moment, I don't know why, something in me let go a little. I felt the ice melting – during those twelve months of silence, she had been getting in, a little at a time. Her burning hands had made their way into my chest.

As she sat, her head bent over the letter, I gathered her hair into a bunch and began to run my fingers through it. I then divided her hair into three tiny pieces and braided from top to bottom. When I finished, I unfurled them and then started again. I must have braided her hair over a hundred times that day but she never told me to stop.

After my fingers grew tired, I moved next to her, and we sat side by side. I looked into her eyes for the first time then, and she smiled at me. They were a beautiful blue – the color of the Indian Ocean.

Chapter Six

WE HAD OUR daily rituals, which the Mothers strictly enforced, but we also had a lot of free time to make friends and enemies.

After breakfast, the Mothers made us wash our bodies. The backyard of the House had a large bathtub made out of stone. From there, we scooped out cold buckets of water and poured ourselves clean. Each boy was assigned a bucket, which had his name on it. Mine had been previously used by "Rajesh," which Mother Jamuna had crossed out and written my name over instead. In big black letters, the bucket said, "Siddharth," which was an incorrect spelling of my name. After I learned how to read, I tried to borrow their black marker and add the letter "a" to the end, but they wouldn't let me. So I was stuck with it, and would've actually preferred Rajesh instead.

During shower time, the Mothers left us alone. I liked this time of the day the best because we were outside, unfettered. We stripped down to our shorts, placing our clean clothes near the edge of the tub. Our clothes were also marked with a black pen, but sometimes the others would steal them. We were given only a few sets of shirts and shorts, and if we soiled them or put a hole in something, we were to fix it ourselves. We only received one new shirt and pant set a year. Therefore, I tried to be as careful as I could with my own clothes, washing them as often as I could and keeping them close. But Jaga-Nai was almost the same size as me, and he would take my shirts. He rarely washed his own clothes, and sometimes if he was feeling bullish, he would make me wash his too. I was left with only one pair of shorts and a shirt. I had to wash them daily.

The fact was, though sometimes it didn't seem like it, life in the House wasn't always so bad, and certainly wasn't always about caste. Most of us forgot who we were. It was as if the sea, for those of us who had come from the sea, had recreated our existence, and we were free to become whoever we wanted to be. The only time our social class was most evident was when the mothers reinforced our backgrounds – almost colonial-like, and their efforts to pit us against each other worked to serve as some sort of self-inflicted discipline, which they did not have to endure. Despite all of that and the fact that our families had left us (we never said they died – they really just left us), we tried to keep the hope of them returning alive by talking about what we would do if they were to return. How would we react? Would we respond like children and start crying and rush into our mothers' arms and never leave? Or would we respond like adults and casually blink our eyes as if they weren't the same people we'd dreamt about seeing again over and over every night?

Most of the time, I listened. It was too painful for me to talk about. I kept that inside.

Golicchio always had the most colorful answers, and they always changed. We relied on him to help us tap into our imaginations and go to the world in which he lived every day.

"My answer depends on whether my father or my mother comes."

"Tell us," Ganesh said. He squatted, and his trunk-like legs stretched out in front of him, leaving none of us room to sit in the shade like we wanted. The House had a huge outdoor area for us to play in, with trees along the border, but unfortunately there was only one tree right in the middle. During the days (such as this one) when the sun was extremely hot and forced its light on us whether we wanted it or not, the heat made us dizzy and tired. I sat crouched behind Ganesh, his big form blocking some of the sun. When he felt the need to pass gas, I also had to take that in as well.

The yard was mostly sand, with a few patches of grass where the tree grew. The side of the House contained a small slab of concrete, which was where the boys typically did their homework or read. Next to the slab was a small wooden "greenhouse" with overgrown plants – a place none of us were allowed to enter. If the Mothers were angry with us, we would get one beating on our legs from a broken tree limb or a stalk from a greenhouse plant for every pinch of sand that they found between our toes, on our legs, in our hair, or on our hands. We never knew when this policy would be enforced, so we tried to be as careful as we could. Ganesh didn't care so much; his skin was so thick he barely felt the beatings. Golicchio and I also felt that his punishments were less severe than ours, but perhaps that was the self-enforced discipline talking again. From behind, I saw that some of the sand had already gathered in Ganesh's dark brown hair. As he scratched himself, the particles flew down his shoulder into my face. I coughed, but no one wanted to hear me.

"Well," Golicchio continued, "if my father came, he most certainly would come in a rainbow. He knew how to build things. He built boats and nets and contraptions to hold fish. He certainly would know how to control a rainbow."

"Rainbows aren't real!" Puni squealed. His real name was Prakash, but he was round and often squealed like a pig, hence the nickname.

"Yes, they are," he said. He used his arms to draw an imaginary rainbow in the air. The way his arms jerked, the rainbow seemed square and more angular in shape. "Rainbows are real for people who believe. And I do, so that is how my father will come. When it is hot, he will travel down the red part for the sun makes his face very red like masala powder!"

"And when it's cold?" I asked.

"When it is cold, he will travel down the yellow part because it is the color that looks most like the sun, and he will get warmth from it."

"Ahh," we all said in unison.

"My father will slide down the rainbow, and he will pick me up at the end. And regardless of what kind of day it is, I will ride back with him on the blue part because that is my favorite color." Golicchio's eyes were a light bluish color, unusual in Tamils, but we didn't know much beyond our region, so most of us just accepted it as part of who he was. Although Jaga-Nai was always one to fiercely attack it. He never left anything different alone.

"And when he comes, what will you say? Or DO?" Ganesh yelled.

"This is what I will do," he said. He picked up a chunk of dirt and threw it on Peepa, whose real name was Nirmal. Peepa meant "barrel" in Tamil. We often joked that even a barrel couldn't hold as much water as Nirmal, who never could quench his thirst.

"Golicchio, you should be eating this dirt!" Peepa shouted, but it was said in fun. Peepa threw sand back at Golicchio. Then of course we couldn't just sit and watch, so I threw sand on Ganesh's hair, and he stuffed some down my shirt. We pelted sand at each other mercilessly and tirelessly. We laughed and laughed and laughed. Together, we could have so much fun. If only we could always do it together.

THE MOTHERS FREQUENTLY took day trips without us. When Ganesh or another would question where they were going, they would lie and say that their visits were to the local government office, to ensure that we continued to receive our rations. They said that if they didn't go once a week, the government would forget about us, and we'd all starve to death. We knew they were going shopping though because they always came back with pink bags filled with clothing. Sometimes Mother Jamuna had small brown sacks with her, the edges coated in grease and oil. We could smell the hot vadai and the coconut chutney, but she never offered us any.

I was not sure if I believed all of what they said to us, but one cannot slap away the hand that feeds him. The Mothers liked to reserve special forms of punishment for those who tried to oppose or question them. Fat though they were, they were unusually strong. And when we were really bad, they used their strength to force us into the "hole," also called the Poor Man's Closet. Golicchio had given it its name – clever for those who had ever visited. It was a tiny closet, dark, no windows, and filled with things Golicchio couldn't even imagine. It was at the back of the House behind one of the Mother's rooms. I had been sent there once for arguing about a book during a lesson with one of the Mothers. I was only inside for ten minutes, but time stopped moving there. Golicchio reasoned that when we entered the Closet, we were in a different dimension, where time didn't exist and we weren't ourselves anymore. He said the room had a lot of power, but unfortunately was being used for evil. He also believed that dark spirits could travel through from their world to ours, and the Closet was a perfect place for them to do it in. Even though I wasn't entirely sure I believed him, his ideas made me fear the Closet even more.

We were lucky to have not been sent to the Closet for playing in the dirt the night before. However, the Mothers, on their way out the door for their "visit" to the local government office, threw wet towels on us in the morning. The cold cloth made us hungry, but they told us that we wouldn't eat until they returned as punishment for our childish behavior. I hoped I would run into Headmistress Veli, the only one of them who was nice to me. She snuck little biscuits into my mouth sometimes as though I were a dog, but I didn't mind. They were sweet, and I was hungry.

After they left, the boys clumped in groups. I typically associated with Golicchio, Ganesh, and Puni. Peepa hung out with us too, but he didn't like me. He tolerated me because the others did. He and Ganesh would've made my life a living hell back on the sea. But in here, they were sort of my friends. I was amazed at how ironic my life had become.

Ganesh yelled, "They're gone," and he grabbed me by the arms. We rushed outside as if we were convicts freed from jail.

When the Mothers left, we were alone and could do whatever we wanted. Some of the time, we were good boys and stayed in the yard. We'd curse and shout and yell and do all of the things that we were not allowed to do. But sometimes we were bad and we'd go through the Mothers' personal items because they lived in the House too.

"No, to Mother Jamuna's," Peepa said, challenging Ganesh. They both nodded in agreement, and the rest of us followed them to her room. She usually locked the door, but we all knew how to pick the lock and get in. That she thought we were so stupid bothered us, but we didn't question our good luck.

I saw Peepa hunched over the cabinet, looking at something. Then I saw Ganesh relaxing, his big body on her bed.

"Aren't you afraid she'll smell you on her bed?" I asked. Ganesh made big impressions wherever he lay. I was sure that once he got up, the bed would be permanently marked with his outline.

"I can sleep wherever I want," he said. He was probably right.

"Yrimal!" someone else called. That was my nickname, which meant "cough" in Tamil. Golicchio had thought of it. I didn't like it because it made me sound weak, but I accepted it just like the others had accepted theirs.

"If she asks, we'll tell her that someone broke into the House and demanded to see the bed otherwise he'd have our arms for lunch. She cannot be mad." I just shook my head at Golicchio. He didn't just make up such outlandish stories. He actually believed them.

"Who would want such sticks as these?" Puni whined and stuck out his arms. They weren't as thin as some of the rest of ours were.

"Look at this." Peepa turned around and was holding a woman's panty. It was big enough to fit Ganesh's whole upper torso.

"Does it smell?" Ganesh asked. Peepa started to sniff it, and I turned around.

"Stop pretending to be the good kid. You know you want to smell this too," Peepa said and held it out to me. I did. I wanted to know what an evil person like Mother Jamuna smelled like. I imagined she'd smell the way rotten eggs would if left in bed for an entire night. I took a whiff, and it brought back an old memory of my sister.

I was very little, maybe four or so. I was playing with Smita, who at the time still liked me. My mother had just finished bathing her. She was naked, and her hair was wet. She was using the ends to slap me in the face. I grabbed it and chewed hard, and her hair tasted the way I imagined jasmine would after a heavy rain.

I began to gasp and couldn't breathe.

"What is wrong? It doesn't smell that good," Peepa said, and Puni squealed.

"What will we do? None of the Mothers are around!" Puni screamed.

Ganesh started opening and closing all of Mother Jamuna's drawers. "She must have something in here. She must considering she hardly ever gets sick."

"She never gets sick because she eats forty-three times a day," Golicchio said, and he was also searching through the drawers. Puni held my head up. I started to see black. I wasn't sure what was happening until I felt something metallic inside my mouth.

"Breathe hard!" Ganesh boomed. I breathed, and I tasted something salty go through my throat. I nearly gagged.

"Breathe again!" Ganesh ordered. I did as I was told, and in a few seconds, I was breathing normally again. In fact, I was breathing better than normally. I actually felt as though my lungs were at full capacity.

"What is that?" I was able to ask without coughing.

Ganesh held out a device that looked like a pipe. "I've seen Mother Jamuna use it when she's coughing."

I started to put it back, but Ganesh stopped me. "Keep it," he said. The others nodded in agreement.

"What if she finds out I've taken it?"

"She won't, and no one will tell her."

"Right," everyone said, and we shook hands as we'd seen the Mothers do with some of the parents who came to query on how to abandon their children.

I felt loved.

Chapter Seven

I AM THANKFUL that we live in a place filled with smog; though I want to count the stars, I am unable.

Chapter Eight

One month, the Mothers left early in the morning, but they did not return at the usual time.

"The government must be giving them extra subsidies this time. They are probably trying to figure out how to smuggle it past us," Golicchio said. I silently agreed. Golicchio was smart. I didn't put it past the Mothers to cheat us.

"This gives us more time to explore," Ganesh said. "We found Yrimal's pipe once. I wonder what else we can find." He pushed open the door to Headmistress Veli's room.

"No, not in there," I whispered. She had never given me any reason to dislike her. In fact, when it didn't hurt too much, I thought of her as my own mother. She wasn't as beautiful, nor was she as slender, but she smelled the same. She also had the same look in her eyes — one that I never really understood — as though she were trying to focus her eyes on an object that she didn't understand, so as a result, squinted. In the end, my mother had suffered from headaches, as did Headmistress Veli.

"She's perhaps the fattest of them all. Maybe she has some food hidden," Puni said. I could see his behind round the corner into her room, and I had the mental image of a very large pig poking its head inside a box that had once contained rice pudding.

"Are you coming?" Golicchio asked. He looked at me, and I knew he wouldn't continue unless I also did.

"I suppose," I said. I looked behind me and saw Peepa waiting for us to go ahead.

"Go on," he encouraged in an impatient way.

When I entered her room, I always noticed the colors. Headmistress Veli had a purple pillow, a bright green sari hanging on the wall, a yellow tablecloth over her desk, and a sea blue stuffed teddy bear. I shivered. It looked unnatural and unappealing.

"Where did she get this?" Peepa said. He picked up the bear and began punching it in the stomach. Everyone laughed except me. I couldn't believe he was touching it.

"There's something inside, boys," he said. He pulled out a bottle that was tucked inside the bear's stomach. Instantly it deflated, and it looked slightly more normal.

"Is that a bottle of love potion?" Golicchio asked. We looked at him funny, but we were all made to feel nervous by his comment. Even though all of us boys could agree that Headmistress Veli was ugly, there was a certain attraction to her that we couldn't deny. In fact, she had aroused me on more than one occasion. I was made to feel guilty by these feelings, but I couldn't deny them always. By the rouge that developed on the faces of the lighter-skinned boys when she was around, I could almost say with certainty that they felt it too.

"No, you dimwit. It's a bottle of alcohol," Ganesh said. He took the lid off and poured some down his throat. He gagged a little, but for the most part, he swallowed it "like a man."

"Give me," Peepa said. He also took a large drink.

"And me too," Puni said. If fun involved food and drink, he was sure to be involved.

"No, you can't have any," Ganesh said.

"Why not?"

"Low castes don't drink alcohol."

"Why?"

"Because your bodies are impure. Alcohol would burn them," Ganesh said.

"And it's expensive," Peepa added.

"That does not make any sense," Golicchio said. "Alcohol is burning your bodies too."

Ganesh thought about his statement for a second and realized he was being silly. "Here, but be careful," he said.

Puni had a sip, but he spit it out.

"You bitch, you wasted it," Peepa said. His eyes were blazing red and his forehead sweaty.

"Calm down, there's no reason to argue," Ganesh said. "There's plenty more." Ganesh revealed several more bottles stuffed inside various other nefarious-looking creatures.

"I'm leaving," Golicchio said. "Alcohol is absolutely the worst thing you can put in your body." As he left, he looked at me, expecting me to follow. I was curious. I saw a bottle filled with blue liquid – I had never drunk anything blue before and wanted to see what it tasted like.

"Sorry," I said. He left without as much as a breath. I picked up the bottle and had a little taste. Although bitter, the sweetness masked most of the flavor. I kept drinking.

After about two minutes, I could feel my head become heavy and knees go weak.

"Peepa, did I ever tell you that you look like a movie star?" I said. Everyone laughed, except Puni who shrieked.

"I almost was in the movies, did you know?"

"Right," Ganesh said, but I could tell that he was interested in this story.

"I'm telling the truth. Vasan came to my house and asked me if I would be in his movie. But see, the thing is, I decided not to because he didn't give me the role I wanted. He wanted me to play the villain, but I was made to play the hero. So I sent him away."

"You sent away the great S.S. Vasan? I don't believe it," I said.

"Believe it, piece of shit. He would have never asked someone like you to be in the movies." Everyone else laughed again, but I didn't find it as funny.

"Why?"

"Because you're low-caste," he whispered.

"Come now," Ganesh said. I was surprised that he said anything at all.

"Then why are you my friend?"

"I'm not your friend. And once we escape this place, we will all go back to our original roles, and you will wash my shoes for me, while I have sex with your mother."

He wasn't far off in his assessment. There had been a time when I had seen my mother disrespected in public by a man. We were returning from the market, this time as a buyer. My mother was carrying a large sack of masoor dhal for sambar that evening. My sister was on her back. I was holding her hand. As we approached the bus stop, there was a middle-aged man standing in front of the bench, smoking a beedi.

"How much?" he asked. He stared directly at my mother's breasts. She knew better than to get into brawls like my father sometimes did. She did not say anything.

"I'm talking to you, dog shit," he said. He bent down and looked me in the eyes. I started to cry. I didn't know why he was so angry, and his breath smelled foul. He also had his hand extended as if he wanted to grab my crotch.

"Leave him," she said. Everyone around us turned and looked the other way. They were not prepared to fight on behalf of a poor woman – a poor, beautiful woman.

"Why, what will you do?" He peered at my sister, just a baby then. He licked his finger and then rubbed it onto my sister's lips. "A virgin," he whispered.

"Get away!" she screamed. She pushed him with the arm she had free. He pushed back, and she fell onto the ground, my sister wailing, and I standing helplessly on the side.

"Someone help this poor woman," I thought I heard someone say, but nobody really said that. That was what I wished I had said. Instead, the man started to feel up my mother's skirt, rubbing her hairy legs up and down. Luckily, the bus came, and the driver chased the man away. As we got onto the bus, however, and as my mom cried, instead of providing us with some consolation, he'd said, "Next time don't travel alone. It's just not responsible for people like you." How that had burned, even at that young age.

"Don't look so serious. I was joking," Peepa said. I knew he was not. Perhaps he had been scared by my face, which I was sure expressed the way I felt about the man who had accosted my mother. Although she had never discussed that day with us or my father, I wondered how many other times something had happened to her – times when we hadn't been there.

"We're all better than that now," Puni said. We weren't. We just pretended that those things didn't exist. Peepa was right though. As soon as we left, it would return to smother us like a sweaty blanket during the monsoon season.

"The Mothers must have a drinking problem," Ganesh said, trying to change the subject. He revealed a row full of bottles inside a cabinet near Headmistress Veli's desk.

"Let's get out of here," Peepa said, clearly made uncomfortable by my scowl. I couldn't figure it out – I thought alcohol made you happier?

Chapter Nine

ALCOHOL MADE ME happy for a time. Amma bought what I wanted because she needed it too. She and I drank together, and when our brains buzzed with an uncluttered hum from the rush of alcohol flowing through our blood, she'd tell me about her husband. He was Indian like me, and an engineer. He had led a privileged life until his parents disowned him for marrying a white woman. She told me that his parents had come to the funeral, and that that was the first time she'd met them. That was also the last time she ever saw them. He had died of an enlarged heart, and she blamed herself. *He loved me too much, and his heart couldn't take it anymore,* she always said. But what she didn't say was that out of his death came a mother.

Chapter Ten

WHEN WE BOYS played Kabaddi, we had no caste.

Because Ganesh was the largest of us all, he was always picked first for teams, depending on who was captain. Captains were chosen by Jaga-Nai. Ever since I had come to the House, it had always been that way. We learned not to challenge his decisions. He took the games very seriously and hated to lose.

On this particular day, the wind was calm. The rain had come the day before, so the sand was moist, and I could taste the dryness in the air. The weather was perfect for a competitive game.

The Mothers had a coil wire stretched out across two large trees that supplied the borders of the backyard. Golicchio mused that it was probably a torture device, by then outdated, that they had used to torment children.

"They would hang our little necks from the coil while our feet dangled, helpless, the birds watching from the trees," he said. I wondered how his mind was able to form the words with such descriptive deliberation.

"With my weight, the coils would tear right down," Ganesh said.

"You wouldn't have had to worry about such things. You are privileged," Puni squealed, and Ganesh kicked the back of his leg. All of us pretended not to notice. We turned the other way, and for us, that meant it never happened.

The birds on this day were lined up on the coil wire, perched in a haphazard fashion, swaying with the light wind. Their beaks were pointed toward us, and their dark, round eyes were calculating. Their feathers were shiny, yet disheveled. They were crows, but they were silent today. They seemed to anticipate our game.

"Who are the captains, Jaga-Nai?" Ganesh asked. His large hands were stretched alongside his body, pointing at imaginary body parts and pretending to touch them.

"Me," he said. He always picked himself as one of the captains. Golicchio and I once talked about the day he would not pick himself.

"That will be the day he is dead, and cannot choose a captain at all," he'd said.

"Don't you believe in ghosts?" I had asked. I believed in Krishna too, and I knew that Jaga-Nai would be reborn into a real dog this time, perhaps as one of Krishna's bodyguards. These spectral dogs were not good or evil, but imposed justice on those who dared come close to the great blue body. The role of captain would not be lost on him after death.

"Yes, but I don't believe in death or Krishna or any of that. If I do, then I will be reborn in the womb of a jackal. That is what my mother always told us. She said that there was no point in doing good because we were doomed from the beginning." I hadn't answered him because I hadn't known what to say.

"The other captain?" Ganesh asked.

Jaga-Nai stood there. He looked at his wrist – at an imaginary watch. The birds continued to observe, their beaks resting against each others' wings, not harming them in any way. He walked around the yard, "examining" all of us, drawing his mouth and eyes very close to the boys and inspecting. He shook his head after a few examinations and then he came to me.

"Open your mouth," he asked. I didn't think twice about disobeying, so I did as he told me.

"You," he said. My mouth was open, and my head completely back, so I couldn't see what was happening. "You, eh?" he said again.

"You can't pick him, he barely knows how to play," Ganesh said with such contempt that I was forced to close my mouth and look down. A bird crowed.

"I didn't tell you to do that," Jaga-Nai said, but he wasn't looking at me. He was looking at the wide open field – the area we had established for the game. I could already see he was calculating his strategies.

I disliked the game of Kabaddi because I felt it was a game of manhood, a game that I was not ready to play. I never won. I was always tagged early, and I knew that it determined whether or not I would succeed in the House, and whether I would live to see what was beyond the confines of this orphanage.

Kabaddi involved two tests: one of stamina and one of courage. I imagined that these two skills heavily defined a man in the working world, and the other boys placed great emphasis on them in our games. In a way, we were fighting for the same job, and our qualifications were how long we could hold our breaths and the boldness of our advances. Caste didn't seem to matter. We were all equal on the court and every teammate valuable.

In an official game of Kabaddi, each team consisted of twenty-four players. At the House, only eighteen boys wanted to play, so we split each team into nine players. Only seven players per team were allowed on the field at any given time. The rest of the players were on "reserve" for when one of their teammates was tagged.

The object of the game was to score as many points as possible. One point each was scored for every opponent tagged and sent out of the game. None of us had watches – we didn't want to keep time because for us, time was the enemy. It moved fast when we didn't want it to and moved slowly when we received a beating. Jaga-Nai had decided one day that we would play until a team had no players left or the Mothers called us inside. Being tired was not a factor. Usually the games ended because of the Mothers, although one time Puni was stung by a bee, and his behind had swollen so large that he had to go inside. The Mothers did nothing to ease his pain, and we teased him after that, pointing out how much more he looked like a pig.

The game began when the starting player, known as a "raider," proceeded to the opponent's area. A line was drawn between two halves with chalk. Sometimes Jaga-Nai would smudge the lines with his feet, but unfortunately there was nothing we could do about that. He was also the official.

If a raider was able to cross the line and into the "anti-raiders" court, he could tag an opponent and send him out by touching him and running back to his own court. The raider's team would then score one point. In order for a point to be legitimate, a raider had to chant "Kabaddi" over and over again while he made the raid. He had to make the capture without taking a breath while he chanted. The moment a player was tagged, another was sent to replace him.

To make the boys even angrier at me, Jaga-Nai let me choose my first player. Of course, none of them wanted to be on my team. Friendship didn't matter when winning was at stake. Everyone wanted to be on the winner's side, even if it meant the evil one's.

I chose Ganesh, who refused to be on my team until Jaga-Nai made him.

"Do as your captain tells you, eh," he said.

Jaga-Nai picked Peepa and a few others. The teams were set, and I was terrified.

"You go first," Jaga-Nai said, which struck us all as unusual. Normally he went first.

"Go on," he said again. As captain, I was to decide the order of raiders on my team. Who would I send out first? Normally, captains sent out their worst players first, saving the better ones for last when the team became sparse. I by far was the worst player on my team, so I chose myself.

"You can't go first. If the captain is tagged out, who will lead?" If a raider did not make it back to his court before taking a breath, he was considered out. No one was safe in this game.

"But who said he will lose in the first round? Maybe he will tag you, Jaga-Nai!" Ganesh laughed, and the ground felt as if it were rumbling.

"What did you say?" Jaga-Nai's dog-like fangs emerged from his bright red lips. His face looked like a disoriented monkey's that had gotten into a woman's rouge kit.

"It fell on your ears," Ganesh said, a Tamil expression that indirectly meant, "You heard me." He pushed his chest out as if the sun were a magnet and his chest were made of metal.

"If Yrimal tags me out, then I will carry his feces for three days, eh?" Our roles were reversing – roles given to me by people I hadn't even respected.

He looked at me and spat on the ground. The saliva was red, and I wondered if he'd gotten into Mother Kalpana's tobacco, which she swore made her teeth whiter. Her claim confused us – her teeth were about as white as an over ripened plantain.

"Is this a bet? Will you follow through?" Golicchio asked. Jaga-Nai didn't answer. He didn't always talk directly to us.

"Will you follow through?" Ganesh asked this time.

"Yes," he said. He spat again and looked at me. "Let's start." The birds began to crow this time, and he yelled, "Shut up!" But they continued. Jaga-Nai threw pockets of sand into the air, but the coil was too far up in the sky, and they weren't scared of us.

"Leave them be," someone said, and Jaga-Nai stopped.

I stood in my court, in the middle of my six other players. Ganesh was to my left, Golicchio was to my right. The other team linked arms. If they broke their chain, one player was automatically sent out. I stared at Jaga-Nai, and I could tell he was repulsed by the other boys' touches. I had never seen a low class person touch a high class person so intimately before I began playing Kabaddi in the House. They felt no different to me.

"Are you ready?" Peepa yelled. His voice was deep but not earth-shaking like Ganesh's.

"Yes," I said. I was remarkably calm for a change. If I could tag Jaga-Nai, I would be the champion of all the boys. But what if I did win? Would Jaga-Nai kill me? No one had ever tagged him, and in fact, most of us deliberately avoided doing so. Should I force myself to lose? The decisions were heavy, but my time to choose was limited. Everyone was looking at me with pity. I was used to that look, and it actually comforted me a little.

"Kabaddi, Kabaddi, Kabaddi, Kabaddi," I droned. I kept my voice low so that I wouldn't stop my cant. Though my head was down, I could feel everyone's presence, even the birds'. They had stopped crowing once I began my chanting. Perhaps I was singing them to sleep.

I looked up and saw that Jaga-Nai was at the end of their human chain. Peepa was in the middle, looking at me, water forming droplets at the sides of his mouth. He was ready to block me. I could see him shouldering one of the smaller boys to his left. If I touched anyone, it would be him.

I turned around to look at my team, and I saw Golicchio. He was now standing next to Ganesh, his face filled with hope. I saw him whispering, and I wondered if he was praying for my safety. I could see the stories he was spinning in his head. He really believed I could do it. He was the only one on my team who did, and somehow that was enough. I stepped over the line, and I heard a shriek. A crow fell down from the sky, bloody and black.

"No stopping the game, keep playing!" Jaga-Nai said. I looked at the bird.

"Yrimal is crying," Golicchio said. I didn't know how he could see me, but I wondered if he could just tell.

"Now isn't the time for your stories," Ganesh said.

"Cry baby, cry baby!" Jaga-Nai laughed. Even though I was crying, I kept up my cant.

"Just come back, Yrimal. You're not tagging anyone." Ganesh's voice sounded quiet, as if he were resigned to losing even though the game had barely started. He was probably right though. Jaga-Nai's team never lost, even if he had to alter the rules a little for his own benefit.

But I kept chanting. Through my runny nose and soft tears, I kept up the cant. Jaga-Nai grew reckless.

"Come on, cry baby, eh? Give up! Your parents did!" he screamed, and the rest of his teammates, even those I had considered my friends, carried on in a similar manner.

Through my tears, I saw Jaga-Nai's arm extend forward. I rushed in and touched him lightly. That was the first time I had ever willingly touched Jaga-Nai, and it burned. I ran back to my court without taking a breath.

"You're out!" Ganesh's voice boomed. We all looked at him, even me. "You're out," he said again, with an incredulous smile on his face.

"He's right," Peepa, Jaga-Nai's own teammate, said. "I saw him."

"You can stop your cant now," Golicchio said. I hadn't realized I was still singing. Jaga-Nai would carry my feces for three days straight. I felt as though karma was finally being realized. He deserved to eat it. I had seen that happen to us before.

I looked at Jaga-Nai, and for once, no one surrounded his canine frame. In his left hand, he carried the dead bird.

Chapter Eleven

IF I WERE to plot Jaga-Nai's life on a graph, it would appear as a bell curve. I could even mark with precision the places where his god had failed him.

A rug in Amma's house always made me think of Jaga-Nai. Handmade in a pueblo in New Mexico, it is covered with geometric patterns resembling a pack of wolves. Amma told me that the rug took almost a year to make, and she had special-ordered it as a gift for her husband. I marveled at how a woman whom Amma had never known had devoted months of her life to making it, and that after it was done, she had no grief over its parting.

During the winter, I always loved standing on it with my bare feet because though the fabric was initially rough on the outside, it had worn down and become quite soft. Standing on it felt as though I had secured a place in the clouds beside all of the birds and the rain.

The rug had resided in an insignificant place in our home, and when Amma died, I took it for my own. I keep it in my closet, so that I can remember him in the mornings while I am in that half-conscious dreamscape where anything seems possible.

Chapter Twelve

We slept five to ten in a room, and only two rooms for all of us. It was cramped during the summers, but comfortable during the winter. Though the government sent us sheets and pillows to use on the floors as we slept, the Mothers found a way to steal them. When I first arrived, I was the only boy who had a full set. Two days later, Mother Kalpana had taken it from me, saying it was because I had looked at her the wrong way. The others would've found a way to have taken it from me anyway.

Though the floor was hard and our elbows useless as pillows, we made do. Sleep came easily for me, and I welcomed it. When I would wake up in the mornings, sometimes having had a dream about my family, the pain of my surroundings would sting. Those days, it was difficult to get back to my normal routine. I preferred to just sleep, and I knew that was why the Mothers served us breakfast so early in the mornings.

I was thankful that I shared a room with most of my friends. Jaga-Nai was in the other room, and especially today, I was grateful of this fact. However, the others couldn't stop talking about my victory in Kabaddi. I just wanted to forget; sometimes winning wasn't winning at all. I wished I had remembered that before I had tagged Jaga-Nai.

Of course Golicchio was the one who embellished the most. Some of the other boys hadn't witnessed the upset, and they were bent forward, intently listening to the "story" of what had happened.

"You were crying because it was all part of your plan, wasn't it? You're more clever than we gave you credit for, Yrimal! Really, you had us all fooled!" he said. I just nodded. I wasn't the creative one.

"Did you give him your feces yet?" Peepa asked. I didn't answer him. Although Peepa was happy that Jaga-Nai had lost, I believed he was disappointed that it was me who had caused it. He would've rather tagged Jaga-Nai himself, even though they were on the same team.

"Yes. Continue, Golicchio!" Ganesh said. He liked to hear Golicchio's stories right before he went to bed. They were like bedtime stories. They helped all of us fall asleep. We didn't really know how Golicchio went to sleep. Maybe he drifted off, lulled by the sound of his own voice, which surprisingly was melodic. His voice seemed impervious to puberty.

"So Yrimal had it all planned, you see. He was going to cry and distract Jaga-Nai. The moment that Jaga-Nai's concentration was spent, you leapt in and touched him! Didn't you? Was that your plan? It was, wasn't it?" Even though Golicchio asked questions, he wasn't looking for an answer.

"And then, it was as if Kumara came down on his peacock and took one of the feathers from his vessel and gave it to Yrimal to use on Jaga-Nai's arm!"

"But that would be cheating," Peepa said. Ganesh sat up.

"Be quiet. I'm listening to Golicchio."

"But it wasn't cheating because it was divine. Nothing that happens with the gods is cheating. And then you should've seen Jaga-Nai's face! He looked like a dog that had just been castrated!" They all laughed. I laughed quietly, afraid that he'd hear us. The walls weren't the thickest. We sometimes heard things we didn't even want to.

"Now Jaga-Nai is probably scooping a handful of crap in his hand and holding it like it was a cricket ball!" Ganesh laughed so hard, we heard one of the Mothers yell from down the hall.

"How do we know if he really carried it?" I whispered, but everyone was starting to nod off, silenced by the rebuke.

Ganesh and Jaga-Nai had worked out the details of the "arrangement." I was to leave my stool in the outhouse without washing it down with a bucket of water. Jaga-Nai was then to carry it (with his bare hands) to the back of the House, turn around three times (in lieu of doing it for three days), and then take it back to the outhouse. He also had to dispose of it. Ganesh hadn't discussed how we would know for sure that he had done it. I didn't blame him – I wouldn't have wanted to see it either.

Regardless of whether he did it or not, I believed the real insult for him was in losing, and losing to someone like me. Perhaps that was why the boys didn't bother verifying that he had done it.

That night I couldn't sleep, and as soon as dawn broke, I heard the little bells that Mother Jamuna wore on her ankles go "chkk chkk chkk" as she walked by our room to go outside. I forced myself up, and heavy as I felt with the lack of sleep, I dragged myself to the outhouse. I needed to see for myself whether it had been done.

As I got to the door, I noticed a cluster of mosquitoes hovering above the toilet. I looked down and saw that Jaga-Nai had not fulfilled his end of the bargain. In fact, it looked as though he had added to it. The sight gave me an uneasy feeling in the core of my stomach.

I heard a knock on the door, and I gasped. "Who is it?" I asked.

"Yrimal, run. Jaga-Nai is coming," Ashandra said. He was one of the weaker boys who had been coerced into being Jaga-Nai's friend. Most of the time, his friendship was beneficial, although sometimes Jaga-Nai liked to take out his aggressions on those closest to him. Even so, I would've much rather been his ally than the boy who had tagged him.

Jaga-Nai wasn't big; that's not what scared us all. It was his psychological control. He was a bully in the truest sense of the word. He could make us shit our pants just by looking at us. Shortly after I'd arrived at the House, when I was still figuring out who to befriend and who to avoid, Jaga-Nai unleashed one of his worst attacks to date. Jaga-Nai had been picking on one particular boy for days. The boy was born half-bald, and Jaga-Nai, sensing his insecurity, called him, "Kolikatta," a plain, bald-like food made out of rice flour. After days of endless taunting, the boy had snuck into Jaga-Nai's sleep area in the middle of the night. No one knew to this day what he was planning to do. The boy had had a knife with him – perhaps to cut off his hair, who knew. Jaga-Nai had woken up in quiet, and almost panther-like, grabbed the boy's neck. The next day, the boy was missing one of his eyes. When questioned by the Mothers and by the rest of us, he'd insisted that he'd done it himself – accidentally of course. None of us believed him, but what could the Mothers do? Even Jaga-Nai had a spell on them sometimes.

That was what we were all really afraid of. We knew he was capable of a lot of things, but we weren't quite sure of what exactly. His range of evil was not comprehendable and far surpassed anything that even Golicchio could imagine.

Before I knew what was happening, I was being led by Jaga-Nai to the side of the outhouse, which wasn't plainly visible from the House. He turned me around to face him. He smiled, and I saw brown teeth.

"Do you know why my teeth are brown? Eh?"

I sat down. I saw his feet, and they didn't look so scary. In fact, they looked rather small.

"My mother used to drink when she was pregnant. The alcohol corroded my teeth," he said without flinching. "Come feel, eh," he said, and he grabbed my fingers and guided them over his front set of teeth. I felt grooves, cracks, slime, and food. He then guided my hand even farther – into the recesses of his mouth. I felt saliva, wet and warm, and then I felt his tonsils. As he threw up on my hand, I almost threw up myself.

"Come," he said. He took me back to the outhouse and made me get down on my knees. "I left a little surprise for you." He forced my face into it. I tried to keep my mouth closed, but I couldn't help it. Feces got into my nose and made its way into my mouth. I tried to spit it out, but it was too late. I could taste the grit on my teeth.

"You're lucky. It could've been worse."

He ran back to the House shouting, "Sid shat his pants! Everyone come and see!" I heard Ganesh's big laugh, and all of the boys rushed out, including the Mothers. They stood there, laughing, except for Mother Jamuna, who scolded me.

"What are you going to do? That is your last shirt." As punishment, I was to remain in my soiled clothing until lunch time.

"No wonder your parents left you. They couldn't get you pottytrained," Peepa said, and Puni squealed. Ganesh pushed him aside to get a better look.

"Yrimal must've coughed so hard, something came out this time!" Ganesh said.

"No, no. Leave him alone," Golicchio said. I looked at him. I could barely see any of them – just their outlines. I could just hear their voices.

"Don't you know? Yrimal was giving birth to a very brown and smelly baby!" Golicchio shrieked. The rest of them congratulated him on his creative story. I sank to the ground, and I could feel the dirt sticking to my shorts.

At the sea, my mother and I had seen a poor boy who worked as a fish vendor get cheated out of a sale. When the other people in the market accused him of lying and asked my mother what she thought, she'd said the poor boy was lying too. I moved to speak, but my mother had covered my mouth.

"Join them when you can," she said.

Chapter Thirteen

I MET MY wife at a pro-life demonstration. At the time, I didn't believe in the horrific pictures of aborted fetuses enlarged on huge white boards, but I believed in the message. She had been carrying a poster, and I had turned my face away.

"Why do you look away? This is what they are doing to our children," she said. I had admired her devotion to the unnamed.

Chapter Fourteen

THOUGH THE MOTHERS claimed that they had degrees in education, they were horrible teachers. Most of the time, they read straight out of a book. The rest was spent lecturing us on ideas and morals that really didn't apply to us.

As we learned about Indian values, two of the Mothers took turns lecturing us on how we were to respect our elders, display good manners, lead a spiritually clean life, love our families (what families were they referring to, I wondered), and retain our culture. The lesson felt completely useless. Most of us had no respect for a culture that let us be washed away without a second thought. The only elders that we knew were the Mothers, and even though we tried every which way possible to respect them, we were still at the mercy of their punishments. They constantly reminded us that we were worth nothing. The worst part of it was that although they told us that caste discrimination had been outlawed, they still reinforced it by telling us that we were to be good boys, else we would be born into the womb of a jackal or worse yet – an untouchable. At that statement, several boys leered at me, sometimes even at Puni and Golicchio. *Bad, bad, bad boys*, some of them even mouthed.

To conclude their lesson, the Mothers reminded us that when they asked us to do something – anything – we were to do it with love in our hearts because they were older than us and now our family. Jaga-Nai snickered, and he was given ten lashes on the palm of his hand. Mother

Kalpana looked down at the rest of us through her peach color-framed glasses. *Anyone else want to disobey me today?* her eyes seemed to say. We remained silent. As if on cue, Mother Kalpana and Mother Jamuna looked at each other, nodded, and then called Puni and Golicchio to the front of the classroom.

"We need you to clean our bathroom stalls," one of them said. They accepted, and were sent to the Mothers' private quarters. Usually Golicchio, Puni, or I were asked to do such menial favors. We never said no or challenged their requests. We had no choice. But they never asked Ganesh, Peepa, or the others. We knew why; when we would return from our "chores," the other boys never asked us what we did. They just accepted that there were some things in life that we were meant to do and that they had no part of. It was the "pretending like it never happened" syndrome all over again.

We didn't receive any special treatment from the Mothers for doing what they asked either, but sometimes we got to see things we weren't supposed to. Once I had seen Headmistress Veli naked. Mother Jamuna had asked me to scour the edges of the toilet because it had been attracting ants. The Mothers, though they preached cleanliness, were notoriously messy when it came to taking care of their personal business. While I was in the process of sticking my bare hand inside the bowl, wondering if the smell would stain my skin, I saw Headmistress Veli enter the shower stall. She had to have seen me – the toilet was next to the stall – but she acted as though she hadn't. She had taken off all of her clothes, and I got to see her body, layer upon layer of fat hanging off the sides as though she were made of lamb cutlets. I had turned away and quickly finished my chore.

After Golicchio and Puni left, we were shuttled outside. The hour after lessons was devoted to homework. We wrote our homework on small, hand-sized chalkboards (again, courtesy of the government). One of the Mothers would check it the next day, and then we would erase the board and start over. If we failed to complete the assignment, we were given three blows to the palm of our hand with a stick. If we got the problem wrong, we were given twice as much homework. The trick was fitting all of the answers on the board without smudging it.

Next to the House was a concrete slab, which was where we were forced to do our homework. Generally, we were not allowed to play or sit there, but for the purposes of completing our homework, it was the only place that contained enough tables and chairs for us to sit on. Even in the dining room, we sat on the floor cross-legged with a banana leaf in front of us and a tumbler of rancid water to boot.

It was hard for me to complete my homework without staring at the greenhouse. Sometimes, if the Mothers were preoccupied, a few of the boys would go inside and stay there. I didn't know what they did, but I suspected that they were more interested in the privacy that the wooden shed afforded than any of its contents. Some, like Ganesh, claimed that they were interested in all of the plants and flowers that were stored there in tiny ceramic pots. Golicchio and I weren't convinced; we believed that he was more curious about the girl who came daily to water the plants than the plants themselves. None of us knew who she was, and she never talked to us. She reminded me of Smita, so I had formed a subconscious attachment to her. Hoping to catch a glimpse of her made it difficult for me to finish my schoolwork.

Our homework was to write at least ten different things we could do to make sure we were good Indian boys. We sat at the tables on the concrete, trying to avoid touching the slab with our bare feet. The sun was intense today, and I felt as though my clothes offered no shield against it. Since my last shirt and shorts had been ruined by Jaga-Nai, I was given a very thin undershirt and a very large pair of shorts. Everywhere I went, I had to hold the shorts up with one hand. I was hoping that the government would send me a new pair soon.

As I focused on my assignment, struggling to come up with answers that seemed genuine and not forced, I saw Golicchio return from the Mothers' quarters. His shirt was soaked, and his hair was wet. He smiled.

"I was lucky. Puni got the hard work. He's still there," he said. None of the others paid attention. The girl had returned to water the plants, and we were all stuck watching her. "She's going to marry someone one day," he said. He sat down next to me and tried to look at my chalkboard. I moved away.

"What's wrong? I'm not going to cheat." He tried to move closer, and I put my hand out. I was still upset that he had joined with the others in making fun of me. I understood why he had done it, but I thought Golicchio was better than that. Deep down, I knew he was a better person than I was, but he was also a victim of his environment.

"She can marry you if you want. I hate girls," Peepa said. He had a tumbler of water next to his chalkboard. He was halfway through his work – the fastest of all of us, but that didn't necessarily mean the best. Golicchio reached over to look at his chalkboard, and he tipped the water. It spilled all over Peepa's homework and erased whatever he'd accomplished in the half hour we'd been working.

"You low-caste pansy!" Peepa shouted. With the strength of a grown man, he elbowed Golicchio onto the floor. Golicchio was no match. As he fell, his jerky body pounded into the floor, while his joints ricocheted off of the sharpest parts of the table. In spite of the pain of his landing, he didn't cry.

I could see the blood drip from one of Golicchio's elbows and by the way he held his face – not in the usual angular way he held it but in the normal way he should hold it but couldn't – I knew that he was in a lot of pain. Peepa didn't stop. He kept hitting Golicchio, yet he didn't yell. He took the blows because he probably felt he deserved them.

I motioned as though I were going to go and help, and Golicchio yelled, "Stop." I assumed he had addressed that to Peepa, so I kept forward, but he screamed. He was looking directly at me. Then Peepa also told me to go away.

"This is their fight. You'll only end up getting hurt too," Ganesh said.

The fighting was practically soundless and without words. The noiseless brawl didn't alert the Mothers. All I heard was the soft sound of flesh on flesh. I felt time had slowed, even though it had probably only been less than a minute.

I saw Golicchio's eyes close, and I yelled, "It was only homework," and Peepa shoved me and returned to hitting Golicchio. Finally after a few minutes, Ganesh intervened. Jaga-Nai stood watching with a smile on his face. The only times I ever saw Jaga-Nai smile was when someone else was in pain.

"He is fine!" Ganesh yelled. Out of the corner of my eye, I saw the girl run to the House. Mother Jamuna came after. I stood back, my shorts running down my legs, afraid she would implicate me in the brawl even though I had nothing to do with it.

She tried to pick Golicchio up by the arms. He was conscious, but his face was bloody. She told one of the boys to run and get a tumbler of water. After he returned, she doused his face with it, reviving him slowly. Peepa stood next to him, not afraid of whatever punishment was to come. She questioned us, asked us all what happened. Ganesh blamed it on Golicchio. He said Golicchio had deliberately thrown water on Peepa's chalkboard, so that he would get in trouble the next day for not completing his homework. Peepa corroborated his story. I tried to speak, to let them know what really happened, but she shushed me. She had heard the version that she'd wanted. She told Peepa that he wouldn't receive any dinner, but Golicchio was to clean the outhouse for an entire month. Not only that, he had to do it during lunch time. Ganesh tried to backpedal then, saying that he didn't really think Golicchio had done it on purpose, that maybe the punishment was too harsh. Mother Jamuna glared at him, and he backed down.

After she returned inside, I was too stunned to say anything. I looked at Golicchio's bruised face and helped him to the bath to get clean. He had stained his only shirt too. I saw Peepa and Ganesh laugh about something, their heads meeting together perfectly as they were similar heights. Anger burned inside of me, but I knew that I couldn't do anything. In order to survive, I had to forget that they had turned on us because they didn't always. And if they did every now and then, that was better than what happened out there in the real world.

Chapter Fifteen

MY WIFE AND I married seven months after the demonstration.

Chapter Sixteen

BECAUSE GOLICCHIO WAS too weak to eat dinner, he decided to wash the outhouse instead. Though that didn't make any sense, I knew he was trying to avoid Peepa.

Cleaning the outhouse was another one of those chores that was usually assigned to me, Puni, or Golicchio. Instead of waiting for the Mothers to get angry and punish us because the bathroom was dirty, we proactively cleaned it ourselves, working out a schedule between the three of us. We each cleaned it every third week. This week was Golicchio's turn anyway, and even though he didn't have to ask, I had planned on taking it over to spare him while he recovered. I was certain Puni, who had been absent for the fight but who had seen Golicchio's face, would have done the same. Jaga-Nai was the only one who complained if the outhouse was dirty, even though he did nothing to remedy it. Sometimes he'd go directly to the Mothers. So we had to be careful about how we cleaned it, sometimes washing it more than once a week if it was especially filthy.

For dinner, we received a small cup of fried eggplant and a bowl of rice. My shorts had extra large pockets as well, so I tried to shove rice and eggplant into them. Eggplant was one of Golicchio's favorites, and I knew by the way Jaga-Nai was staring at my leaf, that if I didn't eat it all or stash it away soon, he would take it away from me. I got up quickly and went outside.

Golicchio lay against the side of the outhouse, breathing heavily. He looked tired, and I saw that he had not finished cleaning.

"I brought you eggplant," I said. He nodded with his eyes closed, and I put it in his hands. He ate it and the rice quickly. After he was done, he belched, and I knew he was happy that I had saved him some food.

"People are strange, aren't they?" he asked. He had regained some of his strength, and his eyes were open now. Because of the bruises, they drooped, giving him the illusion of being very sleepy or having been drugged.

"Yes," I said. I looked up, and I saw the stars. I remembered counting them as a child. My mother said that if I thought that my life was hard, and that I had something to complain about, I should look up and count the number of stars in the sky because that was the number of children out there who were worse off than I was. I began counting in my head.

"I thought Peepa was my friend," he said.

"I thought you were my friend, but you made fun of me."

"You would've done the same thing if you were me. There's nothing like the feeling of belonging. To be a part of something greater than you are. Do you know what I mean?" I did. I couldn't fault him for it because he was right; I would've done the same thing.

We sat together as the night waned, not saying much but not needing to. I counted up to one hundred and was onto almost five hundred before Mother Jamuna came and told us to come inside. As I followed her, I noticed that there were so many more stars that I had just not seen.

IF PRESSED, I would've named Golicchio as my best friend, but I did have a certain fondness for Puni.

From the early days right after my arrival to the House, I remembered my first encounters with Puni the most vividly. He and I had slept next to each other for several months. I envied him then. He had large eyes – eyes of a fish that had long since died and gone somewhere else. He never blinked. He had eyelids, as far as I could tell. But he just never blinked. He could stare forcefully at anyone or anything without so much as a tear escaping his eyes. I knew that he had an unnatural ability, and for that I was jealous. In my mind, if you had a skill such as that, you could see all and nothing could get past you.

Puni stared at Jaga-Nai too. During breakfast/lunch one time, in the middle of a can of spoiled fish and a side of bitter melon, Puni stared and stared at his empty leaf. He had gulped down his food in less than five seconds. Yet he continued to focus on his leaf perhaps thinking food would magically appear if he did so. Jaga-Nai latched onto this weakness and began harassing him.

"Are you still hungry? Eh? Do you want some of my fish, do you?" He held out his leaf, and Puni looked right at Jaga-Nai. Even Ganesh backed away tentatively. When it came to food, none of us wanted to fight.

Puni nodded yes, and he continued to watch Jaga-Nai. Jaga-Nai brought the leaf close to Puni's nose, and then to his unwavering eyes. Puni licked his lips once. Jaga-Nai laughed. Then taking the entire leaf, he smeared it across Puni's wide face. Puni hardly moved.

"Don't stare at me again, eh?" he said. He snapped his fingers (the way Indian movie stars did when they were done with a scene), and his fellow thugs accompanied him out of the dining area. The rest of us turned to look at Puni, who fixated on the spot where Jaga-Nai had stood. He took his fingers and wiped off all of the food on his face and licked his hands. All we could see were his fingers moving, and all we could hear was the sound of his lips smacking in pleasure. The episode with Jaga-Nai hadn't seemed to bother him at all – or so we had thought.

"Can you teach me how to stare like that?" I had asked him once during the night. Most everyone was already asleep, and I had to whisper a few times for him to hear me.

"Like how?" He put his hands up in a gesture to signal that he had no idea what I was talking about. He squealed a little when I poked his eyes.

"What's that for?"

"Your eyes. They never blink. How do you do that?"

"They close when I am asleep."

"No, they don't."

"So you are watching me as I go to sleep, then? That's strange." He turned over. I could see the roundness of his rump in the shadow and marveled how one could retain any fat in this place. Then again, it was still early.

"Please, tell me!"

"Shh!" Ganesh whispered and kicked the wall. He always got to sleep next to the wall.

"I don't know. I don't think about it, it just happens."

"Doesn't it hurt?"

"If it hurt, then I wouldn't do it, would I?" I nodded. I supposed that was a silly question, but he still wasn't being very clear with me.

"I don't think you were born like that. I think you learned it." If he was born with it, I was sure he would've had other birth defects, and as far as we all could tell, he was normal like the rest of us.

"And if I did? Like I am going to tell you. Like I would tell any of you. I am not going to stay in here very long. My family knows. I love to eat. I cannot stay in a place like this. I will go hungry and then crazy. They wouldn't let that happen to me."

"Aren't your parents dead?" I asked him.

"Yes, but someone will come. They are the ones who indirectly taught me how to keep my eyes and my body very still."

"For what purpose?" I was close; I could feel it.

"Yrimal, don't you know that bad things happen when we close our eyes?" he had asked, and he drifted off to sleep with his eyes open. Fear of his power had made me unable to sleep at all.

Chapter Seventeen

I SUFFER FROM insomnia. When I close my eyes, I think of Puni.

When my kids were little, I never begrudged them food. Whatever they wanted I gave them, from the delicate pink cakes shaped like ballerina slippers to the donuts topped with chocolate mounds like cow patties. They could have whatever they wanted to eat. My wife said I spoiled them, but I disagreed. I felt it abuse to withhold food from a child, no matter what.

In time, they grew obese, and in their fat, I felt Puni. In their demands for more and more, I could hear Puni. I began to withdraw as they grew fatter and fatter, and I knew I was hurting them. They accused me of not loving them because they were fat, but they didn't know the real reason. I couldn't tell them because I didn't even know myself.

Eventually, I did tell them. Not only because I wanted to reclaim their love again, but also to tell them about someone who had been important to me, in another life and someone else's pain. They listened, their eyes bugged like his. When I finished, they asked me dozens of questions, of which I had no answers.

"What happened to him, Dad?" they both asked. I looked into their eyes, but I didn't have the heart to tell them.

Chapter Eighteen

PEEPA LOOKED HAPPY on the outside, but they all looked that way when they came to the House. Even though he had come before me, the others (like Golicchio) told me about his early days.

"He glowed like the lanterns set out on Diwali," he said. We were sweeping the cafeteria together after breakfast. Golicchio took one end, and I took the other.

"What happened?" I asked.

"I don't know," he said. I could see that his bruises were starting to fade.

"You can't hide from him, you know."

"I know. I'm not."

"It's been a few days already, and you haven't said a word to him."

"What do you care? You don't even like him anyway."

"That's because he doesn't like me." I took my time in running the sticks across the concrete floor.

"You know, he used to act. He was in a youth drama group, and they performed stories from the *Ramayana*. Sometimes he even got to play Rama because he is handsome." Golicchio smiled. I could tell that his fear of Peepa was starting to dwindle. "He even won awards for his ability. He could've been a great actor."

"Who said that he cannot still?"

Golicchio shook his head. "We all come to the House like lanterns, our flames burning so brightly that we sometimes cannot even see ourselves for what we are. Then after a while, the Mothers with their blowing put it out. Then we are left with nothing but darkness."

After I finished my area, I saw that Golicchio had stopped. He picked up something off the ground. It was a half-eaten chappathi, surely something leftover from the Mothers' breakfast, since we had only received mushy idli and watery sambar.

"But sometimes there's light too," he said. Smiling, he stuffed the entire piece of bread in his mouth.

"Are you done yet?" Mother Kalpana had come up behind us, her pudgy face in a tense scowl. She was wearing her hair in twin braids, which seemed incongruous with the wrinkles on her old face.

"Yes," we said in unison.

"What are you eating there?" She stuck her hand inside Golicchio's mouth and pulled out the chappathi. "Who gave this to you?"

"No one, I found it," Golicchio said.

"Nonsense. Did you steal this? Did you?"

"He didn't. He found it," I said.

"Do you expect to be anything in your life if you steal? Is that a way to gain karma?" Her question was rhetorical, and she didn't wait for a response. She hurried down the hall, I was sure to wash her hands of Golicchio's saliva.

"I swallowed most of it," he said, still grinning.

"Let's leave," I said, afraid that the other Mothers would come too. They were like hyenas; when one smelled vulnerable blood, the rest were sure to follow.

Once outside, we found that the others had already finished bathing. We decided together that no one would know if we skipped showering for one day. Golicchio hadn't been able to rid his clothing of the blood stains from his attack; I was still stuck wearing the oversized clothing that itched like the tickle of hairs on a smooth arm.

As we stood near the water, Ganesh approached with his chalkboard in his hand. "Did you finish the assignment?" he asked us. We both nodded. The Mothers had not checked our answers from before, so the assignment had remained the same – to list how we could be better Indian boys. At the last minute, I had changed some of my answers. Before, I had written that going hungry so often wouldn't make me good, but I decided that that would've warranted lashes, so I had changed it to making sure my chin was wiped after every meal.

"Can I see?" he asked both of us, but he looked directly at Golicchio.

Golicchio was a good student when it came to creative answers. When it came to logic, I was better.

I could tell that Golicchio didn't want to share his answers. If Ganesh stole any of them, he would have to write his assignment over, and class was going to start soon. I was glad that I didn't have my board with me.

"I left it inside." Ganesh sprinted to the House, went inside, and came back with Golicchio's chalkboard. He had already started copying some of the answers. I noted Golicchio's neat handwriting and was jealous. His answers were good too.

"Thanks," he said, and he made his way back inside. He was always the first one to arrive for class even though he disliked learning. Of course his punctuality reinforced the Mothers' view of boys like him and boys like us. It didn't help that he wouldn't let any of the others ahead of him even if we wanted to. He shoved us in the same way he did when we'd line up at the cafeteria for our meals.

"Class!" Mother Kalpana shouted. I saw that she held a chappathi in her hand, and she smiled at us.

"What am I going to do?" Golicchio asked. He panicked.

"Hurry, write something," I said. I knew he didn't work well under pressure; he preferred to be given ample time to come up with his ideas without the Mothers' nasty hands looming in the background. I made my way to the classroom, praying that Golicchio would come up with something.

The classroom was located in one of the smaller rooms, which also contained a sewing machine, a typewriter, and a few bookshelves. The Mothers sometimes went there to read or do their arts and crafts. It also had a cot, which had never been moved. I suspected that it used to be a room for sleeping, but they had converted it. There was no chalkboard, no desks for us, no nothing. We sat on the floor, in order of whoever arrived first. Golicchio and I usually sat in the back.

Mother Kalpana entered still chewing on the chappathi. She surveyed the room and noticed a few of us were missing. She waited a minute, and just as she was about to begin the day's lesson, Golicchio ran in the door. He took his seat next to me. I saw that he had developed a line of perspiration along his upper lip, which was devoid of hair just like mine.

She began the class by calling all of our names. I felt that this was a silly exercise; there weren't that many of us, and she knew who was missing and who wasn't. But we answered anyway. If we didn't say "present" in a loud and clear voice, we were given one lash on the hand. If we laughed as we said it (which happened frequently, since Mother Kalpana had a nasaly voice that sounded like a mouse's and liked to spit when she talked), we were given two lashes. If we weren't paying attention and missed a beat when answering, we were made to stand in the front for the duration of the lesson while the entire class stared at us, made faces at us, or even showed us their privates while the Mother's back was turned.

So as Mother Kalpana called us one by one, our ears strained to hear. Mother Jamuna was especially vicious as she'd switch the order in which she'd call us, which required us to pay even more attention. Jaga-Nai was worse. During roll call, he'd attempt to stick his fingers in our ears or distract us with his threats. Sometimes it worked; sometimes he would get caught. Luckily Jaga-Nai was missing, and both Golicchio and I heard our names and answered clearly and loudly.

"Pass up your chalkboards, so I can check your homework," she said. Golicchio's hands shook as he did. Mother Kalpana spent a minute scanning each and calling us to retrieve our board. I received a check mark, but she scolded me on the penmanship. No lashes though. When she called Ganesh, she paused and turned to the class.

"I'd like you to read your answers aloud," she said.

Ganesh cleared his throat, and he read. And as he read, I looked at Golicchio. He was very sad.

"'The things I will do to be a better Indian boy. Number one, I will thank the Mothers everyday for taking us in when no one else would. Number two, I will look up at the sky and be happy that it is blue because that is how Brahma wanted it. Number three, I will eat only half of what I need so that others may eat more. Number four, when I am feeling down, I will put my hand to my heart and hear its beat and feel lucky to be alive.'" Ganesh scrunched his eyes; he'd had to write in very small letters to copy the wordy answers that Golicchio had written on his board. "'Number five, I will take smaller steps to create less destruction. Number six, I will pray not when I need something but when others do. Number seven, I will not yearn for my parents for they are in a better place. Number eight, I will—'" Ganesh stopped. He couldn't decipher his writing – his own plagiarism.

"That is enough." She dismissed him. "If the rest of you wrote as eloquently as Ganesh, I would have nothing to teach you." She shook her head as she called Golicchio. She skipped over his board and handed it back to him. "Some of you need to start taking more time with the homework, else there may be additional lashes." I saw that Peepa gave Ganesh a little pat on the back. Golicchio sighed.

"What was that, Mr. Goli?" she asked.

"Nothing," he said. But that wasn't enough. He was made to stand in front of the classroom because of his sigh, and I saw Peepa stare at him. Golicchio tried to smile, but I wasn't sure if it was reciprocated.

The rest of the lesson, Mother Kalpana read to us from a novel. She was halfway in the middle of it (she explained) and needed to know what happened. She felt that the way the novel was written and its use of language would teach us a thing or two, so it wasn't entirely about her. But it was.

I tried to follow, but I didn't understand the story. She read straight from the middle, and one character was trying to get another character to go to the market for him. I looked at Golicchio for reassurance, but he was still in front, looking down. His board was next to me, and I saw his second set of answers were short and non-elegant, unlike Golicchio.

After about an hour of reading, she assigned our homework. We were to summarize what she'd just read in a short, succinct paragraph. We were to surmise what we felt might happen next and why.

"Class dismissed," she said. We were happy when our lessons were short. Mother Kalpana's tended to be because she had other things she'd rather do. Mother Jamuna's were longer. Headmistress Veli's were the most interesting perhaps because she posed as eye candy, which made the lesson go by faster.

As we shuffled out of the door, I saw Jaga-Nai sneak past.

"Mr. Jagadesh, please come here," Mother Kalpana said. He stopped, looked around, but didn't move. She got up from her desk and reached her hand out as if she meant to drag him by the ear. A second later, Headmistress Veli appeared.

"Leave him be, he was with me," she said. She and Mother Kalpana smiled at each other, but I didn't have a good feeling about it. I didn't feel it was sincere on either side. Mother Kalpana didn't say anything in response, but let go of his ear. Jaga-Nai showed his teeth and hissed, and then he skipped down the hall.

Chapter Nineteen

I EVENTUALLY RECEIVED my certification and became a high school English teacher. The profession since my start has always felt comfortable in the way a worn belt relaxes around the waist as old age and fat set in.

Mrs. Conrad had been my English teacher in high school, and she inspired me. I disliked her at first, but I approved of how thin she was – she wore it as if it were a condition that just happened without effort or awareness.

I was often late to her class because I had befriended a Pakistani who owned a liquor store near school. He let me buy cigarettes from him in exchange for a few minutes of my company. I was attracted to him because he wasn't from India, but still carried with him a familiarity that reminded me of the people I had grown up with.

My habitual tardiness had landed me in detention with Mrs. Conrad for the third week in a row. No other students were in the room with us, which I believe had given her the courage to ask me without pretention, "What is wrong?"

When I looked at her, I saw that she wanted to help – in the same way those people who had taken us from the House had appeared. I have learned which eyes to trust, and which eyes to avoid.

I gave her the mechanical, rehearsed version of my story, and sections of it brought her to tears. I left out many details, but she was intuitive. After detention was over, she promised that she would spare me future punishments. I was free to do as I wished because she felt guilty for those who had desecrated the profession before her.

I could've abused the power – around those with a deep conscience, victims can become forceful and hungry too. But later, after I thought about how my childhood affected others – even those who had no tangible link to me – and that these others cared about me in a blinding, glaucoma type way, I tried really hard to be better. I needed to prove to myself that Mother Jamuna had been wrong and that I could recover.

Chapter Twenty

THE BOYS WERE catching up in terms of reading level. Some of them had already known how to read before the House – the more educated ones. But many of us hadn't ever learned because we had no use for it. In fact, many of the vendors that my parents used to deal with didn't even know how to read. It wasn't necessary for them; why was it necessary for us?

To say the House had a library was an exaggeration. But to me, it was cavernous – fifty or so volumes in total. The collection was located on bookshelves in the corner of our classroom. Every now and then, books with torn edges and smeared pages would miraculously show up on the shelves. I checked daily for new reads. Sometimes Jaga-Nai would hoard several books at a time. For once, the Mothers actually listened to our complaints (mainly spearheaded by Ganesh, who was angry that Jaga-Nai had taken many sports magazines) and restricted our borrowing to only one item at a time. This was never enforced as the House had no official librarian, but if the Mothers saw us with more than one item, either on us or in our room, we were punished.

I had just finished a book of sayings, many which were not attributed to anyone in particular. I didn't really like the book. It was too hopeful and optimistic. Each day, I read a quote aloud and felt inspired, but then by the end of the day, the quote seemed unattainable, imaginary. Who had written these quotes? Did they live the life I did? I felt that the book didn't touch me the way it could have. It was for people who lived in palaces and who ate orange-colored food covered in sugar. I looked forward to reading something else.

"What are you smiling at, eh?" Jaga-Nai was sitting on the floor in the classroom. He wasn't looking straight at me, but staring directly at one of the bookshelves. I was standing near the doorway, ready to enter and return the book of quotes and check out another. I wanted to read a book called *Revelations*. I didn't really know what it was about, but because one of the boys had checked it out for so long, the rest of us boys needed to read it. I saw that he had finished it because the book was sitting on the shelf waiting for me the way a virginal bride waited for her husband on their wedding night.

"Nothing." I carefully made my way to the bookshelf.

"What are you going to read?" He sprang up and rushed to the shelf. He kept his eyes on it.

"Nothing."

"For all the reading you do, you don't know many words," he said. By now, I had also moved closer to the bookshelf, and he was very close to me, enough that I could smell his underwear. He hadn't washed in days it seemed.

"You see," he continued, "I've been getting so good at reading that I think I'm going to check out *Revelations*. Golicchio told me that I could find it here." He winked.

"It seems long and boring to me," I said. "I was going to check out a book on cricket that Ganesh recommended."

"Puny Siddhartha, also known as Yrimal." He elbowed me and pulled out the book that I had been waiting for months to read. He flipped through it.

"You're probably right. It looks too hard. Maybe I should have you read it aloud to me, as though I were your baby and you were my amma? Hmm?" He kissed me on the cheek. I endured it. I just wanted the book.

"Eh, I don't want to read it. Here, it's yours." He extended it, and when I went to grab it, he pulled it back.

"Wait," he said. He pulled down his pants and rubbed the book all over his penis and between his behind over and over and over until I started to see brown marks on the edges. Then he sat and peed on it. He got up and blowing a kiss said, "It's yours."

I stared at the book and carefully wiping it with my shirt – the only shirt I had left – I carried it back to the room. I wasn't going to let Jaga-Nai take away something that I had waited so long for.

LEARNING TO READ had no order in the House. Those who wanted to learn did well, and those who didn't learned the bare minimum and scraped by. I was surprised that the Mothers were so liberal about education in this regard. If I had known how other orphanages were run, I would've been downright gracious about it. It was as if the Mothers took everything else away from us – our food, our clothes, our pride, our sanity – in exchange for the right to read. We all had it, and it made us free. Reading had such a profound effect on me; I didn't feel lowly or worthless when I read. I had the power to decipher words. That was more than what most people or even kids my age could do.

I was amused by all of the different things we chose to read. We didn't have access to a myriad of items. We were like whores – we took whatever we could because we needed to. I read books about situations, people I could barely relate to. I read a story about a man stranded on an island. I couldn't even imagine what an island looked like or how it must have felt to be physically alone. I didn't realize how much I was like the main character, but maybe I chose not to. I tried to relate the stories to my days near the Indian Ocean, when the vendors would yell and intimidate people into buying cheaply-made goods and roasted pakora wrapped in newspaper. We never cared if the ink stained the snacks; they always tasted so fresh as if they were born from the words in which they were resting. And who could forget the toys? There were always little gadgets either being sold or played with, anything from little trucks to big balloons shaped so ambiguously that it was difficult to tell what they were. There were wagons and trinkets that made noise when you dragged them along the sand.

Golicchio, though he read as voraciously as I did, claimed he didn't like to read much. Instead, he focused on the books that had pictures, preferring to create his own stories. I think his lack of interest had partly to do with the fact that he wasn't as good at it as I was, and the frustration beat him. His case was common – nobody had ever told him that he could learn more than how to clothe himself and earn money. His brain wasn't programmed to read, even though in my opinion he was the most brilliant boy in the House.

"The stories are taking ideas from my head. I can't think anymore," he had said once. I understood what he meant. Sometimes when I read, I couldn't relate to the story and as a result, easily forgot my past, the history that had made me me and that had brought me here. Books tore away whatever kept my past together in my head. There wasn't much to unravel and eventually, I knew it'd all go loose. Maybe I even wanted it to.

Ganesh read books that exuded manhood. There weren't many, but he was the first to read anything related to cricket, baseball, soccer. We had a little radio in our room that broadcast cricket matches and after he had exhausted the supply of sports glory stories, he started writing a journal of scores, stats, and biographies on some of the players. He was creating his own almanac, and would often refer to it when there happened to be a disagreement over a score or a player's skills.

"Let's consult the book," he called it. The concepts were easy for him to grasp. It required no imagination, no thinking outside the realm of his upbringing.

Puni didn't like to read much. He liked to watch us read. His unblinking eyes would move from reader to reader, perhaps trying to glean information from our heads. *What were we reading? Did we enjoy it? What were we learning?* I thought he was lazy. It just seemed like such a loss, that those eyes that could probably take in so many words and comprehend them quickly hardly grazed the text of a book or magazine.

Even Jaga-Nai learned how to read well enough, although I didn't know what he read. I never saw him open a book except when doing his homework or defacing a book to give to me. Even then, he acted as though books, any books, caused him pain – he would open them and shut them quickly, as if the books gave off some noxious gas that could only be tolerated in small doses.

Today, I had gotten to a particularly dirty page from *Revelations* and wasn't sure how much further I could continue. I decided to put it aside for the time being (and disobey the Mothers) while I checked out another. I read a short story about a set of twins, one who was bad and the other good. They got along as well as could be expected, but eventually, over a man's love, the two quarreled. The evil one killed the good one. I couldn't help but ponder whether the author was trying to hint that maybe these weren't twins, but one and the same person. Maybe during times of extreme duress (such as over a lover), this person would physically reveal himself. And this was insanity. Maybe it was just intuition. I didn't know. I felt my thoughts were juvenile, and I wasn't mature enough to understand them.

"Golicchio?" I looked around. I wanted to talk to him about the story, but he wasn't in the bedroom.

"Golicchio?" I said again.

"Shh!" Ganesh yelled. His ear was next to the radio, and he had one pen behind it and another one in his hand. "Get out!" he said. Everyone else glared at me. I noticed that Puni was actually reading today. I couldn't really see what it was, but the cover looked colorful. His eyes didn't move though. I wondered if he was really reading or just pretending to read so as to fit in with the rest of us.

I went outside and looked near the outhouse. I didn't see him. As much as Golicchio was strange, he wasn't a hermit. He preferred the company of others and the others preferred him. He was a charmer, a storyteller, and naturally he attracted people to him. I often thought that if he were more handsome, like Peepa was, and more confident like Ganesh, he could have been so many things. Perhaps even the next Prime Minister. Maybe even Headmistress Veli would have liked him better than Jaga-Nai. She hardly paid attention to him, and sometimes looked at him as if she didn't know who he was.

I came back inside the House. "Golicchio?" I called softly down the hall. I looked to the left and saw that Mother Jamuna's door was closed. We weren't forbidden from walking by their quarters because our bedroom emptied into their hallway. We had no other way to leave, unless we went outside of the House through the door at the back of our room and came in through the front. We were, however, highly discouraged from loitering, especially in front of the room to the far left (Mother Jamuna's room), since we had no reason to be that far to the side of the House. One boy had been caught listening to a conversation between Mother Jamuna and her mother, although we all found it impossible to imagine her having a mother who had suckled her and rubbed her head to make her sleep. He said that she was very apologetic (again hard to imagine), that she would come visit soon, and that she was happy. Lastly, she promised her mother that she would eat less to attract men. The eavesdropper had been caught and hit across the ears with a very thick tree branch. He had also been sent to the Closet for a day. He never did that again.

I walked by the cafeteria, and I saw Golicchio and Peepa talking. Peepa looked as though he had cornered Golicchio; I couldn't see Golicchio's face to see if he was scared. They hadn't spoken since the "incident," and I was worried that Peepa was going to continue to harass him for as long as he felt like it. I knew what it was like to have a nemesis; I prayed that Golicchio didn't have to understand that feeling either. I contemplated whether or not to enter – I had enough to deal with myself – but Peepa spotted me before I could decide.

"Come," he said, waving his hand in a dismissive way. I saw Golicchio's swollen face – he looked as though someone had asked him to choose which hand he wanted to keep. "I'm trying to ask Golicchio to prove his worth to me – to do something so that I know he is truly sorry for destroying my homework. What do you think he should do? He hasn't come up with any good ideas."

I knew Peepa wouldn't move past all of this without getting something in return. That's how both he and Ganesh were. They enabled each other. Even though there were times when Ganesh and Peepa showed remorse and empathy, deep down, they were programmed to use their status against the others. They couldn't fight their need to eat much less their need to lord over us.

Once, in rare form, Peepa had taken the blame for something that he hadn't done in order to spare Golicchio. One of the Mothers had dropped a parcel by mistake upon returning from a shopping excursion. On that particular day, they had spared no expense, carrying load upon load into the House. One small, circular-shaped box had fallen in the hallway. During our afternoon play time, Golicchio had come across it while going inside the House to retrieve a book. His curiosity had gotten the best of him, so he'd opened the package and inside had found the most spectacular looking hat. The hat glistened and was covered in diamond-looking studs. It was shaped like a boat and had a small white bird at the tip. We hypothesized it was something the Queen of England might wear. As we were all busy fingering it, Mother Jamuna came out of her room and saw us touching and defiling her hat with our dirty hands. She screamed, and we jumped back as though she had taken a broom to us.

"Who touched it first?" she asked. She looked tired, and I felt she was too worn down from shopping to punish us all. She wanted us to tell on each other – that self-inflicted punishment again – and she would take care of one.

"I did," Peepa said. I didn't know why he had spared Golicchio. At first I thought it was because he truly cared about him, but maybe he wanted to show how tough he was to both Mother Jamuna and Ganesh.

"Do something bad, and then have Golicchio take the blame, the way you did with the hat," I said.

Golicchio looked confused, but then he remembered. "Why did you do it then?"

"Do what?" Peepa had forgotten.

"When you took the blame for touching Mother Jamuna's hat that time. Why?" Golicchio asked.

"I don't remember that. I think you may have gotten the story mixed up." I could tell that Peepa was busy thinking about what he wanted Golicchio to do.

"No, it was you," Golicchio insisted. It was as though he needed Peepa to remember that he was a good guy.

"No, it wasn't." He stared at Golicchio hard. It was as though he needed Golicchio to remember that he wasn't a soft guy. "I have it. I'll steal one of Mother Jamuna's pens. Then during class, I'll wear it behind my ear and see if she notices. If she doesn't, you're clear. If she does, I'll tell her you gave it to me. Either way, we're even. Right?" He smiled.

"Right," Golicchio said. They shook hands, and then Peepa put his arm around Golicchio's shoulders, both seemingly relieved that their standoff was over. Friendships were so tenuous in the House. Every day I woke up, I never knew whose side I was going to be on.

Chapter Twenty-One

MY LIFE IS quiet by choice, but children brought noise into my world.

I couldn't be with her when she had them, and my wife didn't understand. Why would she think it would be different if they came from her?

The first – a girl we named *Anandakanu* (Happy Eyes) because her eyes twinkled – made me afraid. The other parents worried about pedophiles; I was terrified that she would become a monster. After the second was born, a boy, I felt similar pressure.

When Anandakanu came home from school one day, I was sitting on the patio, grading papers. My kids regularly fought; I was used to their screams. But it was when I heard the sound of pummeled flesh that I panicked and ran into the house. I found Anandakanu beating my boy with a stick because he had stolen her backpack.

My wife later questioned me as to what happened, but I couldn't remember. I had blacked out entirely. She accused me of drinking again, but she could not find empty bottles or glasses marked with its bitter fragrance.

After Anandakanu went to sleep, my wife told me that I had acted crazily, beaten myself with the handle of a skillet, the welts still visible on my legs and behind. She threatened to leave me, and I almost wanted her to. I felt duped – all along, I had been afraid of my children when it was I who had become the monster.

After that day, I made a promise that I would never expose them to violence again, self-inflicted or not. "And if you do?" my wife asked.

"If I do, I will die," I said.

I need her to remember that though much has happened, I am still a good person.

Chapter Twenty-Two

GIRLS WERE STRANGER than a bird trying to fly without wings. That was the conclusion I had come to after watching the girl in the wooden greenhouse. It was early in the morning, right after breakfast, and nothing seemed to be happening according to schedule. Our morning lessons had been cancelled because Mother Jamuna was sick. Mother Jamuna must have been very ill, we all concurred, because it was rare when the Mothers would cancel lessons on us. They had some odd idea that if our minds were left to their own devices, so would our little members. I didn't really see the correlation.

Of course Golicchio was elated. Peepa had stolen a pen from Mother Jamuna's desk and was ready to carry forth their plan. Unfortunately (or fortunately, depending on whose side you were on) the plan would have to wait another day.

With nothing to do to occupy my time, I sat outside, waiting to see if I could provoke some sort of reaction from the girl. Sometimes she smiled and waved at me; other times, she ignored me as if I didn't exist. In some, this trait engendered lust, but it just perplexed and angered me. How dare she think that she could choose what day of the week to be nice to me? She and I had never exchanged words. All of our communication was non-verbal, and I secretly despised her for these games.

I had just finished cleaning my clothing and was forced to put on my wet clothes quickly in case Jaga-Nai tried to steal them. I hadn't seen him for most of the morning, except during breakfast when he made sure to spit on my leaf. I pretended it was chutney. The clothes made me cold, and I was frustrated that every little thing had to be made more difficult for me. So when I saw her, and she was being her usual standoffish self, I grew irritated. I wasn't going to tolerate it today. I thought about approaching her, perhaps scaring her a little. My mother always said I could make a mean face when I wanted. She said I took after my father in that way.

Inside the shed, I noticed that whoever had stocked the greenhouse had piled pot upon pot of plants. Some of them, the more twisty ones, were growing on top and around each other. The smaller ones were suffocating. The jasmine flower, however, was thriving. It grew along the sides of the shed, reaching for the walls as though wanting and needing to escape. Because she was as dark as a burnt dosai, the girl looked sinister against the white of the flowers. As I watched her, she didn't appear to be doing anything. She held a water can, but as far as I could tell, it didn't contain any water. Nothing came out when she tipped it.

She looked at me again, and I waved at her, trying to get her to see my scowl. This time, she stared as if she didn't recognize me, and then continued to "water" the plants.

"What are you doing?" Puni asked. He looked and knew instantly. His eyes couldn't stop staring.

"Nothing."

"How come that girl doesn't ever come into the House? Where does she come from? Who is she? I must know." I had never seen Puni so adamant about knowing something. I halfway felt that it was his eyes that had this power over him. He needed to know about something that he couldn't stop staring at. It was the only way he could create physical balance.

"I don't know. I'm trying to find out, but this girl is not very nice." At this point, she had to know that now two boys were staring at her. I saw her touch her skirt.

"No, she's not. Did Ganesh ever tell you he once shouted at her, asking her name, and she ignored him? Not one word. And you know she could hear him. Ganesh is loud." Puni's eyes fixed on me. I secretly felt a little happier knowing that her meanness wasn't directed just at me.

"Yes," I said.

"I don't like people like that. People who make you feel invisible."

"But the Mothers make us feel like that too," I said.

"That's why I don't like them either. I hate the way they think we can't see how fat their bellies are growing while the rest of us grow thinner. As though we are all invisible to their greed." I saw a little spit fan out from the side of his mouth. I had never really seen Puni this angry or vocal. Most of the time, he was silent.

"Are you all right?" By now, the girl had gone.

"I'm hungry," he said. "I'm so hungry that I can't even think. How do the Mothers expect us to do our homework if our minds are fixated on eating?"

I shook my head. My mind was consumed with Jaga-Nai, so I didn't really understand his pain, although I could partially relate. There were days that I felt so hungry chewing on my fingernails provided some sort of relief.

"Yrimal, when I lived at home, at night when I was asleep, a fairy would come and steal my fat away from me," he said.

"What? You've been listening to too many of Golicchio's stories."

"No, I'm telling you the truth. There were times when I woke up to scars on my body, places where the fat had been removed. My parents always told me it was the fat fairy because too many children in India were hungry, and because I was so fat, the fat fairy would come and take some of my fat to give to those children. I told them to stop the fairy because I would rather have given away my food than pieces of my body, but they said the fairy was divine, and that there was nothing that they could do about it." He lifted his shirt and there were numerous slash marks all across his belly, under his arms, and even on his thighs as he rolled up his shorts. I was shocked that I had never noticed his wounds before.

"Did you ever bleed after she had visited?" I silently thanked Hanuman, the monkey god, for being born skinny.

"Yes, and my parents had to take me to the doctor frequently. The doctors – they never cared about me – we barely had enough money to go, so there came a time when we stopped, and they would bandage me makeshift. Sometimes I would bleed into the night, sleeping in my own blood, my fingers used to stop the seeping."

"What happened?"

"It didn't stop. I had to find out who this fairy was. So I stayed awake one night. She never came. And then another, and another. She never came. I realized then that the moment I slept she would come for me, and I couldn't have that, so I never slept."

"Wouldn't you have woken up to the sting of a knife? How come you never saw her then?"

"Sometimes I think the fairy drugged me. I don't think she was a good fairy."

"I don't think so either."

He looked at me again, and I saw deep sadness and pain in those eyes that I had previously been so much in awe of. I felt pity for his strength.

"I'm sorry," I said.

"Why? I'm still fat, so she didn't win," he squealed and ran off. I could imagine a little curly tail on his round butt.

I HAD RESUMED my reading of *Revelations*. I couldn't bear to not know what happened next. It was better than completing the homework that Mother Kalpana had given us. I still wasn't sure how I was going to write about a story that I had barely been able to follow. I thought maybe I could get inspiration from my book.

I tried not to touch the pages too much as I turned them. I used a rock taken from the yard to hold the pages down as I read. I also tried to hold my nose, but after I became engrossed in the book I forgot, and the stench forced me to remember again. I was getting to a good part though, so it didn't matter. The main character, Amit, had just told his mother that he was superhuman. She didn't believe him, and she threw him out of the house. He was gathering his things when I felt a tap on my shoulder. It was Mother Jamuna, her nose running, her face more bloated than usual. I panicked.

"Siddhartha, come with me," she said. Her voice sounded soft because of the phlegm that coated it. I followed her into her room, my brain relying on its muscle memory to get me there. I was used to her room, the surroundings a reflection of her sloth and gluttony. She frequently asked me to clean it since I had never stolen anything or tried to look through her things. She also liked the way I cleaned: slow and thorough, but she didn't realize that I had to. She kept her room unlike the way bees kept their nests.

The walls were painted a deep yellow, the color of ghee; yet most days, the paint was stained by dust, appearing as though the walls were growing a type of urine fungi. If time had lapsed since my last cleaning, I would find crumbs lining the baseboards, adding to the look of mold. Her clothes often were heaped in piles, and because she was a large woman, it didn't take many saris to form mounds larger than I. I disliked cleaning her room because she took the least good care of it, but because she was the most irresponsible in that regard, I had to do it more often than for the others.

She plopped onto her bed and asked me to grab a wet towel that was on her desk. It smelled like mint and cilantro and was covered in a greenish paste.

"Bring that here, and hold it close to my nose so that I can breathe," she said. So I stood there holding it over her nose as she slept. When my arm got tired, and I brought it down, she woke and scolded me. "Do that again and I'll send you to the hole!" she yelled. I tried to think of something else as I held the rag. My shoulders grew numb, and I became fidgety. I switched hands carefully, and when I knew she had fallen into a deep sleep, I let my arms rest. I waited a few minutes, and then I held it again. I thought of Puni and his story, and I gradually lost track of time. When she eventually woke, the sun was setting, and it was getting dark.

She grabbed the towel from me, and before she sent me away, she told me to open the top drawer of her desk. I did, and I found a box of brown candies.

"Take one," she said. I did, but I wasn't sure what she wanted me to do with it. "Eat it, you idiot," she yelled. "Get out before I take it back." I ran off and down the hall. I found that dinner was being served, and that all of my friends were in the cafeteria. I held the chocolate tightly and walked inside. All of the food was already gone.

"Here," Golicchio said. He waved, and I saw that he'd saved one idli for me on his leaf. "Puni said you were with Mother Jamuna, so I saved you one." I grabbed it.

"What do you have there, eh?" Jaga-Nai asked. He and his friends walked over. Golicchio shrank back. I closed my hands into fists. "Open your hands," he demanded.

"No," I said. The candy in my hand was melting; I could feel it.

"Open your hands!" he yelled. I showed him my palms, and the idli dropped out of one. The other hand contained the candy, its brown goo smeared all over. "What's that, eh?" He grabbed my hand and took a closer look. He sniffed at it. Then he licked my hand and kept licking until it was clean. I giggled. His tongue tickled my hand.

"What's so funny, eh?" he asked. Then he slapped me. I felt my face with my chocolate-coated hand, forgetting, and it left a sticky print.

"Ha," Jaga-Nai said, smacking his lips. He snapped his fingers, and the rest of his friends followed him outside.

"What was that?" Golicchio asked.

"Mother Jamuna gave me one of her candies because I helped her while she was sick. I deserved that. He didn't." I rubbed at my shoulders. They were sore, and my wrists tingled.

"Ask her for another one. I think she's nicer when she's sick."

"I can't ask her for another one. She'll send me to the Closet."

"Ask her, what can you lose? She can't send you to the Closet if Jaga-Nai stole it. Just tell her that he stole it."

"And if he finds out that I told on him? Isn't that worse than the Closet?"

"No," Golicchio said quickly.

I thought about it. I was hungry, and the smell and feel of the chocolate made me hunger for it, even though I knew I would be setting myself up for problems with Jaga-Nai.

"I will try." I hoped that Mother Jamuna's door would still be open. I didn't want to have to knock, especially if she was asleep.

As I crept toward her room, I grew anxious. I was afraid Mother Jamuna would ask me to hold her rag all night. When would I sleep? Would my arms fall off? I hadn't thought about that.

"Sid, come here," I heard a woman whisper. I turned, and it was Headmistress Veli, beckoning me with her finger, luring me into her room. I was happy to be distracted.

"Where were you going?" she asked. Her dark eyes looked glossy.

"To see Mother Jamuna. She gave me a chocolate, and Jaga-Nai took it away, and—" I started to choke up, but I contained myself.

"Shh," she said. She took out a tray of chocolates, similar to the ones that Mother Jamuna had. "Take as many as you want. But eat them here, in case Jagadesh steals more." I looked at her, then down at the chocolates, and then up at her again. We were lucky that not all of the Mothers were mean. So I took one, then two, then three. Then eventually I lost count. I ate so many, I grew full off of their sweetness. As I engorged myself on butter and milk, Headmistress Veli just stared at me, smiling. She liked watching me eat.

After I was done consuming the entire tray of chocolates, she said, "Next time you want something sweet, come here, promise?"

"Yes," I said, smiling. I could feel the chocolate covering my teeth. She put her arm around me and guided me into the hallway.

"Good night," she said, kissing me on the cheek. I felt warm.

Chapter Twenty-Three

THOUGH MY WIFE and I have many friends, I find it hard to be close with any of them.

Can two people find true friendship without the trauma of experience? My life is undemanding. I go to work and then come home. My wife is an artist. The paintings midway – before they are fully completed – look like miniature brains rimmed in flames. She calls me her muse, but I find her work dark, muddied. When I tell her that, she says that is what captivates her.

"To be dark is to be textured," she says, and I find myself longing for Golicchio.

Chapter Twenty-Four

WHEN I LIVED with my parents, we had a dog we named Murukku because he resembled the crispy, rice-flour snack. Murukku was nothing like the dogs they had here.

I had always loved dogs. They were the only creatures I knew that didn't allow anything to affect their love for you. In fact, they put your well-being ahead of their own. I always felt that my parents – especially my father – could have learned a thing or two from our dog.

Our dog was yellow, and he would sometimes curl himself into the most contorted positions that he actually did look like a canine murukku. He never seemed in pain though. He seemed to take pleasure in the fact that the rest of us worried about him hurting himself.

The dogs at the House, however, were of an entirely different variety. I didn't know much about breeds of dogs, but I was sure that these were bred to be angry. They were white dogs, completely white, as if they had been bleached by Fair and Lovely Cream. Their eyes were very dark. Black even. The contrast was terrifying.

The dogs were chained for most of the day while the Mothers stayed inside getting fat. Dogs that size didn't do well being confined, so when they were finally "released" in the evening, they were looking for ways to discharge their tension. They never barked. Those were the dogs that you had to watch out for. Dogs were similar to people in this way. Those who were quiet were the ones to fear because they were the ones who kept everything inside, silently raging. Eventually all that anger exploded, and who would be the unsuspecting culprit?

Mother Jamuna – they must've been her dogs because she was the only one who tended to their needs – was the one who fed and dared to stroke them. She was also the one to set them loose upon us.

"They're for your own protection," Mother Jamuna said when one of us had been bitten in the ear. The victimized boy hadn't made his pre-bedtime pit stop and risked going at night, surrounded by dogs. He was lucky. The attack could've been a lot worse.

"Who do they protect us from? You?" Jaga-Nai asked.

"You boys are so ignorant, think you know what's out there in the world. The real world is scary. You have it better here. Instead of being grateful, all you do is complain and make it more difficult for all of us to take care of you. Do you think we do this for some reward? Do you think we get paid a lot of money? We do this because we care. And if the dogs weren't here, villains would be here. They would snatch you in your sleep and sell you on the black market as laborers, or worse, as whores. Do you want to be a male whore to other men? Do you?" At this, some of the younger boys started to cry. They had no tact. They treated us all the same when it suited them and different when it suited them. Age didn't seem to be a separating factor as much as our caste was.

"The next time I hear one of you complain about these dogs again, I will let them feast on your hands." She walked (or more like shuffled since she was so fat) away, and the rest of us had stared at each other.

"Mother Jamuna," I'd said after her. My voice was clear since the rest of us had grown so silent with our thoughts.

"What?"

"What are their names?" I asked.

For the first time since coming to the House, I saw her smile. Her smile could've set my balls on fire. It was the ugliest thing I'd ever seen, far uglier than the warts that my father had developed in between the lumps of fat that formed around his neck.

"Durga, Kali, Lakshmi, named after the three most powerful god-desses in Hinduism." Then she had left for good. I shuddered. Female dogs were worse than I had imagined.

On this particular day, Golicchio, Puni, and I sat at the tables out-side, debating how the dogs got that mean and why they weren't mean to Mother Jamuna. Our lesson that morning had been arithmetic – double the work – since we had missed the day before. Mother Kalpana was angry that we weren't able to complete her assignment, so she had assigned more math problems than usual. We had plenty to do, but none of us felt like working.

"What did she say the dogs were called?" Puni asked. He looked at them growling at us. They were tied to the fence that ran along the back of the yard. They were given a small bowl of water, leftovers from the day (scraps of our food), and a red ball. They hardly touched the ball. They preferred staring at us.

"They were named after deities. They are not of this world," Golicchio said. "Why did you ask her their names? I could care less."

"I don't know. I had a dog once. They respond well when you call their names."

"Let's try," Puni said. He shrieked, "Parvati, Lakshmi!" Only one of the dogs lifted its head.

"I don't think those names are right," I said. "Durga, Kali," I said in a baby voice. Golicchio and Puni laughed at me. The dogs were confused at first, but then barked in unison.

"Get them to be quiet otherwise Mother Jamuna will come and scold us!" Golicchio screamed.

"Just stop staring at them," I said. "They don't like it." Golicchio and I turned away, but Puni continued to look. "Stop!" I yelled at him, trying to force him around. He didn't budge.

"They have more food than I did today," he whispered.

"So, do you want to become dog meat?" Golicchio asked.

"They'd rather eat human flesh. These aren't divinities – they are evil."

Puni couldn't stop looking at their food bowl and started to move closer to them. We tried to pull him back, but he was too big and strong for us. Mother Jamuna must have heard the barking and stepped into the yard. She clipped Puni on the side of the head.

"Respect for elders includes respecting their things," she said. She grabbed a fallen tree branch and dragged him inside.

"Food will be the end of him," Golicchio said. His prediction was eerie, and I felt shivers run up and down the back of my neck.

"Puni knows his limits. He knows when to stop."

"Since when are you so hopeful?" Golicchio looked at me sideways. I did the same, and we both laughed.

"I don't know. People learn from their mistakes."

"Wrong. History shows that people do not. People repeat the same behaviors over and over and over. That is why a father who is abused as a child ends up abusing his own." He looked serious.

"How do you know that?" The Mothers didn't teach us much about history.

"From watching people. You can learn a lot from observing generations. You don't need a history book to learn from."

"I think people are better than that."

"Perhaps some are. But the overwhelming majority is not."

"And Peepa? In which camp does he belong?"

"I don't know." Since their "agreement," Golicchio had been waiting for Peepa to walk into class with a pen from Mother Jamuna's desk. Since, however, no pen had surfaced – although I knew it was only a matter of time.

"I think he's waiting, when she's really pissed."

"Or maybe he's decided to let the whole thing go."

"I thought you were the one who believed the worst in people?" I asked.

"I don't. I am just saying that most of the time, people turn."

"And in which camp do I belong?" I asked.

"I don't know yet." He looked at me. "I think good."

"You think?"

"You never know. The ones closest to you are the ones that you should be most fearful of."

I laughed. "You have been reading too many horror stories." Headmistress Veli enjoyed gory novels; she was kind enough to leave the discards for the rest of us, however inappropriate they may have been.

"Yes, you're right," he said, putting his hand on my shoulder. We heard a scream come from inside, and we knew that Puni was receiving his punishment.

"Let's get our books and read," I said.

We sat on the grass in the late afternoon, Golicchio enjoying a book on the devil's children, and I continuing to read my dirty book. Amit had left his house, and his mother saw him fly away. My heart pounded so fast I felt I was going to pass out – in a good way. I wished I could fly away, too. Lately, I dreamt of being airborne, floating above the Mothers' fat faces, saying goodbye to the misery that I saw here. Sometimes Golicchio came along, sometimes Jaga-Nai. In the dreams, Jaga-Nai was always gentle. He was my equal, and he listened to me. We talked about things that were important, but I could never remember what when I awoke. How I hated to wake up.

We heard the rustle of shorts on shorts and saw Puni pushed into the yard from inside. He showed us his war injuries. Mostly, Mother Jamuna had contained her beatings to his back, although she'd gotten lazy and the stick had made its way down his backside too. She was careful not to leave any visible bruises.

Most of us, after such an ordeal, wished to be alone or silent. The pain throbbed, and we didn't want to focus our energies on anything other than recuperation. Puni was different though. He needed people afterward. He needed to talk about it, show us. He needed us to listen to him and be sympathetic toward him. It was hard not to be. His soft flesh felt the blows more than Ganesh's rough hide or my thin one.

"She gave me fifteen blows. Five each for the dogs." He sighed. His voice seemed deeper.

"That doesn't seem fair," I said.

Golicchio laughed. "What is?"

"She said the dogs were worth more than I ever would be." We waited. We knew there'd be more to come. "She said she loved those dogs more than she'd ever love any of us, and especially me. She said that when Brahma ran out of good parts, he was forced to make me with the leftover parts, which is why I am so ugly and fat." He stopped to catch his breath. He didn't normally talk so much and it wore him out. "She said all of that while she hit me, and I counted each one. Each one lasted an eternity."

"They always do," Golicchio said. We sat with our books open, not really reading them. I forgot about Amit. Instead, I saw Puni's head, and it was covered in sweat. He was shivering.

"You all right?" I asked. I touched his back. He felt very hot.

"Yes," he said. He stood up. "I'm going to go lie down."

"But dinner?" Golicchio asked. Puni shook his head and walked inside. Golicchio and I looked at each other in surprise.

Chapter Twenty-Five

"Do you think I am evil?" I ask my wife one night. She is covered in paint from head to toe. She had a particularly good day, and on evenings like these, she continues to work all night. I envy her. I wish I could turn my sleeplessness into something productive.

"No, why?" she asks.

"Because one day, a long time ago, some kids thought I was."

She comes to me and wipes her hands, waxy with oil, on my face. "That was a long time ago," she says softly, and I know she wants me to tell her more.

"No, it wasn't," I say, and she crawls in beside me, her papery white skin leaving a trail of flakes on my chest.

She kisses me, and I kiss her back, forcefully. It has taken many years to erase the image of her face. Every now and then, I suffer a relapse, but I try to focus on my wife instead. Her eyes are a gentle brown, and she is tender, in both body and touch.

She is the only woman I have been with who understands why I must cry afterward. She waits, and I can hear the soothing clicks of her tongue. When I am done, I hug her tightly; I need her to be close to me, and sometimes she isn't near enough.

"I love you more than you know," I say, but she already knows that.

Chapter Twenty-Six

"Anyone in there? Please?" I heard a girl's voice begging me to take leave of the outhouse. The voice was deep, dark, and innocent.

"Wait," I said. When I stepped out, I saw the girl – the one from the greenhouse – standing, her face contorted, jumping up and down on both feet. She rushed in past me and didn't bother to shut the door. I saw her squatting, but I turned away. It was funny how people were kind when they required favors.

"Why don't you just use the Mothers' bathroom? They have their own. Rumor has it that it's modeled after the United States. You sit down on the toilet. I think that's unclean."

"Headmistress Veli wouldn't let me use it. I don't like her." She walked away, so I followed her into the wooden house without thinking. I was surprised that someone disliked Headmistress Veli. Most of us boys couldn't get enough of her.

Up close, she was small, but her face wasn't as young as I had thought. I wondered how old she was. She spoke and moved in a carefree way that was unlike what I was used to in the House. I was certain that she was related to one of the Mothers.

"Do you ever wish you were a bird?" she asked.

"Yes," I said. "I dream about flying."

"Where do you go? If I could, I would go up into the sky, as far up as I could go. My father lives there. He died."

"Anywhere but here." I looked at her more carefully. She almost seemed as old as I was. But it was hard to tell with girls.

"But where?"

"Not sure. I don't think about things like that."

"Why?"

"You ask too many questions."

"That's what girls do. We ask questions and expect answers."

"Boys don't talk much."

"That's not true. Nirmal talks."

"You talk to Peepa?"

"Nirmal. Yes, I do. He visits me."

"And you talk to him?"

"Didn't I just say that?"

I looked around. I was afraid that the Mothers would catch us talking. I walked behind the outhouse, hoping she would follow. I was used to Golicchio and Puni's way of speaking, their thoughts, their questions. Speaking with this girl provided a brief respite from what I was used to, the day-to-day mundane. Even if she didn't provide the intelligent insight that Golicchio did, she was still *different* – a distraction.

"Can you give Nirmal a message?" She had a look in her eyes that reminded me of Headmistress Veli: a sort of yearning for something that was forbidden, which was how Golicchio had phrased it. Puni called it the look fat people got when they ran out of fried food.

"We don't talk. He doesn't like me. Why don't you give him the message since you talk to him so much?"

"I don't know when I'll see him next. Sometimes I see him every day, and sometimes we go for days without speaking. He's unpredictable." She kept the same look in her eyes, and I grew disgusted.

"What, are you in love with him or something?"

She slapped me. "How dare you ask me something like that?"

I slapped her back the way I used to do to Smita. My sister liked hitting me on the face all the time because she liked the sound it made. When she was smaller, I tolerated it because it didn't hurt. As she grew bigger and her hands wider, the sting smarted, and I began to hit back. Hitting her grew to be second nature, and when her hand would raise up as if to slap me, I would hit her first. I never knew if she meant to hit me, but I didn't take the chance.

The girl started to cry. Smita did the same, and she garnered sympathy from my father, who would beat my behind until it looked like a slab of date paste. I had learned long ago not to fall victim to her attempts at pity, and I wasn't going to do the same for this girl.

"You are a bad person, just like he says," she whispered. She backed away from me, fear in her eyes. I was not used to this. Smita, though she hated me for what I did to her, never feared me. She knew I was her older brother and that I would never harm her.

I crept closer, putting my hands up like the real Buddha, letting her know through my actions that I had not meant to harm her.

"Get away," she said.

"I didn't mean—"

"Get away!" she screamed and ran into the House. Moments later, like flies to a pile of shit, Mother Jamuna came running, a stick in her hand.

"Did you hit her?" she asked. Her cold had subsided, and she had residual rivers of mucus that fled down her long face.

"No," I said. It didn't matter what I said. I knew that I would get punished.

She dragged me to the very spot where I had been talking to the girl and began whipping me with the stick. I held my shorts up with my left hand, and she yanked it away. My shorts fell, and she hit me on my backside. I smiled.

After her arm grew tired, she made me sit outside until nighttime. She knew that the weight of my body upon my bruises would offer even more punishment than her tired arms could. I sat and the pain throbbed through my body like a bolt of electricity. They were all the same, I thought, as I looked up at the stars. I counted each one and decided that my mother was wrong. There was a star for every woman that could make your life a living hell. I cursed the girl and wished that I had left her pleading, shitting her pants for all the world to see.

THIS TIME, PUNI was the one who consoled me. After dinnertime, he came to use the outhouse and found me sitting next to it. He knew something bad had happened, but none of them knew what. When I told him, he nodded.

"Did you have any sisters?" I asked him. He shook his head no. Getting Puni to talk sometimes required great effort unless he was angry or upset. I forced myself to engage though in order to forget that Puni had brought me nothing to eat.

"And your mother? What was she like?" Puni sat, his eyes staring at the dogs. They weren't unleashed yet. I assumed that when Mother Jamuna came to let them loose, she would permit me to return inside the House to sleep.

"Kind."

"My mother was too. The bits that I remember anyway."

"Yes." He turned his eyes to me. "She was good, and so was my father. I don't have a sad story like the rest." He waved at the House.

"But what about the fat fairy?"

He waved his hands about again. "She had nothing to do with my parents."

"But how come they couldn't protect you?"

"I don't know." He blinked once. "If she wasn't human, then what could they have done?"

"Were you the only one?" He nodded yes. "Lucky," I said.

He shrugged his shoulders.

"You don't call that lucky?"

"No. I don't call being here lucky."

"I didn't mean now, I meant—"

"I know what you meant," he said, cutting me off. "Why must you all live in the past still? We're here now. My parents were good, but my life now is without them. So why talk about them? Why talk about any of that?"

"What do you want to talk about then?"

"Nothing. I just want to sit here and not feel so hungry that I could eat you."

"All right," I said. I looked at him, and in an odd way, he did look happy. His eyes stared, but not at the dogs. Instead, they looked at the trees, the plants in the shed, anything green. He seemed to be taking it all in, reveling in the fact that he was among nature, and this time, it wasn't going to harm us.

Sadly, those sorts of feelings never lasted.

"Come inside," Mother Jamuna said. I looked back at Puni, and his eyes had lost that glow. He looked scared and scurried inside, the way a mouse does when exposed to light. I slowly got up, my bones stiff from sitting for so long. I tried not to moan or sigh. I knew if I did, Mother Jamuna would get some secret satisfaction out of knowing that she'd hurt me. I walked slowly into the House. When I turned to look, Mother Jamuna was stroking the dogs, kissing them on the noses as she prepared to unchain them.

Chapter Twenty-Seven

THOUGH AMMA HAD saved me, our backyard is what nurtures me. My wife is a city person – she grew up in Los Angeles, but the foot traffic and congestion are suffocating to me. There is too much to absorb, and I do not have Puni's eyes.

I prefer the outdoors. Our house has a large backyard, which is where I cultivate my garden and grow trees. When the children play too roughly, I retreat outside. When my wife bothers me with questions, I sit in the rocker that we have on the patio and glide back and forth. I look at the birds and wonder if they were there with me. I particularly enjoy the crows. They look older now, and maybe wiser. They don't caw at me, but instead look at me with surprise. I don't blame them.

Chapter Twenty-Eight

I WAS SURPRISED that we didn't get into as much trouble as we could have. I believed that the amount of punishment it would have taken to quell our naughty curiosities would've far surpassed the manpower and energy that the Mothers possessed, which was why they weren't consistent in enforcing the rules. Whenever the Mothers turned their backs, we were up to no good snooping around their rooms. After we had discovered the immense amount of alcohol that the Mothers – especially Headmistress Veli – stored in their rooms, that was the first place we went, and we took every opportunity we had.

Fortunately, Mother Jamuna's sickness was making its way around the House, which gave us plenty more occasions to be disobedient. We boys seemed immune to the wandering cold – Golicchio said that it was some sort of old person sickness – and his suspicions were confirmed when Mother Kalpana was next. Since she was very ill, she had taken to her bed, and all day, all we could hear was her snoring. The sound of her punctuated breaths of air even made its way down the hall and to the yard. The rest of the Mothers had left in an auto for town because, according to Mother Jamuna, the doctor had prescribed some special antibiotics, which they had to travel into the city to purchase. We were to be on our best behavior, and even though Mother Kalpana was sick, we were told she was still watching us.

Ganesh "tested" her words by visiting Mother Kalpana in her room. He told us he went close to her face, and even waved a hand in front of her eyes. He said she was about as conscious as a dead person. So feeling safe in exploring, we decided to take over Headmistress Veli's room, since she had the biggest selection of alcohol and pornographic materials of all the other Mothers combined.

Golicchio, of course, always abstained. I suspected that his father had had a drinking problem. "They will find out," he said. "They have all of your finger marks memorized and will know which of you touched which bottle. They even have lip marks. They will know whose lips drank from which bottles." Golicchio couldn't be convinced, and because the Mothers could return at any moment, he declined to participate. After he left, we looked at each other, me at Puni, Ganesh at Peepa, wondering if what Golicchio said had any truth to it.

"What does he know," Ganesh said. "He makes up stories." We all laughed but I found that statement strange coming from Ganesh who was Golicchio's most passionate fan.

"Let's try gin." Peepa smacked his lips and reached for the large bottle.

I heard a squeal, and Puni had already made his way into one of the darker-colored bottles. The insides had been filled with peppers.

"Owww, this is hot!" he screamed. I didn't like when Puni drank. His normally opaque eyes would gloss over, giving him the appearance of a person who had died while his eyes were still open. Especially now, with his face and arms bruised from Mother Jamuna's beatings, his pores became larger, making the abuse more visible. I also didn't like how he'd howl for food afterward. Alcohol seemed to make us all a little hungrier. Most of us could handle that. Puni couldn't.

"Just a little at a time, stupid," Ganesh said, and he grabbed the bottle away from his hands. The trick was to just siphon a little bit at a time. The Mothers wouldn't know unless they measured and because of our tiny frames, even a little bit went a long way.

"What should I try?"

"Your own urine," Peepa said and laughed. He was already drunk, but I didn't find that funny at all.

Because I did not consider Headmistress Veli one of the bad Mothers, I hesitated to physically open any of her drawers or sift through her things. I preferred it when she left half-drunk bottles on the table, visible for us to to take, or booklets of naughty pictures scattered on the bed. In this way, I didn't feel so guilty about enjoying her things. She'd left a handful of posters, unrolled and taped to the floor of her room. The images were of men and women, half-naked, holding each other in awkward poses. The women were svelte and light-colored; the men were dark and brawny. My eyes fixated on the men's members, wondering if mine would ever grow as large.

Ganesh came up behind me and put his arm around my shoulders, as if I were Peepa. I suspected he was already drunk too. "She always has the best," he said. I nodded. Sometimes I felt as though she left these pornographic materials in conspicuous places because she wanted us to find them and read them.

I then noticed a small purple bottle sitting next to Headmistress Veli's nightstand. The cap was off, red lipstick smudged along the rim. I took a little taste by pouring a small amount down my throat. It tasted like mint and cherry and salt all rolled into one. I turned to look for Puni, to offer him a little, but he and the others were enamored with her posters. They'd uncovered some more underneath her bed – ones of just women with other women.

I drank a few more drops and stopped. I became dizzy. I knew I had ingested something potentially toxic, and I was afraid that I might get sick.

"What's wrong with Yrimal? He looks like he's ill," Ganesh said. He came to me and slapped my face a few times. I tried to smile, but my face was numb. "Are you all right? Can you hear me?" I heard him mumble, "Stupid."

"Is my tongue still in my mouth?" I asked. I stuck it out. It felt slimy and heavy. Peepa came over and rubbed it.

"Feels like the side of a rough wall," he said. "What did you drink?"

"I don't know," I said. Whatever it was worked fast. I remembered Ganesh and Peepa leaving the room, Puni looking at me and the door, and then leaving too. Before I completely passed out, I made my way into Headmistress Veli's bed. Strands of her hair covered the pillow, and I rubbed my face into it. Her sheets smelled like coconut, and I fell instantly asleep.

When I came to, Mother Jamuna and Mother Kalpana were standing over me. Mother Kalpana had a rag in her left hand that was soaking wet, and Mother Jamuna looked as though she wanted to eat me. She pinched my bruised butt, and I yelped.

"Get out of her bed right now," she said very quietly.

"Let him sleep. It's fine. He's a clean boy," Headmistress Veli said. She was in the corner of her room, holding the posters underneath her arm and fluffing her teddy bears. I could see her reach and tap her fingers against the bottles inside, making a *clink clink* noise.

"You spoil these kids. You do. Leave them alone. They need to learn right from wrong and if you give them everything they want, they will never learn."

"But the street is not one-way, Jamuna."

She ignored Headmistress Veli and said, "Siddhartha, get up right now." She dragged me out of the bed by my ear. Now I felt I had lost my ear as well as my tongue. "What were you doing in this room? What were you drinking? Lately you've become such a bad boy. Beating you doesn't seem to do anything to stop you. Perhaps I need to send you to the hole."

"No, please," Headmistress Veli said. "Just take away one of his books. That'll serve as enough punishment for him. He didn't act alone. Siddhartha is too gentle and weak."

"Get out," Mother Jamuna said and pushed me into the hallway. I then heard Mother Jamuna and Headmistress Veli yell at each other, their sweet voices corrupted by anger. I tried to block out the noise by covering my ears, but I couldn't tell where they were. I was still groggy, and I fell against the cold concrete. I tried to rouse myself awake. My head pounded, and my face felt like paper. I was rubbing myself, trying to find where my body separated and became distinct parts, when Jaga-Nai jumped me. He stuck his face into mine, and I screamed. I didn't know if he was real or a product of my drinking.

"Shut up," he said. He pinched my ears, and I was relieved that I could still feel them.

"I saw them throw you from Headmistress Veli's room. What were you doing in there, eh?" He gave me a chance to answer, but I didn't think he really cared if I did. "Look at what I found in your pockets, you spoiled shit," he said. He lifted out packets of chili nuts. My mouth watered, but I wasn't as hungry as I should have been. I deduced that Headmistress Veli had probably given me something to eat in my semi-state of consciousness.

"What are you doing to her that she treats you so well?"

"I haven't done anything. We were all caught in her room, that's it. The rest of them left me there. She just caught me."

"Why were you in her bed? Eh?" He was asking me with such ferocity, for a moment I had to remind myself that I wasn't talking to Headmistress Veli's husband but a fellow orphan – a very angry orphan.

"I got sick. I needed to rest."

"You are always doing that – always playing up your weaknesses to get what you want. Maybe I should do that." He started howling and whining, writhing in pain on the ground.

"Oh, I'm in so much pain, please help," he cried. I looked on in bewilderment. I wasn't sure what exactly was going on. I felt paranoid.

One of the Mothers walked by. She looked at Jaga-Nai, shook her head, and walked past. Jaga-Nai moaned even louder until we heard Mother Jamuna yell, "Fucker shut up otherwise I will sew your mouth closed!"

He stopped instantly. It wasn't out of fear – no, I was quite sure of that. It was surprise. He was so sure that if he feigned weakness as he thought I did, he would get whatever special treatment I had received. The thing was, I really didn't nor had ever received special treatment. It was all in his head, but I couldn't explain that to a dog.

He ran his fingers along my arm and held my slim wrist between his thumb and index finger. His hands were thick and dirty. I knew he could break my wrist with a flip motion if he wanted.

"You have such slender wrists, like a girl's." He laughed. "So pretty." He leaned down and sank his teeth into my arm. I screamed.

"Will the Mothers answer your calls if you cry? Let's see," he said. He continued to bite down harder and harder. Blood started going everywhere. All I could see was red, red, red. I tried to push him away.

"Someone help me," I said. I saw Golicchio's odd-shaped head in the hallway. He looked scared, but I knew he wouldn't run away. He would help me.

"Stop it, Jaga-Nai. Leave him alone," he said.

"Or else what, ugly eyes?" Jaga-Nai bared his fangs at Golicchio. His teeth were red.

"Mother Jamuna, please come here! Jaga-Nai is attacking Yrimal!" he screamed at the top of his lungs. I was afraid that Mother Jamuna would ignore him the way she had ignored Jaga-Nai. Did she even care if I was being attacked?

"How many times do I have to tell you little..." she stopped cursing enough to see that I was being assaulted. The blood was slowly draining from my body, and the feeling of floating about the House returned. She grabbed Jaga-Nai, slapped him several times, and dragged him away. He didn't utter one sound. As I lay there in my own growing pool of blood, I heard Golicchio whisper in my ear, "Be calm, be calm." He applied pressure to my wrist and rocked back and forth.

When a government-appointed nurse finally arrived, she commended Golicchio on his medical knowledge.

"I'm glad you applied pressure to the wound. If you hadn't, he could've bled to death." The others would have let me die. That was how little I mattered to them.

The nurse, who looked rather young and inexperienced, applied several stitches to my wrist and before she left, said that she didn't understand why kids like me were always getting into fights. If we were good, then maybe we would amount to something. But yet we were destined to always be at the bottom because we put ourselves there. I tuned her out.

IT WAS HARD to eat on my own. I relied immensely on Golicchio's help. For the first time in a long time, I was thankful that he was my friend. Of course the others teased us, making jokes that Golicchio was now my wife and would he lick my this and that. I just shut them out.

Golicchio (with his fingers) spooned soggy pieces of idli and banana onto my leaf, and I, as clumsy as he, used my left hand to eat it. Fortunately for us, most of the boys didn't like idli, especially when no chutney was provided with it. Even Mother Jamuna's dogs didn't like it. The type they served was dry and hard, but if we soaked it in whatever fruit or vegetable curry we were given, the idli broke down and became less like wood and more like actual food. The others weren't as creative with their food, and as a result, the Mothers couldn't get rid of it. We were left with piles and piles of idli. Golicchio had stacks on his leaf; I had stacks on mine. Puni didn't mind either. I kept eating and eating as fast as Golicchio could spoon me my share and eat his own.

"Remember what that nurse said? Do you think she's right? That we deserve what we get?" Golicchio asked me.

"No, I don't believe it. People make excuses for other people's situations. If things changed for us, you know they'd change for people like her too."

"That's true. But there are people who have a lot who don't mind sharing."

"Who are those people? I've never met them."

"When my father would drink, there were always other men who would supply him with alcohol, free of charge. Why would they do that?"

"That's completely different. I'm talking about money and food. Not alcohol."

"Yes, but alcohol isn't cheap," Golicchio said. "Especially for someone like my father. He wouldn't have been able to afford it if it hadn't
been bought for him."

"Do you think these men were trying to deliberately get him drunk?"

"Maybe. But for what purpose? These men, even though they had a
little bit more money, were in the same predicament as my father was."

"I know when we drink, certain boys feel powerful over others. I, on
the other hand, feel very powerless. I have no control over my thoughts,
my body. Anyone could come in and take advantage of me. That's what
happened."

"I told you not to drink. It's your fault that all of this happened."

"Now you sound like the nurse, Golicchio."

"I still think she made sense. If my father hadn't gotten drunk all the
time, we would've been better. He put himself in that situation. He made
himself an invalid, not being able to earn money for us. My mother had
to go work and left us alone in the house. Who was left to protect us?
Who is protecting us now?"

His last question resonated in the air. I turned, and Puni was staring
at us, his eyes unmoving and his gaze unflinching.

"We have each other, that's all we have," Puni said. He rolled up his
leaf and walked away. Golicchio and I looked at each other. Sometimes
the things that came out of his mouth shocked us.

Chapter Twenty-Nine

I HAVE TRIED to find the others. My children – older now – want to visit India, but I am not ready. I need to have a reason to go, so I search.

Chapter Thirty

A FEW WEEKS had passed, and my wrist healed. I avoided getting into trouble, so that I could give my body time to recuperate. The others were growing antsy; ever since my "bust," the Mothers were more diligent about locking away their things. They knew that we had conspired together, yet they used me as a scapegoat and as an example to the others. Ganesh and especially Peepa had become accustomed to the weekly or sometimes biweekly sips of alcohol. Without access, they were more angry and withdrawn, preferring the company of each other instead of Golicchio, Puni, and me. They blamed me for their restriction, saying if I had taken a more moderate taste, I wouldn't have passed out and been discovered. There was some truth to that, so I didn't argue too much. However, the idea had been theirs to break into Headmistress Veli's room in the first place. I did not want to remind them of that.

During class, Mother Jamuna interrupted and asked us to assemble outside on the concrete patio. Afraid that she was going to publicly assault one of us for something, we moved slowly. I stayed close to Golicchio, and Puni walked ahead of us. I saw Ganesh and Peepa laugh at something together. They knew they were immune.

"The government has issued more uniforms for you. I will call each of your names. As I call it, please come and receive your shirt and shorts. Use this pen to write your name on the back. I don't want to hear complaints about missing clothing. If you defile this pair, you will not receive another for one year. Understand?" We nodded. I was happy; I had grown tired of my loose-fitting clothes. My hand was so used to holding up my shorts that I was sure I would need to retrain myself.

Ganesh was given two pairs. When she called my name, she handed me a shirt with a hole underneath the armpit.

"This is torn," I said to her. She just looked at me and called the next name.

"Goli," she said. I turned around, and I saw Jaga-Nai pointing and laughing at me.

"Mother Jamuna," I said.

"Do you want it or not?"

I walked away from her.

"Do you want to trade? Mine has a stain," Golicchio said. He held up his shorts, and there was a large stain right on the backside.

"No, that's okay." I felt better knowing that he had been cheated too.

"Please return to class," she announced. We again moved slowly because Mother Kalpana was teaching arithmetic, and we could all agree that we disliked the subject and the teacher. Mother Kalpana liked to spit when she talked, so those who sat in the front were bathed in her saliva. Usually Golicchio and I were forced to the back, but since Ganesh was always first inside, he tried to take the back seats when Mother Kalpana taught. Peepa, Jaga-Nai and the others joined him, forcing us to the front.

Golicchio had his arm over his face, motioning to me that he was ready for Mother Kalpana. I laughed. After class, Golicchio, Puni and I sat outside again, this time completing our homework. We saw Ganesh and Peepa sit together, and after a few minutes, the girl from the greenhouse arrived. Peepa went to her, and they both sat inside the little shed, talking. Ganesh went and joined them.

"Should we tell on them?" I asked Golicchio and Puni.

"Why? You're the one who will be punished."

"Yes," I said, but it burned me that they were so brazen in breaking the Mothers' rules. "She's a bitch," I said.

"Who? Mother Jamuna?" Golicchio asked.

"Yes, her too, but I meant the girl."

"Yes she is," Puni said. He nodded in the same way he had that night I was punished for hitting her.

We focused on our homework, ignoring them the way the Mothers clearly were. The girl disappeared into the House, and Ganesh and Peepa came to us.

"Let me look at your chalkboard," Ganesh said, putting his arm around Golicchio. Golicchio smiled and happily showed him. Peepa glared at his chalkboard.

"Who is that girl?" Puni asked. He didn't lift his head up from his board.

Neither Ganesh nor Peepa answered.

"She likes Peepa," I said.

"Why do you say that?" Ganesh asked.

"Because she told me."

Peepa laughed. "See. She doesn't want you, she wants me." He rubbed his chest and laughed again.

"And? What are you going to do for her? Bring her barrels of water?" Ganesh roared, and Golicchio and I moved back in our seats. We feared a confrontation.

"She likes handsome men."

It was true that Peepa was handsome. In fact, he was probably the best looking man I'd ever seen in my life, and I'd seen quite a few. He was better looking than any of the Tamil actors who were displayed on the posters that had surrounded my village, but it was hard to describe his appearance without losing some of what made him so charming in the process. His eyes were like an old woman's chewing betel nuts at night, looking for a lost dog. Peepa's luminescent eyes worked in his favor. His teeth were straight, white, and shiny. His hair wasn't very thick, but it didn't matter. There was enough of it, and it was so black, blacker than any that I'd ever seen. Sometimes looking at him I wondered why Head-mistress Veli showered her affections on me. I knew I wasn't attractive. I was painfully thin, with translucent brown skin and buck teeth.

Unfortunately, Ganesh wasn't handsome either. He was big, with de-fined muscles, which gave him some authority, but his face lacked char-acter. He looked like a side actor in a film – one that you would quickly forget. He was one of the lighter-skinned boys in the House, and that was the only appealing quality about him. The girl, who was beautiful in the way a wet hibiscus looked in the morning, probably demanded someone equally as attractive.

"He just said you're ugly, eh," Jaga-Nai said. He always knew when to make an entrance.

Ganesh puffed up his chest and pushed Peepa. Peepa pushed him back. This went back and forth for a few minutes, and I wondered wheth-er either of them would take it to the next level. They were about as close as I was to Golicchio, and I had never seen one of them strike the other.

"Pussies," Jaga-Nai said. Peepa then turned to him and pushed. Ganesh joined in. Jaga-Nai pushed back. I had a hard time keeping track of who was angry at whom.

Finally Jaga-Nai threw the first punch. I didn't see who he had hit first, but Ganesh threw the second. He hit anything that got in his way, including Peepa. Peepa hit blindly, not caring where his fists landed. Golicchio and I tried to turn away. Watching violence, unless it was being inflicted on me, made my stomach heavy. I felt scared, knowing that the punches could easily be showered on me as well. Puni, however, couldn't stop watching. He liked it when others were tormented in the way he felt he always was.

Somewhere in the middle of their fight, Jaga-Nai slipped away. His nose was runny with mucous and blood, and he made his way to the outhouse. Ganesh and Peepa seemed to have not registered this fact, and they continued hitting each other.

"Stop," Golicchio said. "Jaga-Nai is gone."

They didn't hear him. After several more minutes had passed, they grew tired. Ganesh first because he was the bigger one. They stopped, sat down next to each other, and caught their breaths.

"Pussies," Jaga-Nai said again. He'd returned, with his nose cleaned and his body poised for more fighting.

Ganesh and Peepa looked at each other. "I'm tired. I need water," Peepa said. Even though his face was slightly marred from the punches, he still looked handsome. He wandered into the House, and Ganesh followed. Jaga-Nai was left with us. I trembled, thinking that I should've gone inside after the fighting had started.

"How are you finding the shitty book, eh?" he asked me. I was almost done with *Revelations*. I knew what was going to happen at the end and was disappointed by the outcome. Amit had a weakness, and it was a woman. The woman was forcing him to choose between his superhero life or her. I hoped that he wouldn't choose her, but I knew deep down that he would. I was contemplating just giving it up, so that I wouldn't have to be so careful as I turned the dirty pages.

"It's good," I said, hoping to avoid a confrontation.

"Are you still reading it? You have balls," he said with a smirk. I could feel Golicchio behind me, blowing hot puffs of unwelcome breath on my neck.

The three of us were enveloped in some sort of stalemate. We looked at each other, neither one wanting to turn away. I didn't know what Puni was doing, and I was afraid to look. There was an unspoken game being played, and if I was the first to leave, then I would be the first to lose too. Losing would mean suffering at the hands of Jaga-Nai in whatever sick way he crafted.

Finally, after several minutes of feeling like my blood was curdling, Jaga-Nai sighed, and the spell was broken. He sniffed, and pink phlegm dripped down his face. He came close to me, changed his mind, and then pulled Golicchio toward him. He rubbed his face all over Golicchio's and laughed. He skipped his way inside, and Golicchio ran to the outhouse, his hands rubbing at his face as though he were a crazy person.

"He's one nasty boy," Puni said. I laughed.

"Yes, that is very true." Puni and I looked at each other and laughed so hard, we felt as though we were going to pass out. Golicchio came out of the outhouse, Jaga-Nai's marks still slightly visible on his skin. He began laughing too, having no idea what was so funny but finding our contorted faces amusing. Ganesh and Peepa returned, looking a little more refreshed.

"What's funny?" Peepa asked, but Ganesh was already laughing himself. That got Peepa going, and soon, all five of us were grabbing our stomachs, rolling over on the ground, trying not to get our bodies too dirty. I stood up, feeling lightheaded, and I saw Jaga-Nai look at us from the House. He had his hand on his head, rubbing at his hair, and he had a confused look on his face. I couldn't stop laughing though. Seeing his ugly face couldn't stop our fun.

After about ten minutes, we stopped and tried to breathe. Golicchio and I looked at each other, and the fun began again. We laughed so hard we cried, and I promised God that if we could laugh like this every day, I would be willing to forgo my place in Nirvana this time around.

WE WAITED IN line for dinner and despite our camaraderie earlier, Golicchio, Puni, and I were still pushed to the back. I could see Jaga-Nai's pointy hair sticking up; I knew he was in the front, along with Ganesh and Peepa. The cafeteria was empty, and we could see the food assembled along a narrow table, but the Mothers had yet to give us permission to eat. Mother Kalpana waited near the food, a spoon in hand, ready to dish out unfair amounts to each of us.

"Why is it taking so long?" someone yelled. The voice came from the front of the line. I hoped that the voice belonged to Jaga-Nai.

"You boys need to learn patience." The thing was, we *had* learned about patience, the week before. Mother Kalpana had taught us about it in class. She insisted that in order to achieve the "ultimate karmic experience" (at this statement, some of us chuckled because it sounded like a type of yogurt drink), we had to periodically abstain from things or people or places that we really liked. If we could forgo some of life's little pleasures, she said, then we could give up the material possessions of this life and be ready for the next. Ganesh had groaned. I felt the same way. She had no clue how much all of us had already sacrificed to get where we were. In my opinion, we all deserved the super ultimate karmic experience, but some of the higher castes would've probably disagreed.

I didn't know how much time had passed waiting for our food, but my knees felt sore. Most of us began sitting down. Golicchio rested against the wall of the hallway. He had a hard time getting up once he sat, so he preferred standing. Finally, Mother Jamuna approached from the tail end of the line. I smelled fire, and when I looked, I saw that she held a cake with lighted candles.

"Today is Headmistress Veli's birthday, and in honor of her, we will have cake. She has insisted that we all have a piece." Mother Jamuna smiled from ear to ear, and I could feel the earth trembling as her thick legs made their way past us and into the cafeteria. After they let us inside, we were served the usual – cup of dhal and rice – but I didn't care. I couldn't wait to try a piece of cake, and I knew that if Headmistress Veli had chosen it, it would be delicious. My heart warmed at the thought; she deserved a special place somewhere up there.

Headmistress Veli came into the cafeteria about halfway through our meal. She looked splendid. She was wearing a blue sari dotted with brown flowers, and in her hair she had clipped a red hibiscus, tucked neatly behind her ear. She wore makeup; most of us had only seen movie stars apply such paste, and we were surprised to see it on her. She had painted bright purple shadow on her eyelids, and her lips were colored a ghoulish red. The contrast of her lips and sari was electrifying. I saw her smile at someone, and when I turned to look, she was smiling at Jaga-Nai.

Mother Jamuna made us stand, and we all sang "Happy Birthday" to her. Afterward, Headmistress Veli herself cut slices of cake and served us all a piece. We didn't have to wait in line, nor did we have to battle for front position. She came to where we were, as if we were her masters, and placed a piece of cake upon our bean-soaked leaf. I noticed this time

Ganesh and Peepa received smaller pieces, and I received a very large one, complete with pieces of candy stuck to the frosting. I used my finger and licked off a dab.

"Enjoy," she whispered to me.

Enjoy we did. After I had my first piece, Headmistress Veli offered us all seconds; there was that much cake left. Mother Jamuna and the others were served last, and Golicchio and I chuckled at that. We knew they were burning inside, their fat shaking with desire for the buttery dessert. I hoped they finally understood how we felt whenever they dangled treats in front of our malnourished noses. As retribution, Mother Jamuna made Puni and Golicchio clean up after everyone. Bits of sugar and cake were stuck everywhere, and they had to get on their hands and knees with a wet towel in order to clean up the mess. I waited near the hall for them to finish before we linked arms and went outside to sit on the small patch of grass, letting our bellies – our full bellies – settle.

We saw the girl come outside with a piece of cake in her hand. She saw us, almost went back inside, but decided to approach us. I backed away slightly.

She completely ignored me and Puni and instead directed her comments at Golicchio. "Nirmal says you tell amazing stories. Do you have one for me?" Here was a girl used to getting what she wanted. I hoped that Golicchio would refuse her, but how could he refuse a beautiful woman?

"What kind of story?" I saw Puni's eyes – lecherous for the first time – look this girl up and down slowly. She shivered, and I saw her pull her sari closer to her body.

"How about a horror story? I like to be scared." She sat down, but had her back to us. I was afraid to tell her to bug off, and I was also afraid of her being so close to us. Either way, it was a poor situation. I stood up, ready to go inside.

"Good night, Golicchio," I said, and I motioned for Puni to follow. His eyes didn't register my finger movements at all.

"Puni, come. Let's go," I said again. Golicchio looked at me, and the spell she had cast was broken. He too stood up.

"We can get five lashes for even being seen with you," he said. Both he and I walked toward the House, and we left Puni. He couldn't be persuaded. We saw the girl and Puni talking, her head tilted forward slightly, and I wondered if he was telling her the horror story about the evil fat fairy. I hoped to God that Mother Jamuna didn't see them together. His fatty body could only handle so many beatings at once.

We were settled into our resting places when Puni came inside. Mother Jamuna had him by the ear, but whether it was the cake or fatigue, she seemed to be in good spirits. She let him off with a warning.

"But she approached me," he said. She closed her ears and moved away.

"What did you talk about?" Golicchio asked, but I knew he wouldn't tell. He needed to unravel stories on his own, in his own time.

"Nothing. Mother Jamuna came before we really could talk much at all," he said. He held his hand over his eyes, but I could tell that they were still open.

I was glad that Peepa and Ganesh were absent. I didn't know how they would react if they knew that Puni had been talking to the girl who was obviously the object of both of their affections. But I knew, in the same way I knew Puni was smart, that the little girl was to be avoided. She was like a spider, spinning her web for as many suitors as she could handle, but who would be left when she pitted them against each other? I didn't want to find out.

Chapter Thirty-One

FOR MY FORTIETH birthday, my wife tries her luck with kesari. Though it's an easy Indian dessert to make, you must have patience. My wife, as forgiving as she is with people, is not so accepting with food. By the time we are ready to have a spoonful, the cream of wheat has spoiled, and the butter has left a black stain on the pot. But she is not the type of woman to cry over failure; she just laughs it off, and we drive to McDonald's and pick up a couple of apple pies instead.

In the car, enjoying a brief moment without the children, she hands me an envelope.

"Happy Birthday, Sid," she says. "I have been waiting a long time to give this to you."

I open the envelope and inside is a newspaper clipping.

"That's the orphanage, right?" she asks. I had mentioned the name once to her, in passing, and had regretted it.

I don't finish the article because I black out. When I come to, I am in bed, and her arm – as white as how I imagine the drapes to be in someone else's heaven – is sprawled across my chest, her hand in a secure fist.

Chapter Thirty-Two

THOUGHTS OF AMERICAN-STYLE toilets, outhouses, and the girl in the greenhouse with hair like the waterfalls in Kootalam flooded my head. I needed to use the bathroom, but I was afraid. The outhouse was about ten meters away, so it was often difficult to run fast enough to avoid the dogs. Most of the time, we did. I believed they were trained to give us a head start, but sometimes it wasn't enough.

One night, Ganesh had smuggled really strong whiskey from Head-mistress Veli's room, and we all had had way too much to drink. My bladder was small, and I had to go to the bathroom three times in succession. The dogs were not trained to wait at such regular intervals. After the second time, they didn't even bother. They latched onto my ankle and tore a large piece of flesh from it, but I couldn't scream. If I were to get caught, the Mothers would have known we had been drinking. If the dogs mauled me or an infection on my ankle grew where they would have to amputate my leg, I'd become disabled. I decided to keep mum and cried through the pain. I stayed in the outhouse until the morning, waiting for Mother Jamuna to chain them before I crept back to the room. I kept the wound covered, and for one of the few times in my life, I managed to get lucky. It healed without incident, but after that, I dreamt of dogs with five arms and hundreds of teeth.

I pushed on Golicchio's shoulder. "Can you walk me to the out-house?" I felt that there was power in numbers. Having someone with me gave me courage, and I needed it badly. Yet Golicchio would not wake up. He was asleep so soundly it was as if he were dead. I didn't know if he was faking it, or if he really was asleep, so I continued to knead his shoulders until Ganesh growled at me. I couldn't hold it in any longer, and I knew I had to go out on my own.

I stepped outside of the room and before I unlatched the hinged door to the back, I peered through it. I saw large, dark shapes move across the dirt near the outhouse. I slowly unlocked the door. The hinges creaked as though it had rained, but the dogs didn't hear me. I took a breath. The air I took in was like a slap on my neck, and I almost fell back from it. I hunched over and looked at my destination. All of a sudden, I felt as if I were in a tunnel. I saw nothing else. And as I ran, I couldn't feel or see anything but the outhouse. I felt a tongue on my leg, but other than that, I felt nothing. I made it to the bathroom and counted my blessings.

After I was done, I looked out and saw the dogs pacing in front of the fence. They generally avoided the outhouse, and I wondered if it was because they were afraid that their feet would get stuck in the hole in the ground in which we pooped. Or maybe they were repulsed by the smell. Even though we cleaned it as often as we could, sometimes the stench was so awful it made my nostrils burn.

The dogs' pacing reminded me of my father; he had been the master of pacing. I remembered a time at home when I had been curious about the differences between boys and girls. Smita was younger than I, and against her will, I pinned her down to examine what was underneath her training shorts. I was completely appalled by what I saw, and instead of letting her go, I continued to hold her, trying to make sense of what was before me. Her screaming brought my parents, and right after my father slapped my behind, he stood pacing back and forth, trying to figure out what other punishment I deserved. The waiting was agonizing. I wanted him to just beat me and get it over with. I felt that the longer he paced, the worse the punishment. I was right. He didn't speak to me for a week.

Now, waiting, I pondered what the dogs would do to me if I were to leave. I could now see the outline of the dogs' fur, and I wanted to touch them. The space we shared was so intimate; I couldn't understand how in one minute we could share this space so peacefully, yet in another we could be at each other like wild beasts. I grew cold.

I couldn't do it. I couldn't leave. I knew I had to stay, huddled near this foul-smelling hole, and wait until morning. I leaned against the wall and wrapped my arms around my body. I thought of the woman who used to help clean fish with us. Sometimes when Smita was scared because the fish were alive and writhing, she'd sing songs to appease her. I remembered one in particular about a woman who spent an infinite amount of time taking care of her feet. When it came time for her to get married, no one wanted her because her face was so ugly and unkempt. The lyrics came to me:

The more she clipped, the less she looked.
her face had grown to the size of a jackfruit, but her toes – Vishnu
would be so happy.
She says she could get a man to lick her feet,
but why won't he marry me?

I laughed and felt a little less scared. I sang to myself, trying to remember all of the songs that I had learned from the woman. After I ran out of songs, I tried to remember if my mother had sung me any. Nothing came to mind. I couldn't remember if she had ever sung to us. Though she was attractive, her voice was the kind that made me want to pierce my eardrums.

I didn't like the way she sounded, but she was my mother, and I loved the things she'd said and the way she'd said them. She didn't scold me in the handsome voice that my father had. She loved me and told me so, often. I missed her voice. The Mothers here had voices like angels, which was hard to stomach sometimes when they would beat us or tell us that we were worth nothing.

I slowly closed my eyes, trying to picture my mother singing. I could hear her voice, but not how she sounded. I also couldn't conjure her image. Every time I tried to recall her face – her beautiful face – Headmistress Veli's came to mind. I tried and tried and tried, but my mother's face was gone. I wasn't sure if I would ever remember what she looked like again.

When I finally felt that she might be coming to me, whether in a dream or for real, the sun was rising. I opened my eyes, putting my hands out, thinking I'd reach her. Instead, I saw Mother Jamuna. She chained the dogs, and as she made her way back to the House, she saw me, my fingers groping the thin air.

"What are you doing here?" she asked.

"I had to use the bathroom."

"You know you are not to leave the room at night. Bad things can happen to boys who go out at night. You know this." She came closer and then stepped back, repulsed by the outhouse's odor.

"I went this morning, after the sun had come out," I lied. She covered her nose and came close to my face.

"You look like you have been awake all night."

"No, I just came this morning."

"And the dogs didn't get you?" She smiled.

"No, they didn't."

"Hmm. All right, then I want you and Goli to clean the entire House today." All I wanted to do was sit. Enduring class even sounded appealing. But manual labor didn't, and I was not sure if I could muster the energy to do what she was asking me to do.

"And class?"

"You'll be fine missing one day." She put her finger underneath my chin, and I felt myself wanting to recoil. "Come. I will give you both your assignment."

We were given our breakfast first, despite the line. Jaga-Nai and Ganesh snickered at us, but the Mothers silenced them. We had to get an early start since they wanted us to clean all of the Mothers' rooms, including their closets and crawl spaces. We were to launder their sheets and some of their clothes even. I was glad at least that Mother Jamuna had assigned Golicchio to the job too. Life's insignificant rewards were all that we had.

Between the two of us, we divided our chores straight down the middle. I was to take Mother Jamuna's room, but in exchange, I was given Headmistress Veli's room. Sometimes she left us little treats in a small bowl on her desk. She told us that we were welcome to whatever was inside, and sometimes she had candy, shiny with different colors, arranged in a rainbow. Golicchio was to take the other Mothers' rooms. We were told that we must finish by night time; otherwise we would not have dinner. Not wanting to risk it, we avoided speaking to each other unless absolutely necessary.

THE SUN BEGAN to set, and I was finished. Golicchio was almost done; he still had to rinse Mother Jamuna's panties. We were aware of the inappropriateness of the task, but mitigated its impact by playing a little game. We had to state a number, and then the next person had to state another number and then its sum, and then the next person had to state another number, and then the sum of all three and so forth. Whoever faltered first would have to wash the Mothers' undergarments. Golicchio lost. As good as he was with his brain, he didn't have the best memory.

"Next time we're going to play a game that involves words," Golicchio said. He was throwing Mother Jamuna's extra large panties against the ground, trying to shake off the soap and water. Both of us could've fit into one leg. I thought of that and laughed.

"What? Looking at me and laughing?" Sometimes Golicchio could be so emotional. He was like the battered wife, and I had to make things better before I disappointed him again.

"No, I was thinking about how these look like elephant knickers," I said. Golicchio laughed too, but I shushed him. I motioned toward the House. We knew that she'd come to check on us soon.

"You need to hurry," I said.

"Then help me! I still have another four to do!"

"You owe me," I said. I grabbed a pair and began to rub soap into the folds. I tried not to get too close to the fabric as sometimes the Mothers left us their monthly surprises.

"Ganesh said that you were caught in the outhouse this morning. Did the dogs get you?" I could see Golicchio's eyes brighten.

"No, obviously I am fine. I tried to wake you, but you were dead."

"I was? I don't remember."

"Right." I didn't believe him. He was more afraid of the dogs than I was to the point where he would dehydrate himself so he wouldn't ever have to pee at night.

"I don't."

"One day you'll have a stomach cold, and then you'll have to go there on your own, in the dark. You'll ask me, and I will say no, and tell you to remember that time."

"That's mean."

"Right." I was about finished with my set, but Golicchio was slow. He was still working on the first. "Hurry up."

"Yes, yes," he said. He shut his mouth and feverishly tried to get the last of the soap out of Mother Jamuna's underwear. "Done," he said a few minutes later. He wouldn't have survived as a fish cleaner – he had too much of a one-track mind.

As if on cue, Mother Kalpana came to the yard, and she collected the clothing. They hung the wet ones on lines in their room. They didn't trust their clean underwear hanging in the yard for us boys to defile. I was sure that there was a story behind that, but I didn't have the courage to ask.

"I left you dinner in the cafeteria," she said. Light-headed, with the smell of women and So Clean EZ Soap on our hands, we headed inside, anxious to see what we were to be served. I was starving. The last I'd eaten was a stick of candy from Headmistress Veli. Golicchio and I had skipped lunch thinking that we'd probably not finish in time if we gave ourselves a break to eat. Two leaves were set aside on one of the tables, and we looked: fried moong dhal and a small bowl of rice.

"What was lunch?" Golicchio asked. I shook my head. We took our leaves to the floor and sat cross-legged, sighing together as we did. My feet were sore, and my wrists ached. I hoped that I would sleep well tonight.

Unfortunately, the quantity of food they had given us wasn't enough to compensate for the amount of labor that I had just performed, so I gnawed on the side of my leaf. I didn't realize I was doing it until Golicchio said, "Don't you know, leaves are bad for you. The green in plants drug the good parts in your body into thinking it's a vacation, so your body rests. And then when a cold comes along, the parts that are supposed to protect you are too busy napping."

"What are the good parts?" I asked. I knew that I would get the "imagination-coated" response from him, but it would be closer to the truth than anything that I could possibly know. The House wasn't big on biology. The Mothers were more focused on values and etiquette. The idea was to educate us enough about home life, so that our lack of parental upbringing would not harm us when we had our own children or if we ever left.

"They are living things inside our bodies that protect us from things that are bad, even from ourselves," and he became quiet as he whispered his last thought.

"Well mine don't work very well, otherwise I wouldn't have problems with Jaga-Nai."

"They don't always know the difference between right and wrong. Sometimes we have to teach them. But if we teach them wrong, then they act wrong. Do you understand?"

"How do you teach what you do not know?" I asked. When I first came to the House, how was it possible that I would have known that Jaga-Nai was bad? How could I possibly have known that at birth? Bodies weren't fair.

"We always know what's right or wrong. That's not something that our parents teach us. That's what we already know."

"Then shouldn't our good parts know too?" I didn't understand Golicchio's reasoning.

"Your brain may know, but your good parts do not. That is the sneaky thing about our bodies. Sometimes they work against each other, and that's when we get cancer."

His was an astute, if not entirely precise observation, and I often wished that life were able to be reduced to such easy explanations. How Golicchio possessed such complicated knowledge confused me.

"Who determines whether our bodies work against each other or not? Brahma?" I was very curious. "Does this mean that we can train our bodies to protect us against pain?"

Golicchio shook his head. "No," he said. "If we don't feel pain, then we never learn how to be better people. If nobody ever treated you with meanness, then you'd never learn what it feels like to be treated with kindness, and you'd never treat someone else like that." Golicchio was smart, but naïve.

"I believe it is possible to be kind without being treated badly. I think when you treat people badly, that's when they become bad people. Didn't you say that once before?" I'd seen it happen most intimately with my father, and now with the other boys. They would come into the House, bright-eyed and as rosy-cheeked as any dark Indian boy could be who had just lost his entire family to the water, and months later, would join Jaga-Nai's group or wish to be more like him and emulate his bullish ways.

"Yes, but not always. My mother was the nicest woman in the world. And when my father would beat her, she only became nicer and nicer to the point where she would allow any of us to do whatever we wanted. She never scolded or hit us." His bony head jerked back and forth like a bird's.

"By your logic, that means Jaga-Nai was treated with nothing but kindness."

He moved his hips around as he began to get up to leave. "Like I said already, our bodies don't always do what we tell them to do or even what they're supposed to do."

I thought some about what he had just said. I agreed that my body certainly didn't do what I wanted. Sometimes I dreamt of larger muscles or even better lung capacity. Even so, I didn't think that Jaga-Nai's body was meant to be kind, and that somehow, the forces inside of him were working against that. As if to prove my point, Jaga-Nai readily appeared, wearing a serious look on his face, not unlike the one Golicchio had had earlier. But his provoked fear in me. When Jaga-Nai was serious, something bad was going to happen.

"You, eh? Leave." He pointed to Golicchio and made a motion with his head. His hair had grown long, and the ends were falling into his eyes. He didn't bother brushing it away. I looked at Golicchio, and he put his hands out as if to say, "I'm sorry, Yrimal," and got up to go outside and wash his hands. I got up too, hoping he'd become distracted and forget what he wanted me for.

"I didn't tell you to leave," he said. "Listen, you have to listen to me." I expected him to shove another letter my way (he hadn't shared any in a long time), but I saw nothing in his hands. In fact, what I did notice was his shirt half-tucked and his shorts not pulled taut over his stomach, but rather hanging about loosely around his thighs and knees. He then pulled his shorts up and tucked his shirt in, as if he had read my thoughts. "Look, you're going to listen to me, eh, even if you don't want to. Do you understand?"

"I'm sorry," I said. I didn't know what else to say to save myself. I was beginning to understand why he was so fierce in his revenge. It was important in the House to look forward to something. Golicchio looked forward to his stories, and Ganesh looked forward to hearing them. Jaga-Nai looked forward to hurting us. If you didn't look forward to anything at all, then you ended up dead inside.

"What?"

"I'm sorry about the game, about Headmistress Veli's bed..." My voice trailed off. I looked up at him, and he was completely confused.

"Listen," he said, and it was as if any mention of the game had never happened. He held up a piece of paper, and I could make out a short letter. "I was with Headmistress Veli." He paused. He showed me the piece of paper. "A letter from my mother. She said that they have moved and want me to return now. I am so lucky."

"Your mother?" I remembered the letter I'd read for him so long ago.

"What about her, eh? She wants me to come. Fuck my father."

"When are you going to leave? Soon?" I hoped. I wanted him to go. I wanted his parents to come and take him, or I wanted him to die. Even when the other kids taunted me on the sea or my father's hate paralyzed me, I never wished for them to die. This was the first time, and I felt like a bad person for thinking it. I took it back.

"She said she won't give me their address until the time is right." He smiled brightly and even all of his decayed teeth shone.

"Why are you telling me this?"

"She said not to tell anyone, but I don't care. She can't keep controlling me the way she does now. It'll end soon. Then my parents will come and close the House."

"And what will happen to us? You cannot close the House." I didn't really believe that his parents could do that, but I didn't really know. I'd never really thought that I would end up here with my parents dead either.

"You really think that I care about you?" He smoothed his hair, and I noticed white dandruff flaking off of his scalp. I also smelled a faint odor of coconut oil and a sweet fragrance I couldn't really place. He smelled like a girl, but I didn't think that it was the appropriate time to say aloud such an observation.

"No," I said.

I remembered a time in my village when a man like me was killed by a man like Jaga-Nai. This man was killed because he was said to have joined the Naxalites – a rebel group that raged against the upper castes in power. My mother had told me that the Naxalites were a bad cadre of men, wanting to annihilate all of the higher castes and divide their wealth equally.

"Why should you be rewarded for killing others who kill? Then you are doing the same as they are," my mother said to my father. I could see it in his eyes – my father wanted to join this renegade group, but he was too afraid.

"If someone is going to kill you anyway, then you kill to get them first. It's logical," he'd said, trying to appeal to my mother's practicality.

"Shh…" she'd said, covering my ears. I never got to hear the conclusion of the story, but the Naxalites hadn't seemed as bad as my mother had made them out to be.

Jaga-Nai came closer to me. Then I saw it – a smudge of pink on his neck and some on his shorts as well. "What are you looking at?"

"You're wearing rouge," I said.

"Where?" He began to rub himself everywhere. He started with his lips; they were already dry, and he rubbed them until they cracked. Then he rubbed his chest and neck, and finally his crotch. He scratched as if he had an insatiable itch.

"It's okay," I said, but it was too late. He was obsessed.

"You didn't see anything, you fuck, eh," but his assertion sounded like insecurity. "I have to do it," he said. He kept repeating himself, but I was too scared to ask him what he meant. I started toward the exit, and this time he didn't stop me.

"Fine, leave. But I'll be the one leaving for sure."

Chapter Thirty-Three

AMMA HAD DIED waiting for cancer to play its final card, and when the doctors explained to me what was happening to her – inside of her body – I nodded.

"The body is working against itself," I said.

"I'm sorry," they whispered, but I had known this was coming.

Chapter Thirty-Four

THE FIRST TIME the strange man visited, I thought he was Jaga-Nai's father. He arrived in an ornately-decorated car that gave off puffs of smoke whenever it braked.

After the driver parked the car, a dark man with glasses and a mustache like the hangers Mother Jamuna used to hang her blouses stepped out and walked to the front entrance as if he'd been here before. I instantly thought *doctor* but the only "doctors" we saw around here were the female nurses they'd send from the main hospital thirty-two kilometers away, if they even bothered to come. Most of the time, the Mothers tried to fix us as though we were dolls made out of rice – a snip here, a nip and tuck there, and all would be fine.

After we were sure the driver was fast asleep, we crowded around one of the front windows and stuck our heads through the metal slats, careful not to expose our heads to their eyes. I was surprised to see Mother Jamuna come and greet him, and I wasn't the only one. The moment she arrived, we let out a universal gasp. I grinned. Sometimes we boys did do things together.

"Who is that?" Puni asked. "Another food delivery?"

"No," Ganesh said. "It's not the usual van. This is a regular passenger car."

"He looks familiar," one of the boys said. "I know I've seen him before."

"Could it be Jaga-Nai's father? Does anyone remember what he looks like?" I asked.

"Why would it be his father? His father doesn't want him, like most of us whose parents are still alive." Leave it to Ganesh to let all the children know that fairytales didn't really exist.

"Jaga-Nai told me that his father would come and get him."

Ganesh looked at me with renewed respect. "Why would he tell you that and none of us?"

Even though Ganesh would never admit it, I secretly suspected that he wanted to rule the House jointly with Jaga-Nai. Together, they would be invincible. I quivered at the thought.

"What did you say?" I heard Peepa ask. I didn't immediately answer.

"He said that Jaga-Nai's father has come to get him," Ganesh boomed. Soon everyone heard, and some of the weaker boys started to cry. I tried to get Ganesh to lower his voice.

"What are you crying for? No one wants you anyway," Peepa said, but that sentiment didn't seem to bother any of us anymore. We had heard it spoken so many times, either from the Mothers, from our parents, from other boys, and even from ourselves. It was like throwing a grenade into an already burning van.

"This is cause for celebration," Ganesh said. I could see him flexing his big forearms, which were already too big for a boy his age.

"How do you know for sure?" Golicchio asked.

"You don't verify facts," Puni said. Puni sometimes surprised me with what his mind caught.

"Shut up," Ganesh said.

"I've seen this man come and go many times, and he has never taken any boys with him. They all come to visit Mother Jamuna. Our fathers, as strong as they were, couldn't have braved the sea. They just couldn't." I didn't want to think of her kissing a man.

"Golicchio, you are full of stories as always," Ganesh said.

"Let him speak," Peepa said, and surprisingly, Ganesh didn't challenge his retort. Golicchio smiled at him.

"I am just stating what I've seen. I'm not telling a story." His bony head lapped against the metal bars, struggling to see where Mother Jamuna and her mysterious male visitor had disappeared to.

"I think that he is right," I said.

"Really?" Golicchio looked at me, and his eyes twitched. Sometimes I wanted to hug him. Sometimes I wanted to stick his head underneath a piece of glass and examine why his head moved the way it did, but I didn't have a microscope through which to examine it.

"Yes. Continue," I said, trying to deflect the attention away from me. I didn't like having an audience, and in that way, Golicchio and I were drastically different.

"She is mean to us, but who says she is mean to him? We are boys. If we were men, perhaps she would try to charm us. She has nice-smelling perfume – we all smelled it when we stole Yrimal's pipe." Peepa nodded in agreement, and I recalled that day with fondness. I wished that we could all go back to that day. It was as perfect as days here came.

"What does she do with this man?" Peepa asked. Everyone crowded in closer, and I saw Golicchio's chest rise a little.

"Maybe that's her lover. He comes to make her feel good. Do you ever notice how sometimes she is in a very good mood and won't make us throw away a cookie if we happen to be eating one when we're not supposed to? Sometimes men make women feel good. They touch their hair, sing them a song, and sometimes even cook for them. That's what makes women feel good. That's what my father never did for my mother. But that's okay. I don't mind." He added the last few sentences as after-thoughts, but most of us were already so engrossed in what he'd said earlier. The personal affectations didn't mean much to us. Sadly, most of the boys didn't care very much about Golicchio anyway.

"What do you know about love?" Ganesh asked. "The most that you've ever come to love was when your mother washed your special finger when you were little," and we all laughed. Golicchio laughed too.

"Yes, but that's not the kind of love I'm talking about. I mean real love – the love that you feel for someone when you don't have to feel anything for them. We have to love our mothers; it's inside of us. But do we have to love a stranger? If we do, then it is true love." He nodded his head as if he were agreeing with himself. In rare form, his nod seemed well-connected and seamless.

"Yes, but what do you know of real love?" Ganesh asked. And I was curious too. It was hard enough for us to find "real love" inside the House from the other boys. Golicchio and I were about as popular as a married woman at a bride-viewing.

"I know." He stopped talking and sat down. The rest of us were on the edge of our invisible seats.

"What? Come, tell us!" Puni squealed. I really wanted to know about this love that he'd experienced. Sometimes I thought I felt it for

Headmistress Veli. I really loved her, and I barely knew her.

Golicchio shook his head, and the rest of us lost interest. We scrambled down to the main verandah and stood, waiting for the man to leave. Some of the bolder boys went and examined his car.

"He has gloves," Ganesh said. In the front seat, there was a pair of black gloves folded neatly, new and unused.

"What do you suppose he uses them for?" I asked Golicchio. He had also come out to look at the gloves, and I knew the story wheels were turning in his head.

"He uses them before he sees her so that his hands are pure and clean when he touches her," he said. I felt goose bumps.

"Where does he touch her?" one of the more lewd boys asked. I'd often seen him touching his "finger" in the outhouse. It sickened me. I had the urge too, sometimes, but I held back. That's what it meant to have self-control. I was afraid if I allowed myself that temptation, then there might be other temptations that I'd allow myself that were way more dangerous.

"I told you, her hair. Perhaps the end of her sari – the part that is so fragile, it is often the part that wears down as the sari gets old. It is the most exposed." I felt goose bumps again. I wondered where Golicchio had learned this secret – this weaving of words to make them so sensual. His words were so moving, yet he had no idea of their power. The rest of us drank them like sugar water.

"He has money," Peepa said. I saw him eyeing the bottle of water in the car. I'd seen a thermos before, but I'd never seen a water bottle intact. The bottle was exquisite – the sun reflected light off of the plastic, and it looked like it was covered in jewels.

"I want to open this car. I'm thirsty," Peepa said. He and Ganesh looked at each other, and I felt fear. I could see Golicchio slowly backing away too. There was something that wasn't right about the situation, and I didn't want to be implicated. I knew it was only a matter of time before the driver awoke or the man returned. For once in my life, I went with my instinct and left, deciding not to care if they thought I was a coward. I heard Peepa ask, "Where is he going?" But I didn't bother to turn around. I ran so fast that I plowed into Headmistress Veli.

"Sid, watch it," she said. Her lips were wet, and I wanted to know what she was eating that had made them so. "Would you like a mango?" She took a bite from a mango and spit out a piece into her hand. I took it, and the meat was like divine nectar. The mangoes the Mothers gave us were dark, bruised, and moldy. I wasn't used to this sweetness.

"Do you know where Jagadesh is?" she asked. "I wanted to offer him some of my fruit." She smiled, and I could see the dimples in her cheeks. My mother said that dimples were a sign of good fortune. I thought they were a sign of being fat.

"Why do you want to give him something to eat? He's not a good person," I said. Then again, nice people were nice to everyone. Maybe he was different to her.

"He is," she said. "You boys play differently than we do. He is such a sweet boy. He reminds me so much of my younger brother, who died when I was eighteen." Her eyes moistened, and they matched her lips. She looked as if she had stepped underneath a light shower.

"You promised to send him home?" I asked.

"It is possible that his parents are alive and want him to come home. I'm simply making the arrangement."

"That's not what he said." She shushed and hugged me.

"Don't listen to anything he says," she said. "Sometimes he talks much but listens very little. I never told him anything beyond what I've told you." She continued to hug me close.

"Veli," Mother Jamuna called. I panicked.

"Run," she said. As I started to move, she asked, "Would you like one last taste?" I nodded. She took a bite of her mango, and then she kissed me on the lips. I could taste the juice and pulp and although it was sweet, it was not ripe. She left, and I vomited. I used my shirt to wipe the contents, angry that I would waste such a delicacy like that and confused as to why I threw it up in the first place.

PENALTY FOR SNOOPING was two days in the Poor Man's Closet.

As a game back home, some of the more privileged boys had challenged me to climb into a waste well that was about two meters deep. I was young, so young then.

"You'll get to be just like us if you do it, we promise," they all said.

When I looked at them, at their tailored pants, callous-free feet, I wanted all of that too. I really believed what they told me.

"How long do I have to stay in there?" I asked.

"For four days. But you can't leave. Even if you get hungry, tired, or you can't breathe."

The well had been deserted for years and had never contained fresh water. Originally, it had been used to store trash but had been abandoned in favor of other larger waste wells. Sometimes people burned their excess in the well, but for the most part, it was empty.

When I looked inside, I could detect movement. I reassured myself that it was just a leaf, nothing more. I could see other foul things too, such as fish bones, old clothing.

"It will be like a new home," one of the boys said.

I climbed inside and was able to stand fully upright without my head coming out over the top. I was also able to sit because it was wide enough.

"We're going to cover you with the lid, so you can't come out, okay?"

"Right," I said, not really thinking it through. Once the lid came over me and the darkness set in, I lost it. I yelled and screamed, tried to push away the cover. It was too heavy. I cried so loud my throat felt scratchy, and I began to cough. I coughed and coughed until I was certain that my lungs were coming out through my mouth.

The hours dragged by slowly, then the minutes, then the seconds. I didn't know how much time had passed. I knew that I slowly began to withdraw. My eyes blinked rapidly. My mind cleared itself. I listened to the sound of my own breath and the waves crashing so close but not nearly close enough. I grew heavy and fell asleep. When I woke, my father was carrying me. I looked down at myself; my body had shriveled, and my skin had grown masses the size of jackfruits. Yet I didn't have the clean clothes. I was still poor and unprivileged.

"Has it been four days?" I asked my father. He shook his head, and I demanded to be taken back. I yelled and tried to pry myself away from his arms, but I was too weak.

"You'll die, is that what you want?" he asked me. Even though he knew who had done this to me, there was absolutely nothing that he could do about it. When I saw the boys the next day, they tried to throw sand at my open sores. They just laughed. I never found out how many days had elapsed while I had remained hostage in the well.

I had survived then, and I knew I could survive in the Closet again if I had to, but I preferred not to try.

I made my way to the outhouse to use the bathroom and try to rinse my mouth of half-digested mango. Jaga-Nai blocked my path.

"Eh, what. What are you looking at?" I could have gone around him, but I didn't dare.

"Headmistress Veli is looking for you," I said, hoping he would be lured by her request and leave. I looked him in the eyes, but he wasn't moving.

"You are a low-caster, but you're not entirely bad. But still." He punched me in the arm and laughed, and I was tired of his laugh, which sounded like an army of small birds being driven through a meat grinder.

Before I knew it, he smacked me so hard I almost fell back, the bottoms of my feet crumbling underneath me like rotted wood.

"What..." I trailed. The pain didn't hurt as much as the shock did.

"For trying to win favors with Veli." He stood over me, and the proximity of my head to Jaga-Nai's made me nauseous. I stared at his face, and he rubbed at his cheeks, looking at his hands afterward.

"You don't understand what I have to do to get what I want." He started circling me, and I flashed back to that night with the dogs. "I'm sure your mother had to do things too, to get food on the table." He winked, but I didn't give him the response he craved.

"You go using your failing breath as an excuse for people to be nice to you. Nobody picks on you because they see you as weak and not worth it. Imagine if you were me – a big strong boy. Who defends you? Who takes care of you? You have Ganesh, Peepa, even Golicchio." His rationale made no sense to me. I would much rather have taken care of myself. Those other boys didn't protect me. They turned on me in a second if it meant something extra for them to gain from it.

"If you are strong, you should take care of yourself," I said. "It's not up to others to take care of you. Everybody does your bidding. Even Headmistress Veli likes you." I cringed again. I could still taste the mango in the back of my throat.

He laughed. "I don't want her affections. It's too much." He whispered, "She does special things for me when the others are not looking."

"I hate you," I said quietly, and because he was so focused on his thoughts, he didn't hear me.

"She touches me," he continued to whisper. I flashed back to that kiss, and I felt myself get nauseous again. Those very lips that had touched mine had probably touched his first.

"Do you like it?" I asked. I hadn't liked it.

"Of course, why wouldn't I, eh? She's attractive enough, as far as I've seen. My father would like her. She looks like my mother," he said.

"I don't know," I said, my voice again trailing off.

"Tell anyone any of this and you're dead," he whispered. He stepped closer, and his feet were dangerously near mine. I wheezed.

"If you like it, why?"

"Because she has said to keep it a secret, and that's what I intend to do. It's our arrangement. My secrecy for information on my parents. It won't be for much longer, eh. So no need to tell anyone else."

"So why tell me?"

"Because I saw her kiss you." He kicked me right in the scrotum, and I could hear the breath escape me. I saw stars around Jaga-Nai's head, and he looked like he was wearing a wreath of flowers.

"Just because she kisses you, doesn't mean she likes you. She LIKES me. And don't think that because you've kissed her, that she will be special for you and stop being special for me," he said. I hoped that the moment I passed out, I'd forget what I had just learned.

"She is special," I whispered, but I shouldn't have spoken. The words took the last breath I had, and I fainted. I felt the hard form of a pipe being inserted into my mouth, and some air forced through my lungs. I looked up and saw Jaga-Nai's hand outstretched, his mouth shaped like an "o" in despair.

When I woke up, I was in the Poor Man's Closet. I screamed. Then I heard Mother Jamuna's voice outside.

"You will stay in there until tomorrow. Do you understand?" I shook my head. Once my eyes adjusted, I saw that there was a tumbler of water next to me.

"What for?" I screamed.

"All of you – I saw you looking at Mr. Ragendran's car. Touching it, eavesdropping. You are all to serve one night in here. You are first." I heard the tiny "jingle jangle" of her ankle bracelets as she walked away. I screamed again, and I heard "two days now total," and I had to force a hand over my mouth to stop the shrieking. To say the Mothers were unfair was an understatement.

I sat up and drank my water. I looked into the bucket that was provided to me – someone hadn't even bothered to empty it. I could smell it, so I moved it as far away as possible. I tried to calm down and think about my situation logically. I had never spent two nights in here. I had to come up with a plan in order to survive. Boys like me had learned how to survive in worse places than this, so I had to learn.

While in the dark hole, I thought about the well and instantly felt stronger. I stiffened and tried to keep my body as still as possible. When I felt something tickle my toes, I didn't think about it. I focused all of my energies on keeping still. I tried to think about nothing.

I then gradually faded from my body.

I was in an outhouse, but not the one at the House. This one was much cleaner and nicer. There was a bar of soap on a tray in the corner and a plastic blue bucket instead of a rusty metal one.

I dropped the bar of soap into the toilet and poured water over it. I was mesmerized by how the water dissolved the soap and created little bubbles that broke the surface. I stared, hypnotized, and then fell into a deep sleep. When I came to, I was back inside the Poor Man's Closet. But I wasn't still this time. I was alert, my body jerking in a way I'd imagine a nervous man would awaiting trial for murder.

Although the room was dark, it was light. I could see everything. The wall had initials carved into it. Mostly vulgar, but there was one that touched me. It said, "I love my Amma, even though she left me."

The bucket was rusty and crawling with tiny black bugs. They didn't move, but I could tell that they were alive. They formed a static strand on the rim. There was also a pile of dried feces in one corner, and almost as if to counter it, pages of the *Ramayana*. I wondered why someone would've bothered to sneak such a thing in here. It was so dark – it was impossible to read anything or even count one's own toes. But then again, maybe it wasn't the words but the actual existence of the holy text that had comforted the owner. Perhaps the book's presence offered some sort of protection against what lay in the darkness of the space and the mind.

I wasn't in the mood for reading, and the brightness of the imaginative light prevented me from getting sleepy. I measured myself against the wall and found that I could barely stand. I had to hunch over otherwise my head would hit the top of the ceiling. Bent, I pretended that I was a scary monster coming from the depths of the Closet to scare little boys into using the bathroom every day. I laughed so hard that I couldn't keep up the façade and decided that it was more of Golicchio's style anyway.

I looked at my hands, and my fingernails were too short to etch something into the wall. I thought – what would I inscribe if I could? My initials seemed too boring. I thought of my sister's name, thinking that making her place permanent in this world might help me unload some of the guilt I felt at being so cruel to her for so many years. Even though I didn't logically believe that my parents had been taken away because I had been mean to my sister, emotionally I felt betrayed. She hadn't kept her mouth quiet enough. She had been too vocal when I was misbehaving, and the gods had heard her and perhaps decided to punish me. She didn't stick up for me when they were listening.

Most of the time, it was my father who had been the protector of my sister. Perhaps seeing himself in Smita, he constantly held her hand and always touched her hair tentatively as if it were made of egg shells. My sister was so spoiled; it was understandable that any brother would resent the situation.

I never realized how much my father cared for Smita until the day I let her touch his razor blade. I didn't "make" her do it, as my father later accused me of, or even subtly guide her in that direction. I was outside, brushing my teeth. At the House, we used black ash. Back home, we used real toothpaste, given to us for free by some of the upper caste women whom my mother knew and helped. It wasn't expensive, and sometimes in exchange for cleaning services, my mother received toothpaste. I knew she would have preferred money, but I was always excited when new tubes would appear.

That morning, I had been actively brushing my teeth and eating some of the toothpaste. It tasted like candy, and it was good for my mouth. I saw Smita looking for me, and she followed me outside, her little pudgy hands reaching over the top of the little table that my father used for all of his toiletries. Normally, he was quick to put them away after shaving because he didn't want us little ones in his stuff. This morning, my father had gotten up late and was moving slowly. My mother had asked me to set out his things, so it would be easier for him to finish getting ready. I did, and Smita was busily grabbing what I had laid out for him. The mornings were mine, and I ignored her. She was my father's responsibility.

Before I knew it, she had grabbed the razor and put it in her mouth. I heard a loud wail, and when I turned to look, blood and saliva were dripping from her mouth. The razor dropped to the ground, and I stepped on it, anxious to hide it because I smelled my father close by. Then I saw him.

"What happened," he said, but he didn't ask. He knew, and he grabbed Smita and pushed her into my mother's arms.

"How could you," he said, but again, not a question. He asked me where the razor blade was. I didn't show him, but he knew it was under my foot because the force I used to hide it was driving the blade into my flesh, causing blood to seep from underneath. He stepped on my foot so hard, I thought that the bones would break from his crush if the razor didn't slice through them first.

"Don't do," was all he said. He didn't even finish the sentence, and before he left, he punched me in the stomach. How that punch had knocked the wind out of me. I fell to the ground, and my father accused me of being a girl. The razor was still stuck to my foot, and my father had peeled it off, skin and all.

"The first time you learn how to shave, I will remind you of the pain you put your sister through. Understand?" I never wanted to grow hair on my face after that, and he died before he ever had the chance to teach me.

For years he made me believe that I had something to do with my sister's disobedience. Why hadn't he or my mother been watching her? Here, in the light/darkness of the Poor Man's Closet, I finally realized that it was not my fault at all – none of it was my fault. I should've been relieved, but instead, it made me depressed. My father would never have the opportunity to right the wrong he made. The both of them would never have the chance to love me more than they loved Smita. Smita would never disobey her parents again, and I would never get in trouble again.

I found myself back in the darkness of the hole, but this time it didn't seem so mortifying. The thoughts in my head seemed a lot worse, and somehow I wished that I could take those thoughts and make them into something tangible, so that at least I could physically push them away.

I used my hands to navigate the wall and found the inscription of the lost boy who missed and still loved his mother. Oddly, I felt comfort in someone else's pain. I would never love my mother the way I had, and certainly not my father. Perhaps the only person whom I could continue to love in the same way was Smita. She was just too young to realize what she had done to me, and I wondered at that moment if, before she died, she had thought about the guilt of hurting me as I have carried around the guilt of hurting her.

Chapter Thirty-Five

THESE DAYS, I DON'T think about Smita very much. I can hardly remember what she looked like anymore.

When I first taught my son how to shave, I thought of the kind fathers at the last orphanage instead.

Chapter Thirty-Six

My eyebrows were different when I emerged from the Closet. I had always had straggly eyebrows, giving off a distracted and weak look. Now, they seemed straighter and stronger, if possible. They gave my entire face and body a sense of purpose and even urgency. I had somewhere to go, something to do. I was going to be somebody, is what they said.

"Did you dream at all while you were inside?" Golicchio asked me. I was sitting near the row of eucalyptus trees that lined the yard, watching the others play Kabaddi freely now that Ganesh was in the Closet and Jaga-Nai was nowhere to be found. Spending time in the Closet made me see things differently. Besides Smita, I thought about Jaga-Nai and his situation for a long time. If he had sexual contact with Headmistress Veli, that was between her and him. Why should I change my view of her because of what Jaga-Nai said? He could've been lying for all I knew. I also didn't feel it was any of my business anyway. Indians didn't really value and respect privacy; my father was British in this regard as he left us alone to live our lives, sometimes too often. Perhaps being left here was a result of his belief in a privacy so pure that it could only be achieved through death.

"How do you mean?" I took a twig and broke it in half. I continued to break it in half as I listened to the boys yell, "Kabaddi, Kabaddi, Kabaddi..."

"Did you dream while you slept? And if so, did you dream about our futures? Some have said that the Closet allows normal people to become fortune-tellers – to be able to see into the future by way of visions or dreams." His open, slanted mouth looked strange as he tried to make himself comfortable against the bark.

"I don't remember. I don't think I slept at all." I looked at him, and his mouth remained open. I could see the edge of a chipped tooth. I wondered if he had fallen or if someone had done that to him.

"If you didn't sleep, what did you do?"

"Why are you asking? You will find out for yourself soon enough. But good for you, you'll only get one day in there."

"You were only in there for one day, Yrimal. Time must have stopped in there," he said. I felt as though I had been inside for two weeks, but was it possible that Mother Jamuna had a heart and didn't prolong my sentence?

"I thought a lot." By now, my twig had disintegrated, and my hand searched for another.

"About what? About us?" His leg was twitching to the point where it pained me to watch it.

"Please stop, stop moving your leg."

"I can't."

"Why not? Just will your brain to stop your leg."

"It won't. I can't." He put both hands on his leg, and it still kept shaking.

"What is it shaking for?"

"I don't know." He stood up, and the shaking lessened to a tic.

"Are you afraid to go into the Closet?" I stood up too. I felt an unnatural maternal instinct toward him, and I put my hand on his shoulder, the way I'd seen my father do to his friends when telling a joke or agreeing that their wives were either ugly or beautiful.

"It's not that bad. The worst is the smell. But Golicchio, you're the inventor – convince yourself that this place is magical, that it's on the way to somewhere even more extraordinary. I tried to do that, but it didn't work. I know it would work for you." I smiled, and for the first time in weeks, I felt good about myself.

"You don't know my fears," he said. He walked around the tree trunk in circles. He kept his face down.

"What are you afraid of?"

He stopped circling and slumped against the trunk. This time, however, his leg stopped shaking. "I am afraid of myself, most of all," he said after a long silence. "Being alone with myself for that long of a time with no one there to occupy me. That is what scares me."

"Why? It was almost a relief to me. No one I had to constantly keep an eye on. No Jaga-Nai to steal my food or beat the crap out of me."

"Maybe when I am alone, I will see exactly the reasons why my parents were taken from me, and then maybe I will also learn to hate myself. I am starting to. The Closet might solidify that feeling."

I nodded.

"What? You think that I'm a failure?" he asked me. I had to be honest.

"Golicchio, everybody has their strengths. Yours are your stories." Golicchio tucked his head down so it looked as if he were using my body as an umbrella. Even though he was taller than I was, I felt as though I were the bigger and older one, protecting him from a bully. In this case, the bully was the Closet.

"My inventions are just that – made up. I don't believe any of what I say."

"That's not true. If you didn't believe it, you wouldn't tell the stories with such conviction."

"You don't believe them. Then why should I?"

"Does it matter what I think? All that matters is what you think since you're the one who's going to be in that Closet alone."

"It does matter. A story is only true if the listeners believe it. What's the point of fabricating when no one is seduced?"

I took a moment to understand what he had just said. It was clever, and certainly way over my head.

"So are you saying in order to seduce, you must lie?" I looked at him. This time, he was standing up straight, gazing at the sky.

"Yes. Any victory of power over another, whether it is seduction, sports, or politics, is contrived in lies. Some bigger than others."

"How do you know this? How did you know this?"

"Look at us. At how we compete. Look at the Mothers. Remember our mothers with our fathers."

Golicchio seemed to understand that we were much older than our years. The circumstances afforded us no folly. We couldn't be children. And cliché as it was, we were forced to grow up way too fast, and forget the dolls and toy cars and games in the hot sand for something even larger than us – something that didn't even really involve us. It was our parents. We were living the lives that they should have lived, shouldering their responsibilities and mistakes.

"But what is the fun in observing when one can be a part of the action?" I asked. He was done. He let his body slump until the back of his behind hit the bottom of the tree. His leg began to shake again.

He always knew when to stop talking. Perhaps that was the sign of a great storyteller.

I turned my focus to the game of Kabaddi, this time trying to pay attention to the subtleties that I might have missed the first time around.

Chapter Thirty-Seven

WHAT HURTS ME now is the sacrifice. I had to be reduced to nothing in order to gain everything. If I had not lost my parents, I would not have earned Amma. Without her, I would not be here, in the States, humbled by my family's love for me and my devotion to them.

I try to teach my children what it means to fall. They are older, out of the house, carrying on their own lives independent of me. I see them making the same mistakes I did – my son, entangled in various affairs with no future, and my daughter, so desperate to win the affection of others that she postpones her own happiness. But they have something that I never had – the knowledge that there will always be someone who will care for them, and I believe that will be enough to see them through.

Chapter Thirty-Eight

I REMEMBERED ONLY one time at home when food had been deliberately taken away from me.

My mother had been lighting a candle to place in front of one of the many deities that she and my father collected. It was a Hindu tradition. Place a flame, say a prayer, smear your forehead with red powder. I didn't understand it all.

"Why are you doing that?"

"If we pray, maybe things will be better for you when you are my age," my mother said.

"But why are things the way they are? Why aren't they better now?"

That was when she gave me a short historical lesson on how the caste system came to be. It wasn't necessarily born from religion, but from land and wealthy men devising ways of keeping it from the lower classes. Religion was the excuse that was used to perpetuate it. If you were bad in your past life, you were born into a lower class. If you were a good person, you were born into a higher class. It was a form of a control. Even at my age, I knew this.

"Why are you praying to a god that is bad?" She didn't say anything and instead sent me to sleep without any food. People like her who were victims of a system that failed to support them were often its most passionate supporters. I never understood why.

Since, I had seen sleep many times in the House without anything to eat. It was commonplace here, and I didn't have to speak out against anybody or anything.

The next morning, I almost expected an empty leaf, my memory of my mother's punishment so fresh in my mind. Lately, the Mothers seemed to randomly withhold food from us, as if we were animals not used to regular feeding schedules.

"I think he's finally learned how to tie a knot and has hung himself from the rafters," Golicchio said. We were enjoying breakfast without the threat of Jaga-Nai's viciousness, and Golicchio in particular seemed to be in a good mood.

"Where is Jaga-Nai?" Ganesh asked.

"How was the Closet?" I asked him. He did not answer. He looked relatively unchanged, but his voice seemed softer, somehow lighter.

"The next one is Peepa," Golicchio whispered. I felt nothing.

"Go, look for him," Ganesh said. He pointed his finger at me, and I felt as though I were his prostitute and he were a wealthy man telling me to undress and get on all fours.

"Why do we even care what his fate is?" Puni asked. Nobody answered him.

I went "looking" for Jaga-Nai, but was hoping to find Headmistress Veli instead. In the mornings she seemed less affectionate, but always had something sweet in her teeth, which she was quick to share.

I came to the hallway which led to her room. Her door was slightly open, not enough to welcome me into it, but not enough to warrant trepidation. I approached and peered inside.

Jaga-Nai was underneath her. She looked as though she were suffocating him with her weight. They were both naked and rolling into each other's bodies. Their dance looked painful, but Headmistress Veli was smiling, sweat and saliva dripping from her mouth and onto Jaga-Nai's firm nipples. Jaga-Nai was scared. I almost had to look twice to believe it. He looked as if he were about to cry, but without the tears. I feared for him as I crept away. The others didn't need to know. In this, Golicchio was right – the House was meant for secrets.

"She told me that Peepa, she calls him Nirmal, wants to marry her," Puni said. It was dusk. Most of the boys were inside, already lined up, waiting for dinner. We felt no rush since we knew we'd be tossed aside as though we were spoiled korma.

"The girl?" I asked.

"Yes."

"What else did she say?" I waited, but I knew I shouldn't ask too many questions. He shrugged his shoulders.

"Not much else. Why would she want to marry him? He's an asshole."

"Ganesh wants her too."

"Is that right?" he asked. His eyes looked sad.

"Yes."

"I want her too," he said. He licked his lips.

"Why?"

"She's pretty. And nice. She talks to me and looks at me like I am real."

"So does Headmistress Veli."

"No," he said, shaking his head. "She doesn't look at me. She looks at you."

"Is that right?"

"Yes."

We were silent. I put my hand on his shoulder. "She's trouble," I said softly. "I just feel it."

"So is Headmistress Veli."

"You're probably right," but I didn't believe it. She hadn't done anything to harm me. And if she harmed Jaga-Nai, didn't he deserve it?

"If you don't talk to Headmistress Veli anymore, I won't talk to the girl. Can you do that?" He knew I couldn't.

"I can't do that."

"I can't either."

Puni knew things that the rest of us didn't, but it was virtually impossible to get information out of him. I wanted him to tell me why he thought Headmistress Veli was bad, to convince me that she wasn't as good as I felt. Deep down, I knew he was right. A good person would be good to everyone, not just to a few people. But given my situation, why should I care if she was mean to someone who was mean? Perhaps this was what Mother Jamuna meant when she preached about karma. Who was I to turn away karma that was deserved?

"Tell me why is she bad?" I asked. He shrugged his shoulders again and got up.

"I need to eat," he said. He looked at me. "You coming?" I knew he secretly hoped I wouldn't because it would mean more food for him.

"Yes," I said.

MY FATHER HAD once told me that in certain parts of the world, crocodiles were a symbol of protection. The occasion was rare – he normally saturated Smita with stories of his wooden gods, but instead he was talking to me. He had shown me a statue of a crocodile, its mouth gaping. It looked more menacing than loyal.

"What have I taught my boy?" he asked, but not meanly. I shook my head no, knowing deep down that he would find that endearing. And he did. He patted me on the back and drew me in closer.

"The smartest people in the world have learned how to take something that should be feared and use it to help them. In some places, crocodiles are worthy of fear, but in the hearts of those men who are truly wise, crocodiles are just a part of nature. Ultimately, Brahma expected us all to live together in harmony, no matter who or what we are."

"Crocodiles are scary though. They have large teeth and are only concerned with eating." I kept up my childish farce. I didn't often get to play the child with him.

"Sometimes looks can be deceiving. Things that appear to be the strongest are often the weakest inside." I remembered thinking about the boys who had forced me into the well. Were they truly cowards inside, and was I the victorious one?

I bared my teeth. "Aaarrhh," I said. Even though it seemed as though I were imitating a baby, I wasn't; instead, I wanted to see what it felt like to have the semblance of power, but to truly be scared inside. I could see what my father was saying. Baring my teeth – posing as a terrifying coward – only made me feel weaker inside. I felt duplicitous.

My father stared at me for a few seconds, and then he slapped me hard. "This is what I get for trying to teach my own son something about life. Mockery. Smita!" he called. He got up and left. I felt my face, and it was hot. I was calm on the outside, but inside I was fuming – my own father didn't understand me. How could he understand the world any better?

I saw my mother cross the room to come and sit with me, but I realized that this was not a time for pity. I shunned her, in the same way that my father had shunned me. My mother stared at me leaving her, unable to do anything about it, but knowing that it was necessary. I had to find my own way, somehow, with or without them.

If my father were here today, I wondered what he would think about Jaga-Nai. Would he embrace him as having the qualities in a son that he'd found always lacked in me? Or would he find him to be a crocodile in hiding?

Chapter Thirty-Nine

I DON'T BELIEVE in God, and when followers ask me why, I don't have an intelligent answer. They take it to mean ignorance, but I take my silence as proof of a belief so instinctual, it cannot be reduced to words.

"Does that mean when we die, we won't go to heaven?" my son had asked, years ago when he was still a child.

"There is nothing to be afraid of," I said.

"But after death, there can't be nothing," my wife said. She believes in Christ and in having mature conversations, adult as they may be, in front of our children. I used to hate how she wanted them to grow up too fast.

"But in the nothingness, there is everything," I said.

"You sound like Buddha," my wife said, and laughed.

"Who's Boota?" my daughter had asked.

Chapter Forty

GOLICCHIO WAS WRONG; Peepa hadn't forgotten about their deal. With pen in mouth, Peepa said, "Today. We are going to do it." He smiled, and the pen fell out of his mouth. It made a clatter as it landed on the ground.

"Do what?" Puni asked. Peepa ignored him.

"Okay," Golicchio said. He looked as though he'd been defeated in a multi-day struggle. His eyes bulged, and the veins under his eyes were red, making them appear even more blue.

"Do what?" Puni asked again. I shushed him.

"I'll put the pen in my hand and spin it. If Mother Jamuna notices, I'll say you gave it to me, got it?"

"Yes," Golicchio said.

"Why would you do that?" Puni asked again, and Peepa pushed him down on the ground.

"Listen to your friend and shut the hell up!" He closed his mouth, and I knew he wouldn't speak for the rest of the day.

"Don't forget otherwise," Peepa said as he made his way outside for a few minutes of sun before class. As we stood in the hallway leading to the cafeteria, Ganesh walked by, chalkboard in hand, looking.

"Quick, hide," I said to Golicchio. "Ganesh is looking to copy more homework."

We had been asked to write a story in first person. It was to be short because there was no space for a long one on our chalkboard. I had already seen some of the others copy passages from the books they were reading. I was tempted to do the same; *Revelations* was about to end, and I couldn't get the book out of my head. Amit had not chosen the girl, and I wasn't sure where the story was headed. I had drastically slowed down my reading of it because I didn't want to finish too soon and not have anything else as interesting to read. I rarely looked forward to much these days; Amit's adventures were something that I relished with a passion. But for the sake of integrity, I had opted to draft a few lines about a girl who had a mean brother who tormented her. In conclusion, the sister and brother reconcile. The story was about as pathetic as my body, but I lacked the imagination that some of the others had.

Golicchio's story was more interesting than some of the books that the Mothers read aloud to us in class. He had drafted ten lines about the fate of a flower. Nothing much happened in the story, but the way he described the flower and its struggle to get sun and avoid the bugs that trampled the little garden in which it lived was beyond my realm of thinking. I would never have thought to write a story about something that wasn't human.

I knew that if Ganesh read the story, he would make fun of it, but secretly realize the genius of the prose and copy it for himself. Golicchio had spent hours working on it while Ganesh pored over a cricket match. The tradeoff was not fair, and I felt territorial about Golicchio's work.

Golicchio hid behind one of the tables in the cafeteria. Because he was thin like a long piece of rice, he was able to completely conceal himself behind one of the legs. Being still, now that was a challenge for him. I hoped for once he could restrain his jerky movements.

"Where's Golicchio? I thought I heard him." Class was to begin soon, and Ganesh was nervous. His eyebrows were wet, and he clenched his chalkboard so tightly I could see drops of sweat smear the edges.

"We don't know," I said. Puni shook his head no as well.

"Are you lying to me?" Ganesh came closer. Even though he was large, I wasn't as scared of him as I was of Peepa and Jaga-Nai. Deep down, I suspected that he had a warm heart. But because of his stature, he was forced to play the part of a high class bully. He had never hit me out of turn, and the most violent he'd ever been was to kick me once when I had rolled into him during the night.

"No," I said. I smiled at him. Without the others, he could be a good guy.

"I haven't finished the homework. What am I supposed to do?"

"Do it now. Hurry," I said, coaching him. I suggested he write a story about a sports hero, since that's what he was so interested in.

"Good idea," he said, slapping my arm in jest. He sat down, and he completed his homework. Just then Mother Jamuna called us to class. Ganesh ran as fast as he could; he couldn't lose his prime seat. After he left, Golicchio came out of hiding.

"He almost," he said.

"Why don't you just tell him no next time?" I asked. Puni nodded.

"It's not worth it to make enemies. Better to make friends," he said, and it was my turn to nod.

We headed to class, arms linked. Our mood quickly dissipated when I saw Peepa in the front row, right underneath Mother Jamuna's nose. She had come prepared; on top of her desk were three sticks, each of varying widths and lengths. Sometimes the fear of being punished was enough to keep us disciplined, and she knew that, which was why she often presented us with various torture devices. Sometimes we didn't even know what the items were used for, but our imaginations running wild were sure to placate us. Mother Jamuna was smart in that psychological way. She could have worked as a police interrogator.

We made our way to the back, nearly tripping on Jaga-Nai's extended feet. He lacked ingenuity; he often played the same trick on us day after day after day. We had caught on early, yet he continued to see if he could make us fall. As we slithered by, he coughed, and I felt something wet on my leg.

"Sit down," Mother Jamuna said. She began by calling our names, out of order of course. I was called right after Jaga-Nai, which I was sure was no coincidence. When she called Peepa, she stared at him, but since we were in the back, we couldn't tell what exactly she was looking at, and if she had noticed the pen in his hand. He had chosen to steal a bright yellow pen – no shocker – and we knew it was only a matter of time before Mother Jamuna's cat eyes would notice.

"What is that in your mouth?" she asked him.

"A pen."

"Yes, I see that. Where did you get it from?"

"Golicchio gave it to me." He turned around, and we saw the fluorescent pen sticking out of his mouth, looking like a torpedo about to be fired.

"Goli, where did you get this pen?" She looked at Golicchio, but I could feel the heat of her glare on me too.

"I don't know."

"Yes you do," Peepa said.

"What is happening?" Mother Jamuna looked confused, and she hated to look confused. She was the puppet master, and we were her puppets. If any of us went astray, she was sure to know. Puppets didn't do anything without her knowledge. She grabbed the largest stick on her desk.

"I took it, from your office," Golicchio said.

"But that pen was not in my office, it was in my nightstand," she said.

"Idiot," Peepa mumbled.

"Quiet!" she shouted. She yelled at both of them to come to the front of the class. As they stood at the head, the three whispered as if they were conspiring for evil. Then Mother Jamuna called Mother Kalpana and Headmistress Veli, who took both of them away. Golicchio turned to look at me, and he mouthed, "the Closet." I shuddered.

"If we catch you in our private quarters, you will spend two days in the hole. Understand? Goli and Nirmal, since they conspired together, are being sent there together. If you think the hole is too small for one, imagine the space for two." She laughed. I could feel goose bumps popping up all over my arms.

"Now, back to class," she said in a sweet, cheerful voice. It was as if nothing had happened. I worried about Golicchio, and more so, I worried about the two of them together, in that small confined space. I wondered whether Peepa would eat Golicchio alive.

THEY WERE RELEASED two days later as promised. It was night, and I had gotten used to the empty spaces on the floor. My head felt less itchy, and I wondered if the absence of extra bodies was abating my lice problem.

Golicchio squeezed in next to me, and instead of Peepa returning to his usual space – near Ganesh – he lay down next to Golicchio. Ganesh was already asleep, so I was hesitant to talk at all. I wasn't sure what to say or even what to ask. I decided to let Golicchio speak first, if he wanted to. Puni beat me though.

"How was it?" he asked.

No one said anything. Golicchio rolled over, and in the light shining through the window from the dark moon, I could see that his face was pale and his nose runny. But he smiled.

"Good," he said. "Better than I thought."

"What happened in there?" I whispered.

"A lot, Yrimal. A lot." Golicchio's punctuated speech puzzled me.

"Are you going to tell me?" I asked.

"There's too much to tell, I don't even know where to begin," he said, still smiling.

"Mind your own business, fuck," Peepa said. That was his only contribution for the night.

I closed my eyes and tried to think about a place that was expansive. As I was about to drift off, I heard Peepa and Golicchio whisper to each other. Then I heard a small laugh and a rustle. I figured I was dreaming, so I ignored it. Later that night, when I got up to stretch my limbs, I saw that Peepa had his arm on Golicchio's shoulder, as if he were protecting him from some unknown harm. I was jealous.

Chapter Forty-One

WHEN MY SON tells me he is gay, I am almost relieved.

He expects an argument or at the very least a discussion. I know he thinks I am conservative, but that is because of my accent.

"Who is he?" I ask.

"Balram," he says, and I am surprised he has taken an Indian lover.

"I'm happy for you," I say. "Promise me something, yes?" I ask him. I know the pleading in my voice will ensure his submission.

"No more secrets," I say.

Chapter Forty-Two

I HAD JUST finished *Revelations*, and I was anxious to talk to Golicchio about it.

Golicchio never did tell us what happened in the Closet, and I never bothered to ask him again. I knew it drove Puni insane to not know, but I didn't have a lust for curiosity like some of the others. I figured whatever happened was best not known, but things had changed. Golicchio and Peepa became almost inseparable after that. When I was around them, I felt the way I did when Smita was born, and all of my parents' affections were showered upon her. I didn't feel wanted. As a result, Puni and I became a little closer, even though I didn't always like his one-track mind and his insatiable appetite. But orphan boys in abusive situations couldn't be picky.

On the last page of *Revelations*, Amit dies at the hands of his very own father. I was shocked. I couldn't believe how it had ended, and I needed to talk to someone. I wanted to understand how a father could do that to a son. As much as my father despised me at times, he never would have killed me. What did it take to put someone over the edge like that? I knew I could pose these questions to Golicchio, and he would respond with something introspective, which would cause my brain to spin for days. I needed that stimulation. Lately, all Puni wanted to talk about was the girl.

"Golicchio?" I called softly down the hall. Even though Peepa seemed to be his new best friend, he didn't abandon me. I felt grateful for that at least. He could've – he had Ganesh on his side now permanently too – but inside, I believed he got something out of our friendship the way I did, though it was more limited now.

I looked to the left and saw that Mother Jamuna's door was closed. Headmistress Veli's door was closed as well. I walked by, and I could hear murmured voices. I was afraid to see her and Jaga-Nai together again, so I tiptoed along. As I got to the main dining hall, her door opened and she whispered, "Sid?" I looked back, and her hair was unbraided, her sari barely hanging above the top of her shoulder. I couldn't help but stare at her fat neck and how the area between her left shoulder and neck was so exposed.

"Will you come here, please?" She motioned with her head as I went into her room, and she shut the door.

"Yes?" I looked at her, and she smiled at me.

"My head has been feeling very itchy lately. Will you look for lice?" I always preferred doing chores for Headmistress Veli because she always rewarded handsomely. Once, for massaging her feet with talcum, she had given me a handful of pork samosas, still steaming from the hot oil that dripped from the sides.

She allowed me to sit on her desk chair, and she sat on the floor in between my legs. She rested her head, and I moved the chair back a little. Penalty for improper touching? I could imagine a lifetime in the hole.

"What's wrong? You can't look for lice if you are that far away, silly boy! Move closer!" She giggled and slid back into my pants. I looked down and with my fingers, separated the hairs on her scalp, so I could see if any of the lice had laid eggs. Her hair was incredibly oily, just like my mother's had been.

I tried to remember her face again. I knew it was buried somewhere, and I just needed the right trigger to release it. Finally, after several minutes passed, I concentrated on the back of Headmistress Veli's head, and my mother's face came to me. I had not forgotten her after all.

Her eyes were light, not blue like Golicchio's, but a lighter brown, the way perfectly-cooked molasses banyarum looked right out of the fryer. Her nose was peppered with black moles, and her mouth was thin but shaped like a small bow. Her face was like a wedding present for my father – a caramel-complexioned gift.

I leaned down and put my nose against Headmistress Veli's hair. When I combed my mother's hair, I would carry around her scent for days. My father would make fun of me, teasing me that I was a girl, but his taunting was never hurtful.

"You like the smell?" she asked. She tossed her head to the side, and again, I was given free view of the side of her neck.

"My mother," I said, but I had to stop. I didn't want to cry.

"What's wrong? Are you crying? You boys are so soft these days, nothing like the boys of before." She stood up and glared at me. I couldn't remember ever having angered her.

"What boys?"

"The boys who used to live here. They were rough. They were manly. You all are so mushy. I have to constantly reassure you with my words and my touch and my food before you will do anything for me. What do I get out of it?"

"But you are the one who works here. You chose to work here."

"I didn't choose to work here. I am enslaved just like you. And trying to make it as bearable as possible, just like you. Now get out."

"Enslaved? Like us? How…"

"Get OUT!" she shouted and pushed me. I nearly landed face first into the wall across from her room. I turned to look at her, and she shut the door.

As far as I was concerned, she was not like one of us. Deep down, I felt as though she used that as an excuse to act in inappropriate ways, especially with Jaga-Nai. I feared for him, but had no sympathy, so I let these thoughts pass. But thoughts were like bad memories – they left you sometimes, but they always returned.

ON MY WAY to the outhouse, I saw Headmistress Veli leaning against the side of the building, holding back her sari. When I looked a little closer, I noticed that she was vomiting onto the ground, getting her hair wet in the process. She turned to look at me and snarled.

"Hate is a force that creates tension inside of you," Golicchio said once. I remembered this conversation vividly because it was one of the few times that he didn't seem to be making up fairy tales. I really believed it because I felt it.

"What about love?" I asked.

"Love eats away the tension until you are completely at peace like the Buddha – ey, like your namesake!" He laughed. I laughed too. For someone named after such a great spiritual leader, I sure lacked the insight that Golicchio had.

"Why do you think that people are so mean though? Why in here especially?"

"Haven't we had this conversation before?" He yawned. He was probably right, but I never tired of talking about people's motives and their desires.

To change the subject, I jokingly asked, "What is there to not like about me?" I didn't expect him to take me seriously, but Golicchio looked me up and down and showed me two fingers.

"What?" I asked.

"There are two things that I don't like about you. Do you want to know?"

"Mmm. Okay."

"Your solitude and your frailty. The others are always picking on you. And I wish you wouldn't keep so many things inside. I think you know more than you share, and sometimes you don't speak up for yourself when the Mothers are unjust."

I wasn't sure how to respond. The frailty I understood. I didn't like that about myself either, but the House wasn't going to do anything to change that. I knew it was easier to be a soft cushion for the Mothers and let them sit on me whenever they wanted. I didn't think standing up to them was the best use of my energies. But solitude? I was not one who preferred to be alone, and I certainly talked more than Puni.

"Why do you say that I like to be alone? I like talking to you. I tell you a lot."

"No, you don't. There is a lot that goes on in your head, Yrimal. You know a lot more about this House than you say, and I wish you would just tell me."

"Why do you want to know? I suppose I just tell what is relevant."

"But who are you to decide what is relevant? Why not let me decide?"

"But it's my information to share," I said.

"Aren't we friends?"

I laughed. "Yes, but Golicchio it's impossible for me to tell you everything anyway. You'd have to live inside my head."

He didn't look convinced, but he took that as an answer. He had sighed in response.

He was right. I kept many things from Golicchio. He shared openly and freely, without expecting much in return. I wanted to tell more, but

I didn't know how. It was as if I had a third limb, but had never been told how to use it. In a way, I felt a little happy for Golicchio. He had found perhaps a better suited friend in Peepa – one who shared many things, and I with Puni, who shared very little. I wondered if a sense of order was finally coming to the House.

Inside, Mother Jamuna was in a very bad mood; someone had torn a hole in several of the pants parts of her salwar kameezes. She was outraged at the manner in which they had been damaged. Someone had made big holes in the crotch area, which Mother Jamuna hadn't discovered until sitting down this morning to scold a boy in her office. The boy had been unable to stop laughing hysterically, and it wasn't until she looked down that she knew why. I didn't know who exactly had done it. No one wanted to take blame. Ganesh puffed up his chest acting as though he knew (or was the culprit), but I didn't think it was him. I had a feeling it was one of us weaker boys. Some of us were destined to play the roles that were made for us. It was a self-fulfilling prophecy – tell a lower class boy in the House to act like he was meant for the bottom rung, and he will not disappoint. Sometimes it was easier to act the way you were expected to act. That way, there were no surprises on either end.

As I approached the outhouse, I overheard voices in the stall. As I got closer, I realized the voices belonged to Golicchio and Peepa. My instinct told me to turn away and leave, but I couldn't. I was frozen.

"Do you regret it?" Peepa asked.

"No, but—"

"Let's run away." Golicchio laughed.

"To where? You heard the Mothers. We'd be sold into slavery."

"Is that any different than here?"

Silence.

"I can't leave. What I know is here, my friends…"

"Who? Yrimal?" I heard Peepa groan.

"Yrimal, Puni, some of the others. They're all the family that I know."

"And me?"

"You too." I could hear a smile in Golicchio's voice.

"I don't understand why you like those pieces of shit. They're so low class and dirty."

"I'm low class too, you know. Or have you forgotten?"

"You don't act like they do. You're different."

"Am I really that different? You choose to see what you want to see. Why can't you see the good in Yrimal and Puni the way that I do? We all have our weaknesses. You have yours as well."

"I don't use them to get special favors, especially with the Mothers."
On this point, Golicchio remained silent.

"We don't have much time. We should leave soon," Peepa said, after being quiet for a few minutes. I heard a shift of clothing.

"Why?"

"See, and this is where you are stupid." I imagined that Golicchio was hurt, but he'd probably pocket it because he cared a great deal about Peepa. Power in numbers, Golicchio had once told me. "I can feel it. Something is about to happen. And if we don't leave now, we won't ever leave."

"Let me think about it."

"What is there to think about?" Peepa screamed. I shrank back in fear.

Golicchio sighed. "A lot. A lot more than you think." Now it was Peepa's turn to sigh. I had heard enough. I crept back to the House, holding my bladder as if it were a safety blanket, hoping and praying they would be done soon, so I could relieve myself.

Chapter Forty-Three

WHEN I AM ready, I retrieve the article. I go to the basement where my wife paints and hides things, and I find the clipping stuck to the back of one of her canvases:

Pooveli Boys' Home was burned down yesterday in what appears to be arson. Unfortunately, one casualty remained...

The orphanage was shut down when government officials discovered that the Mothers running the operation were laundering money meant for the children. Mother Jamuna, the head matron, was captured ... trying to leave the country. The others...

The article shows a picture of a body, scarred and black, resting in one of the rooms. I recognize the half-burnt colorful bears and the charred posters still pasted to the wall.

Chapter Forty-Four

"Yrimal," Golicchio said. I looked up from my supper. Mother Jamuna still hadn't figured out who had cut her pants. I thought she'd punish all of us by taking away our food, but that hadn't happened. I nodded at Golicchio.

"Did you finish your homework for tomorrow?" He sat down next to me.

"No," I said. I tried to force myself not to act as though I'd heard their conversation, but I couldn't help it. Though I concealed much, I couldn't hide my disappointment well.

"What happened? Tell the truth for once."

"What? I am always honest. You are the one who is keeping secrets."

"What?" Golicchio looked at me sideways.

"I heard your conversation with Peepa in the outhouse. What were you doing in there anyway?" Golicchio sighed. It was the same sigh that I had heard earlier.

"What were you doing listening to us?"

"Answer me first!"

"No," Golicchio said. He didn't cross his arms like I did. He reclined, with his hands out behind his back.

We both sat quietly for a while. I finished my dinner and was about to get up when Golicchio shrieked, "Answer!" The rest of the boys stared, but none were interested enough to intervene. Golicchio rarely lost his composure. I chuckled.

"Why are you laughing? How dare you listen to us?"

"The outhouse is a public area. I had every right to listen. If you wanted to speak in private, you should've gone elsewhere."

Golicchio let this idea settle, and I believed he realized it made sense. "I don't really remember how we ended up there. We were talking about something and then started walking..."

"I don't care."

"Yes, you do. Otherwise you wouldn't have listened. It's easier to shut our ears to nonsense." Golicchio stared at me, and he looked pained. "What all did you hear?" he whispered.

His question gave me heartburn. "What happened between you two in the Closet?"

"You wouldn't understand." I saw Peepa cross the room, and Golicchio looked down. "I can't," he said.

"Did he hurt you?" He looked toward Peepa as he sat next to him. He hadn't heard me, and I wasn't even sure if Golicchio had. They began talking, laughing, and I felt foolish for caring the way I did. I stood up and went to lie down. Bed time was an hour away, but I didn't care. I wanted to be left alone with my dark thoughts. I needed time to let them come out on their own, and I needed to be sure that I was ready to listen.

I SAT UP, gasping for air. An image of my father kneeling came to mind. He was praying to one of the many false idols my mother had constructed near the stove. He asked for forgiveness and for money. My mother came and shushed him. He kicked her away, and he continued to pray for forgiveness.

"Do you think this is a hotel?" I heard Mother Jamuna say. I got up, and Jaga-Nai was pointing at me, laughing.

"No, I was tired."

"You are to clean the cafeteria today. Who do you think will do it?"

I started to get up, but she pulled me by my armpits.

"A good boy is mindful of his chores and doesn't waste his days sleeping." She left, and I went to the cafeteria. As I passed Jaga-Nai, I could smell his foul breath on my neck. He patted me on the back.

THE CULPRIT FINALLY revealed himself. It was Peepa who had torn Mother Jamuna's pants into shreds. No one knew what he had done with the crotches. Golicchio said he'd seen some of the dogs with colored pieces of thread hanging from the sides of their froth-dripping mouths. The image was symbolic of what we all thought of the Mothers and their sexuality. Feed them to the dogs!

As expected, Peepa was sent to the Closet for three days. Instead of being released in the morning like usual, he was released at night.

"Go to sleep," I heard Mother Kalpana say. Her voice was soft, the way it sounded right after one woke up and tried to use vocal chords that had gone unused for most of the night. I turned my head and noticed she was wearing a night dress of sorts. As she moved her body in a circle to leave, I saw the back of it sweaty, sticking to her body and all of the fatty folds that lined her spinal cord.

Peepa crawled into the space next to me and used his arms to cover the top of his head.

"Ey," I said. Peepa didn't say anything. I repeated myself.

"I heard what you said. There's no need to talk so loud," he said. I had barely whispered, but after days of silence, even a hush could sound deafening.

I tried to move away from his warm body and focus on the ochre-colored spots that topped the ceiling. Sometimes if it was hot and we were lucky, water would drip down in a slight mist and cool us off. When it was cold, the leak was a curse and one that the Mothers didn't care about. As I watched the yellow turn into white and then back to yellow again, my eyes relaxed and I drifted off into a place that served lunch twenty-four hours a day.

"Yrimal, can you hear me? Wake up!" He clenched my hand so tightly that I finally did wake up. I shrugged him off.

"What's wrong?" I looked over at him, and he was grabbing his stomach.

"I need to use the bathroom. Really bad. I feel ill." He got up and went to the corner of the room. I looked around, and every single boy was fast asleep.

"Ask Ganesh." I pointed to the big round mass heaving in and out. "Or Golicchio."

He looked at Golicchio, peacefully sleeping. He shook his head. "They didn't give me enough water in there. My body shrunk." He lifted up his shirt to show me his ribs protruding in the moonlight.

"So? When did you get so skinny?"

I noticed that severe dehydration had caused his pores to grow markedly larger than before, and the hollows in his cheek were more transparent, which made his eyes look bigger.

"Drink water then." The one and only thing that the Mothers didn't begrudge us was the water. We were allowed to drink as much or as little as we wanted, but at our own risk. Sometimes we got sick from the water, but it was rare.

"I did, I drank too much. Now I feel ill," and as he doubled over, he threw up a slew of liquid near the back door to the yard.

"I'm going to call the Mothers."

"No, no. I just need to use the toilet. Please come with me." I looked and saw the silhouettes of the dogs roaming. I could tell that they smelled our fear. They knew we were about to step out into their territory. I thought I even heard one of them growl.

"I don't want to," I said. I looked at him. His face was water-logged; large bags were hanging under his eyes like bananas on a branch, and his eyes were covered with red veins.

He looked at me in anger – as much as he could possibly muster. "You owe me," he said.

"Why? What do I owe you for?"

He took out a picture from his shorts pocket, which I noticed had no holes. I was jealous.

"Look," he said. I did, and I saw a black and white image of a man who looked a little like Peepa. There was a man standing next to him.

It took me a second to register who it was. As every day went by, the little grains that made up his face were slowly fading away.

I didn't even know what to say.

"Is your father's name S. Vikash?" Peepa asked.

"How did you know…?"

"Golicchio told me." He turned the photo over and my father and his father's names were imprinted on the back – including the date the photo was taken.

When I first came to the House, Golicchio had asked me what my father's name was. All of us were intent on establishing some sort of link to our past. We held onto the hope that perhaps our families hadn't died after all and someone knew of their whereabouts. We questioned each other then, asking if our families knew each other. Did we recognize each other's name? No one had known me or my family – or so I had thought. Golicchio hadn't recognized my family's name, nor I his. I was surprised that he'd remembered my father's name at all – that was many years ago.

"If you want to know more, come with me," he said. "Please."

He had something to bargain with, and I couldn't say no.

"Fine," I said. I grabbed his hand, and we ran as fast as we could to the outhouse. As we closed the door on the dogs and the night's own light, Peepa asked me to help him with his pants. I couldn't unfasten them in time. And after he vomited into the hole, he slipped into unconsciousness.

"Peepa?" I called over and over. "Peepa? Answer!"

Waking the Mothers at this hour for something that might have been as mild as dysentery would warrant several beatings. And that didn't even scare me as much as the idea that the dogs would get to me first – hungry, and probably nutrient-starved, they'd attack my heart first because that was the place where most of my blood was (or so I thought anyway). I didn't know if Peepa would survive until morning.

I left Peepa's side and peeked outside. I could see the dogs moving around the yard. The sun was still a few hours away.

"Tell me about my father," I whispered, but I knew he couldn't hear me. I studied his face, thinking that for as big as India was, for my father and his to have known each other, it really wasn't any bigger than the back of my hand.

I rolled his dripping head into my lap and rocked it. "Wake up, wake up," I said.

He didn't, so I slapped his face. I punched his arm for all the times he had been mean to me. I pulled on his hair, envious of how shiny it was. I felt shameless, attacking a defenseless, sick man.

"Yrimal," he said, and I was so startled that I dropped his head to the floor.

"Are you awake?" I held my hands up, afraid that he knew I had hit him.

"Will you rub my head?" he whispered, and I had to ask him again. He repeated it, almost apologetically, as if he were asking me for my right leg. I kneeled next to him and rubbed it.

"Why are you so angry with me?" I asked him.

"I'm not."

"You're not here because of me." My shirt was covered in something that looked like mustard seed paste. I was cold.

"The Mothers don't pick on you. You yelled at Mother Jamuna, and you didn't get extra days in the Closet. I ask for more water, and I get none!" he screamed. The dogs barked outside.

"You upper castes are all the same. The moment we get a break, you complain when all your life has been easy."

"You play up your weakness. Golicchio is weak too, but he doesn't act as you do." Peepa tried to swing at me, but he was too sick and fell against the inside wall of the outhouse.

"Why did you hit me? Hit me while I was too weak to do anything about it? That's a coward, that's what," he yelled again, and I cringed not because of his voice but because he was right.

"We should be friends. We're all in the same situation." The moment I said that, I knew it was a mistake. We weren't all in the same situation. Jaga-Nai and most of the upper caste boys were treated differently than I was. But in the difference, there was sameness. For those of us who weren't shipped here directly at birth, we knew that in order to be treated the same we had to be treated differently as that was how the world was, and we were all different people who reacted differently to different things. The thoughts and words mixed around in my head.

"We both had mothers and fathers," I said.

"How dare you speak of my mother on your tongue," he said.

"Golicchio told me that—"

Peepa yelled at me to shut up. I looked at his arm, and it was very hairy, like the skin on the monkeys I'd seen in the little temple near our house, the one in absolute ruins. We weren't forbidden from attending ceremonies at the larger, nicer temples, but we weren't welcome either. So we prayed at the dilapidated one instead, risking death by falling rock or attack by hungry monkey.

Peepa stopped talking. "You owe me information about my father," I pleaded. I was a mirror image of my placating mother in all ways, even in looks. I had the full eyelashes and the bottom-heavy nose sprinkled with black dots. My face was very sensual and soft; I would've made a beautiful woman.

"Why must you always ask the questions?" He looked at me, and even in the darkness, I could feel the contempt in his eyes.

Peepa survived. I couldn't say that I was happy or sad. He owed me information about my father, and I wasn't going to ever get it.

The next morning, when the Mothers discovered us, we were still awake. They weren't angry. They saw how sick Peepa was and let him sleep. I got to take a bath, but was forced to go to class and study afterward. Maybe that was their punishment for me.

Today, we were learning about the afterlife. Golicchio and I were afraid of dying. If the Mothers were right, we'd be born into a far worse situation than we were in now. The upper caste kids were bored; the Mothers told them that in Hinduism, once you were up, you couldn't go down, but I didn't believe that. However, I couldn't pretend I wasn't riveted. For once, the topic was intriguing and I hoped that we'd learn what dying felt like. In the middle of the lesson, Mother Kalpana came in to announce some news. I booed inside.

"Children, I have something wonderful to tell you." I couldn't remember if I had ever seen her so happy before. Her fat seemed to glow from underneath her neck. She lit up like a burgeoning fertility goddess on drugs. "Mother Jodi got accepted to a higher post in New Delhi, running a girls convent there, so she will be leaving us. This is such a high honor, so please congratulate her when you get a chance." She turned to leave, and then swung back around. "Oh, no more class the rest of the day. She has brought treats to share. Gulab jamun and burfi in the cafeteria!"

Someone unleashed the cows from the gate. We all got up at once and rushed toward the door. Too many of us caused a jam, and we were stuck in the bottleneck. Finally Golicchio, one of the skinnier ones, inched his way through, and then the rest of us were able to pass. The Mothers made us wait in line, and although I was pushed to the end, it didn't matter. There were so many treats to choose from, I knew there would be enough for everyone twice over. The Mothers had also taken care to arrange the delicacies in an artful way on the cafeteria tables, heightening the sense of desire that we felt. The spread looked like a page from one of my fantasies. I looked at Puni, and I could see his mouth salivating. His eyes were brimming with tears.

Because there was so much of everything, we didn't fight over any. We took our shares like civilized men and sat down next to each other, engaging in jovial conversation.

"Do you even know who Mother Jodi is?" Puni asked. We looked at each other and laughed.

"I didn't even know there was a Mother named Jodi here before today!" Ganesh yelled.

The Mothers morphed together and looked like one. Ghosts were what they reminded me of.

"Have any of you ever seen a ghost?" I asked.

Most of the boys nodded no, but we were all eager to hear stories. Golicchio started to talk, but Ganesh cut him off.

"Only real stories today, Golicchio. I want to hear a real ghost story."

"Who said that I don't have one?" he asked, but I could tell that his feelings were hurt.

"I have one," Puni said.

"Go on," Ganesh said. I could tell that Puni liked the attention because he blinked once.

"At night, ghosts came to haunt me. I've told Yrimal this story already."

"About the fairies that come to steal your fat? Those were fairies."

"They were fairy ghosts," he said. Everyone gasped.

"My parents always said that I was too fat. So at night they warned me that if I didn't lose weight the ghosts would come and take it. I never knew why they needed it."

"Maybe they need it to be real like the rest of us," Golicchio said.

"Every night, I would wake to find cuts in my flesh and fat to be missing."

"How could you not wake up?" Ganesh asked.

"It's as if they put a spell on me. I never felt the pain and never woke up in the middle of the night. But one night, I did see something."

"I thought you never saw anything?" I asked. Ganesh pushed me and asked, "What?"

I saw Jaga-Nai out of the corner of my eye. He was making his way closer to our group to listen. I hadn't noticed him earlier, and his leaf was piled high with sugar. I wondered where he had been, but my mind quickly returned to focus on Puni.

"I forced myself to stay awake one night. The ghosts were making me sick. My parents didn't have money to take me to the doctor, and I was afraid I was going to die. I need fat to live. I need to eat. But I refused food that day. Maybe they wouldn't come if I didn't eat? And I forced my eyes to stay open. I never saw the fairy. But I saw two men – they looked like they had come from a different time. They were dressed in rich clothes and had black masks over their faces. I screamed, and they ran away. I never saw them again. Nor did I ever close my eyes again. My fat was now safe."

He finished his story, and I was letting it settle.

"Those don't sound like ghosts," Jaga-Nai said. "Maybe those were fat traders come for your body."

"What are those?" Ganesh asked.

"They sell fat to make soap and candles and other things. Human fat lasts longer. Your parents probably were trying to make money and sold your body to those thugs. Eh, do you blame them?"

"My parents were worried about me. If they had sold me, why care?" Puni stared at him.

Jaga-Nai didn't answer. He just smiled.

Golicchio finally was given his chance to talk about a ghost, and he regaled us with a tale about his dead aunt Thirumma, who visited him regularly for an entire year. He always knew it was her because she had a large nose, which she'd use to tickle the insides of his toes at night. We laughed, but Puni stayed silent.

After we had our fills, most of us disbanded for the day, suffering from diabetic comas. Puni stayed on in the cafeteria, eating and eating until the Mothers had to kick him out.

Later, I found Puni vomiting in the backyard near the outhouse. Every sugary delicacy that he'd put into his mouth now surfaced, and I could tell that he didn't want to cry.

"The waste," he said. "I wasted it all." I patted him on the back and felt it best not to speak. After a few minutes had passed, I saw the girl from the greenhouse walk by with a plate stacked with candies. She saw Puni throwing up and came over.

"Are you all right?" she asked him directly. She put a hand on his back and rubbed it.

"No," he said, sniffing. He'd pause for a second, as though he did feel better, but then he'd return to the ground, the lurches overpowering him to the point where he could barely hold himself upright.

"What do you need? Can I get you some water?" I detected genuine concern in her voice, and my stance toward her softened.

"Water, yes," I said.

She ran back into the House and returned carrying only a tumbler of water. Puni drank it and then five minutes later, vomited it and some more yellow jaggery.

"Do you want me to get Mother Jamuna?"

Both of us shouted no in unison. She smiled. "We'll just wait until you're better then," she said quietly. She and I took turns rubbing his back as he threw up, and Puni thanked us each time. After his episodes calmed down, he put his back to the outhouse, wiping his nose and breathing heavily.

"I think that's it," he said. The three of us sat in silence, enjoying the cool air. I rubbed my stomach. It felt good to be full. I looked sideways at the girl, and whatever animosity that she'd felt toward me seemed gone. I remembered that we weren't supposed to be talking to her, but the draw to remain near her was fierce. She was pretty, but not breathtaking. I wasn't sure what it was, but nonetheless, I was attracted to her. As were all of the others. Ganesh, Peepa, and Golicchio soon came outside with a ball in hand, ready to play some sort of game. I saw them look at us and start to approach.

"Why are you talking to her?" Peepa asked. I saw Golicchio look on with curious eyes.

"Puni was sick. She helped."

The girl stood up, and at that moment, she had tunnel vision. All she saw was Peepa. She smiled, and I felt butterflies in my stomach.

"Nirmal, a long time has passed since I've seen you."

"I was in the hole," he laughed, but the girl seemed concerned.

"For what? Are you all right?" She put her hand on his arm, and he shrugged it off.

"Yes, I'm fine."

"Anyone want to play ball?" Golicchio asked. I knew he was trying to avoid a confrontation.

"No," Ganesh and Peepa said in unison. Golicchio nodded at me, and I went off with him. Puni stayed behind as well.

"Does Puni want to die?" I asked no one in particular.

Golicchio and I threw the ball to each other across the dirt. I wasn't paying attention and grew tired of the ball frequently hitting me in the face.

"Stop," I finally said. Golicchio kept deliberately aiming the ball right at my nose.

"Do you want to play or no?"

"What do you suppose they are talking about?"

"I don't know. But whatever it is, it will not end well." We saw Ganesh shove Peepa and vice-versa. Puni looked on, scared, but he refused to leave the girl's side. The girl didn't stop her staring at Peepa. "She will marry one of us someday," he said.

"Who?"

"I don't know."

"I think she likes Peepa." Golicchio's face darkened.

"How do you know that?"

"Just guessing."

"If I were you, I'd stay out of it."

"Why? Because it involves Peepa?" I knew better than to revisit our prior conversation. At this point, I didn't care anymore.

Golicchio nodded yes. We saw the girl and Puni try to pull Ganesh off of Peepa, who was now on the ground, his hands in his face. He was yelling. "Not my face, you fuck," but that's exactly where Ganesh aimed his punches. Soon Mother Kalpana came outside, and she called Mother Jamuna. The two of them wrestled the boys apart, and we saw them take Peepa, Ganesh, and Puni inside. The girl was left alone, with not a slap or a rebuke to boot. I felt my animosity returning.

"Why do you fight all the time?" she yelled across the expanse of dirt that divided us.

"Because they all want you. Who will have you? Which one do you want?" Golicchio asked.

"Nirmal, of course. I've never been deceitful. I've always expressed my clear desire for Nirmal. I am just waiting for him to ask for permission from one of the Mothers." She smiled. "Soon he told me." She was fearless for expressing her desires so openly to us.

"When did he say that?" Golicchio asked. He had moved closer to her, his blue eyes staring, perhaps finally being seduced by her as the rest of us had been.

"I don't remember, but he did. Why would Ganesh think I want him? I don't even talk to him. And Puni's like a brother." She laughed. "I could never marry someone whose eyes are that way."

"Peepa has other plans – plans that don't involve you."

For a brief second, I saw a flash of hurt cross her teardrop-shaped eyes. Then she rebounded. "What plans?"

Golicchio remained silent. I wondered if he was still planning to run away, and I motioned to speak, but then decided against it. She kept asking him.

"Let's go inside. The Mothers will return with even more hate," I said. Golicchio agreed, and we left the girl with her questions. Even with our backs to her, she continued to ask.

"Why don't you leave us alone? Don't you see that you bring nothing but hurt every time you come around?" I asked her. She just stared at me, and I could tell that she didn't understand what I meant, and why I would say such mean things to her. Most people liked when she came around. She didn't seem to care that the Mothers forbade us from talking to her.

All she cared about was Peepa and her need for male attention. Though she called Puni her "brother," she even lavished the way he looked at her.

Before I walked inside, I spit a large yellow wad onto the ground. I hadn't done it to spite her; I realized, though, that I looked at her after I did, and it appeared as though I had done it on purpose.

Chapter Forty-Five

HIS STORY IS one that I cannot easily forget.

Late one night, before I was married, I started typing random queries into an internet search engine. I remember trying various strings of indiscriminate words from my past – "Kabaddi rules," "*Revelations* and Amit," "female dogs white." Then I typed in "selling human fat." I found several stories of gangs in India that went from village to village, abducting mainly poor people – women and children included – and hacking their bodies for profit. The fat they sold to cosmetic companies in Europe. They put human organs on the black market. It is a huge problem in India and other countries, especially in places where economic sustenance is a dream rather than a reality. I could almost envision Puni's parents making a "deal" with a gang like this. How he had survived I don't know. Some would call it luck, but I don't think it was.

Chapter Forty-Six

HEADMISTRESS VELI'S TEDDY bears would have been cute had they not smelled like rainwater mold. The stench was the first thing I noticed when I entered her room. She had asked me in, but I was worried. I hadn't spoken to her in a long time, and I had avoided her as much as I could. In the past, I had sought her out in hopes of obtaining a snack or a kind pat. But since her mean outburst last, I was scared that she didn't like me anymore.

"Wait inside," she said. She half-shut the door while she and Mother Kalpana continued their conversation.

"He's not good for you. Love marriages never work." And with her final words of advice, Mother Kalpana left. She turned to look at me, and in her eyes and twitching mouth, I found pity.

"Are you in love with him?" I asked. I was sitting on the floor, looking up at her.

"Who are you talking about? My suitor? I have many," she answered. She finished braiding her hair and was applying powder to her face. Afterward, she opened up her closet and showed me all of her saris. "I have so many," she said again, and I didn't know if she was referring to her saris or her men.

There had always been a certain attraction and energy that drew me to Headmistress Veli besides her generosity and willingness to share. She was fat, but her face was decent. She had tiny beady eyes that provided a wild contrast to her bushy eyebrows. And her lips were her best feature – they even made one forget that two chins loomed below. Her lips looked painted on by a very soft and very fine artist's brush. They were very shapely, and even when she was eating (which was frequent), they remained uncorrupted.

"You are a bad, bad boy, Siddhartha," she said. She rubbed the part of my neck under my chin. "Why were you mean to me last? You hurt my feelings." She picked at the bright green teddy bear and then cuddled with it.

"I didn't. You were to me."

"Those are just words. You are not like the others. You are too sensitive."

"Do you need me to do something for you?" I hoped she wouldn't ask me to wash her floors today.

"Why must you ask? Have I not given you enough, done enough for you? You boys are so selfish, only thinking of yourselves."

"You do, but—"

"But what? If I ask one small favor of you, why is it that you cannot do it? Would any of the others dare question me when I feed them mangoes and ginger pickles?"

"Dare?"

"Those are just words," she said again. "You could show your appreciation in other ways, you know."

"But I do appreciate you. I tell you thank you, and I always speak highly of you to the others. I don't know what else I can do?" I was flummoxed. What was it that she wanted? Then it came to me.

"Oh," I said. "I know what you want."

She just smiled. She didn't say yes or no, but I knew I was right. I was uncomfortable, but somehow, that word wasn't quite strong enough to describe how I was feeling then.

"Do you know how?" she asked. She leaned forward, and I could see that the teddy bear was still in her arms. "Should I show you?"

"No," Jaga-Nai said. He came into the room, his hair standing up even higher than before. I avoided looking at him directly, but was quietly relieved that he was there.

"Don't do that to me, you promised," he said.

"Take off your shorts," she said to me. She started to unwind her sari. Her fat folds were everywhere.

"You promised!" he shouted. "You leave, eh? Leave or else I will bust your nose." I was frozen, but he knew that I wanted to leave, which made it harder.

Finally, Headmistress Veli's awareness of Jaga-Nai broke the trance. I was able to move and started toward the door when she grabbed me by the back of my shorts.

"Jagadesh, this does not concern you. Please leave right away otherwise I will never help you find your parents. Are you listening to me? Go!" She stared at him with such intensity it almost seemed as though she were in love with him.

He left like a robot. She had a spell on him, and he did as he was told. She turned to look at me.

"Should we continue?"

I WAS BACK in Headmistress Veli's good graces, but there was always a trade-off when it came to friendships in the House. I knew it was all mental. Let her do what she wanted if it gave me special privileges and perks. She promised that if I did what she asked, she would rescue me from any of Mother Jamuna's future punishments and would let me use her toilet if I needed to go during the night, but only in exchange for an evening meeting as well. She said that I was not to say no to her whenever she called upon me, and that if I were to tell anyone of this "arrangement," she would deny it and have me sent somewhere far worse than the House. Although it was hard to picture anything that was worse, I didn't want to find out.

Even though she deemed it an "agreement," I didn't feel as though I had any choice in the matter. Do as she says or sell me to another who will do the same. I thought I would feel special for her selecting me, but I didn't. Why not lust after Ganesh or even Peepa? They were bigger, stronger, and more likely to hurt her. I was puny and small-boned. I could do no harm.

"You think you can get away so easily, eh?" Jaga-Nai.

I didn't say anything and waited.

"Why so quiet? What did she ask of you? Eh? Tell me!"

"Please don't shout or the other Mothers will hear."

He dragged me by my ear to the back of the House. Unfortunately for me, the boys that had been sitting with their backs to the House scattered like passengers exiting a bus.

"Tell me everything she told you. If you ruin this for me, I will kill you." He spoke with such evenness. A true psychopath.

"She asked me for favors and in return she'd protect me from the Mothers, that's it."

"What favors? Did you accept?"

"What?" He had his hands still on my ears, so it was hard to hear him.

"What favors? Did you accept them?" He pushed me back so as to look at me closely.

"I don't think I have a choice. Believe me, Jaga-Nai, I'd rather not. She forced me."

"'She forced me,'" he imitated. "Please. Any man would pay to have her. You are not even a man. What does she see in you? Does she make you wipe her butt or clean her armpits?"

I tried to recall what we had done, but I couldn't really remember. It was a blur, and I preferred it that way.

"I don't remember, honest."

"Did she say anything about me?"

"No."

"I love her, you know." He looked at me, and I could tell he was lying. He was scared shitless. What could be more horrific than a hundred kilos of flesh grinding into your body the way raw goat meat and rice mesh together? I couldn't think of anything.

"What? You don't believe it?" I didn't say anything. "She is helping me, so I help her. I like it. That's what men do. That's what they're supposed to like, eh?"

"Right."

"You didn't like it?"

"No, I don't think so."

"That's because you're not a man." He stepped on my foot. "And to think that I was threatened by you. You are nothing but a distraction to her. Go, leave." He waved me away, and I was happy to oblige.

I wished that that had been the end of it, but Jaga-Nai refused to let me alone. Now that he knew about us, we had become companions in the loosest sense – conspirators in a deadly game of mind and body. Whenever he would see me, he needed to talk to me about Headmistress Veli. Sometimes he'd yank me away from the others to talk alone, so that he could share some more about their meetings. The other boys were intrigued, but so far, none of them had said anything to me about it. I was waiting. It was only a matter of time, and I was afraid the truth of Headmistress Veli's penchant for young boys would leak, and I would be tossed out of the House faster than I could say "save me."

Chapter Forty-Seven

I USED TO think only men could disfigure and be disfigured.

But just as the spectrum can lead one to hate unimaginable, the other side is compassion. Amma had bent toward a magnanimity so powerful that she eclipsed those she cared about. I cannot even whisper the other's name – her self-loathing was so sovereign that it was like a disease.

When I finally told people what had happened to me, they didn't believe it. They saw me as the aggressor – the wicked face, bulky shoulders, triangle chest. How could a woman damage me?

I never told Amma about my ordeal; she would've mourned for her kind in the way the white man feels remorse for being privileged.

When I told my wife for the first time, she asked, "How long?" The movement of time is unclear in my mind. I cannot recall how many years it continued or even the intensity of our exchanges. I told her that at times I did enjoy it, in a perverse way, although I would have never admitted it to myself then. I had found her attractive, and she possessed a power so great that it had burned inside of me.

Chapter Forty-Eight

IN A SICK way, I grew used to Headmistress Veli's molestations the way one gets used to wearing old clothing. I didn't always like the situation, but I knew that it was better than not having any clothes at all. Sometimes I even looked forward to our meetings because I knew that my physical needs would always get met. If I pleased her, I never went hungry, and I was given extra uniforms whenever I wanted. I didn't have to worry about rushing to the cafeteria or trying to avoid Jaga-Nai. I had underestimated the amount of stress these activities had caused me, and now that they were absent, I felt a little lighter.

Even so, there were additional stressors to be worried about, but I tried to ignore those. My life was different now, but who said different meant worse?

Though Golicchio and Peepa grew closer and closer by the day, Golicchio refused to accept that our friendship had changed in turn. Now that I also harbored a deep secret, I thought we could be even. Yet I didn't feel that way. I felt more of a kinship with Jaga-Nai than with any of the other boys in the House. Golicchio didn't understand what I went through, and I couldn't explain it to him. In this way, both of the private lives we led drove a wedge between us.

With Puni, I was comforted by knowing that there was a deeper intelligence beneath those unblinking eyes. Even though he never asked me many questions and I never offered information, I just felt he knew things. Through that understanding, there was a peculiar closeness that I hadn't felt with him before. He was also too distracted with his own inner battles to pester me about my secrets. Food became his number one interest, and though I never held it against him, I knew he envied me because I had access to whatever foods I desired.

Once, Puni and I had been cleaning the outhouse together. It was my turn, but Puni needed something to do, so he joined me. We were in the middle of carrying buckets of water to wash the floor when Headmistress Veli came and asked to speak to me privately. Puni stared at her, his mouth open. In both of her hands, she carried packets of almonds. I could see Puni's tongue lap at the corners of his lips.

"Do you want some?" she asked me. I took a bag and as I opened it and was about to give half to Puni, she intervened.

"No," she said. "These nuts are only for you. Come," she said, waving her hand in the same dismissive way that Jaga-Nai sometimes did. As I left, I told Puni that I'd bring him back some, but I was lying. For Headmistress Veli, generosity without anything in return was not part of the arrangement.

EVEN THOUGH I wasn't allowed in the cafeteria when no meals were being served, I went in there anyway. As I sat and waited for food I no longer needed, I rubbed the sides of the walls for fun, coating my hands in a filmy chalk – the color of some of the whitest sea shells I'd ever seen in Madras. I didn't collect them, but Smita had. They were her prized possessions, which she never let me touch; my father put it in her head that divinities were trapped inside, waiting to be released. She guarded those shells as though they were gold, but no spirits ever escaped them. Where were those gods now? How come they hadn't broken free of their shells and saved her?

My hands became as white as a widow's sari as I ran them in circles across the wall.

I looked over my shoulder (afraid the Mothers would catch me) and instead saw Jaga-Nai in the corner, huddled over a pile of letters. As I walked closer to him, he was sifting through a pile of missives, all of which were from his family.

"Do you need help reading them?" I asked. I took a step closer, and he growled like a dog.

"I know how to read, eh? You think I don't?" He knew how to transform every statement into a question. It was the "eh" that did it.

"What are you doing?"

"You think that because you know things about me, that you and I are friends?" He stood up, and I took a step back. I didn't want to end up in the Closet again, this time with a bloody nose. I knew that Headmistress Veli offered "protections," but she couldn't save me always. I wasn't invincible, and Jaga-Nai wasn't wearing any shorts.

"No."

He reached out his hand, and I couldn't back up anymore. I had reached the wall. His hand touched my shoulder, and he embraced it.

"They said they were coming. They said that in the letters. Why haven't they come? She lied to me." He gasped, and I wondered if he was having an asthma attack. He could barely talk.

"Do you need a pipe?" He just shook his head. And then I realized. It hit me the way the warm ocean felt on a very cold day – he was crying. It barely sounded human. "You're crying," I mumbled.

"No, I'm not," he was barely able to get out. He was; I knew it. I wanted to run through the House and announce the news to everyone I could find. I wanted them to see a fallen bully.

"Then what is it that you're doing?"

"I'm mourning," he said.

"Did someone die?" I asked.

He didn't answer. He placed the pile of letters in a bunch, tucked it under his arm and went the way of the Mothers' corridors. I wanted to follow him and tell him no. I wanted to warn him against going into Headmistress Veli's room. But I didn't.

"WHAT ARE YOU and Jaga-Nai doing? Everyone wants to know, but no one wants to ask."

"Nothing. We're sort of friends now, that's it." I remembered what Jaga-Nai had said earlier, but weren't friendships formed of common bonds? Headmistress Veli was it. Good or bad.

"You know what the rumor is?" I nodded. "That you and Jaga-Nai are doing special 'favors' for the Mothers. You are absent a lot. No one ever knows where you boys are. Yet the Mothers never seem to bother you anymore. Even when you laughed at Mother Jamuna the other day for walking into class with her blouse unbuttoned. That would certainly have warranted at least ten lashes on any normal day. What is it you are doing? How can you live with yourself? Don't you feel disgusted?" I was not used to Golicchio's judgments.

"That's not true. None of it is true. You can ask Jaga-Nai. I help him read his letters sometimes. That's it. He's one of the few of us whose parents are still alive. Sometimes the letters are difficult, so I help him."

"How is it that his family can write a letter that he cannot read?"

"I don't know. Why don't you ask him?"

"I'm asking you. See, this is what I mean. You keep secrets. I know you're lying. I saw you leaving Headmistress Veli's room the other day with oil on your hands. What was it that you were doing?" I knew he wanted to unveil the secret, and perhaps drive the wedge between us away. I wanted that too, but I wasn't sure if what I told him would do that or drive him farther away.

"You wouldn't believe me if I told you, and I can't tell you. I promised."

"If she's making you do things against your will, you need to—"

"Do what? Tell who? The Mothers? Please, Golicchio. Please."

"Maybe you could tell the others? We could help?" He looked at me with such pity. I supposed there was a first for everything.

"The others would kill to be in my position. I should be so happy. But I feel so dead inside." On good days, I felt normal, maybe even optimistic about my future. On bad days, I felt as though Headmistress Veli was slowly sucking the livelihood out of me through my nose. And as strange as it was, my conversations with Jaga-Nai helped me stay alive. I used to loathe them, but now I looked forward to them. He understood what I was going through even though he lied about his feelings.

"No, it's a betrayal of trust, you need to do something. If she continues, she will have your baby. Is that what you want?"

I didn't know how babies were made, but I trusted that Golicchio knew what he was talking about. He didn't seem to be exaggerating.

"It's only for a little while. She doesn't like us when we grow up," I said.

"That's disgusting." Golicchio shook his head, but I knew that he wasn't going to tell anyone or the others. I trusted him, and what would he say besides? The information was not gleeful – who to share it with? I also felt he was burdened by my confidence.

"Perhaps you shouldn't ask so many questions." Golicchio nodded. He knew I was right, but he felt too sorry for me to even care.

I ALWAYS KNEW Peepa enjoyed drinking water, hence his nickname. Sometimes I wasn't sure if he drank out of enjoyment or pure necessity. The water seemed to evaporate when it touched his lips, and he always needed more, and more, and more. His addiction (which was what I called it) brought to mind Smita's attachment to one particular Hindu figure my father had given her. It was of Shiva gracing his son, Ganesh, before he went away with his monkey friend, Hanuman. Shiva looked sad – not really common for the fearless destroyer. Maybe Smita sensed that, which was why she had latched onto it so. Back then, I thought she was too young to understand the feeling of loss. Instead, I thought she was drawn to his bright blue color – the shade of the gaudy saris our mother would gawk at in the shop windows. She claimed the fabrics were hideous, but she stared at them nevertheless.

Whatever the reason, Smita carried that figurine around with her wherever she went. Seeing her had reminded me of my own obsessions, namely of trying to win my father's approval. I was burdened by the knowledge that sooner or later, all addictions came to an end. I knew the time would come for Smita too, and it finally did. She lost her Shiva doll and cried for days. She had never been quite the same after that; a piece of her went missing along with the figurine.

"What to do? What to do?" Peepa slurred. He was alone in the greenhouse, drunk as an alcoholic at the end of a three-day binge. I hadn't talked to him since the day he showed me the picture of our fathers together. I decided that if I wanted to find out anything, I had to ask him now. The Mothers were preoccupied; they were crowded in the cafeteria, having some sort of party. It was someone else's birthday this time, but they offered us no cake. Through the shut door, we could hear loud laughing, cups and spoons clinking together. We could also smell roasted tomatoes and chicken seared in black pepper. I advised Puni to stay away, but when I left him, he'd had his nose pressed against the door.

"Are you drinking?" I always hated when people asked questions that they knew the answers to, and here I was doing it myself.

"Yes." He nodded and even gesticulated.

"What are you drinking?"

"Whiskey," he said. I noticed a bit of gray in his beard. Was he prematurely aging?

I picked up the thermos that lay next to him and took a drink. It tasted worse than ginger juice. I almost spit it up.

"Do you like it? Not as good as a mango lassi though," he said, grabbing the thermos from me and taking another drink. I felt a little lightheaded, but dangerous.

"Can you tell me more about my father?" I asked.

"Don't think you'll get that so easily," he said. He looked at me very seriously and wiggled his finger. I came closer to him, and he said, "You are certain you want to know everything?"

"Yes," I said. My face was close enough to his to almost kiss him.

"Okay," he said, but he remained silent. I wasn't sure if he was thinking about how to say what he wanted to say, or if he had forgotten what we were talking about. I waited.

"Are you jealous because I am so handsome?" he asked. He stood and strutted around the shed of plants; his actions were absurd against the flowers that surrounded him.

"Peepa," I said softly.

"Yes?" He turned to face me, and even though he was in the middle of doing something comedic, his eyes expressed deep sadness.

"Nothing," I said.

He sat down again and began tracing imaginary kolams into the concrete floor. "My mother," he began, and I sat down too.

"My mother, she used to draw a kolam in the sand in front of our house every day. She said the signs protected our family against evil. And she hated when any of us would talk to her while she did it. So what did my father do? He'd talk to her. He would even sing to her when she was drawing. And every time, she'd use the back of her sari and wipe away the marks, only to start over again." He wiped his mouth with the back of the hand the way a mother might wipe away a kolam. "She'd sometimes be drawing until nightfall because my father wouldn't leave her alone. Why couldn't he leave her alone?" he yelled and then stood up again. I stood up too.

"Did your dad hit her?" I asked.

"No," he whispered. "I did."

"Why?" I could feel the alcohol rising up at the back of my throat.

"I needed to eat. She was more interested in the stupid kolam than in feeding us. Everywhere in my life, I've always had to worry about someone else taking my share. When I was at home, it was my brother. When I was in school, it was someone else. And here, it's you and Jaga-Nai and the others. I am tired. Stop drinking my whiskey!" he yelled and snatched it out of my hand. I was beginning to get used to the dark taste.

"How many times did you hit her?"

"What are you, a khaki-shirt?" The Tamil equivalent of police was "khaki shirt" because the policemen in India wore camouflage shirt-and-pant sets. Their uniforms made them official, but they were far from it.

"I just want to know, that's it."

"So you can feel better about why you are here? Golicchio doesn't know the truth about you."

"What truth?" I felt panicky, but I wasn't sure why.

"You've changed since you came here. I remember helping you with your homework once. That seems like so far away."

"That's so unfair," I said. I could feel the tears surfacing in my eyes, but I brushed them away, much like how I imagined Peepa brushing his mother's face with the back of his hand. "We've all changed since being here. Golicchio and I used to be close, until you both came out of the Closet."

"I was always Golicchio's good friend. I never pretended otherwise." I covered my ears. I didn't want to face the fact that I may have changed, may have become less trusting, less eager to help. But what purpose did it serve? Did I gain anything from being friends with these boys? We all thought we did, but I didn't know if that was true or not anymore.

"No one ever wants to hear the truth. Everybody is so scared that it will expose them."

"And you? What is your truth? How do our fathers know each other?" If anyone was hiding anything, it was him. He was trying to deflect the attention away from himself, and people only did that when they were trying to conceal something.

He closed his eyes and leaned back, and he looked like he was going to pass out from the copious amount of alcohol he'd consumed.

"Don't fall," I said, but he didn't hear me. He slumped to the floor and curled up in a ball. Sometimes he took my breath away with his handsome presence.

"I wish I looked like you," I said. He said not a word, and we both sat in silence, taking sips from the thermos.

Chapter Forty-Nine

THOUGH PEEPA NEVER told me how our fathers were connected, I have my theories.

Chapter Fifty

THE MOTHERS WERE nowhere to be found. They seemed to leave the House frequently these days as if being around us was bad for their health. This time, they left early in the morning – before serving us breakfast. Luckily for me, Headmistress Veli fed me mini masala dosais before she left to join them. She even let me drink the leftover sambar from a cup.

"Where do they get the money to buy things?" Puni asked. "They always return with big bags that say 'ISP' on them. What is that?"

"Indian Stupid Pigs," Golicchio said. We all laughed.

"No, it is 'Indian Sari Palace.' My mother used to come back with bags from there and new saris. She said it was one of the best places to shop," Ganesh said.

"Your mother shopped a lot? Was your family rich?" Golicchio asked. We looked at him. It wouldn't have surprised me. He was certainly the most arrogant of all of us, except for Jaga-Nai.

"Yes, they were fairly well to do."

"Don't you have a sister?" Golicchio asked.

"Yes, I have three. Had three," he corrected. I looked at Golicchio, and he smiled at me.

"What?" I said.

"Nothing," he said, and that was that.

"Let's go to Mother Jamuna's room and find ladoo," Ganesh said. The Mothers, perhaps because they were away more often, had become a little less vigilant about keeping their items stowed away safely. Head-mistress Veli never seemed to care that much since her room was a private playground for many of us anyway. Mother Kalpana was the worst; she'd specially ordered a series of safes just for storing her private things. The safes were guarded by a five-number lock combination. We'd never found much of use in her room anyway, so her excessive paranoia didn't bother us. She seemed the most prudent of all of the Mothers – she never had alcohol or dirty magazines in her room, and the most we'd ever found of interest was a series of letters written to herself about how she was going to try to be a better person. Those had amused us for an entire month.

Though we looked and looked, we never found what we secretly hoped to find in their rooms: sweets and treats of every shape and size, enough to overload our bodies with sugar. Headmistress Veli had the best selection of hidden goodies, but the boys could only take pieces, afraid she would discover the missing food and send them to the Closet. I just went along for show since most of what was hers was mine too – but the other boys didn't know that.

"Yes," I said, excited to be doing something together for once. I clapped my hands, and everybody stared at me and started toward Mother Jamuna's door. I felt a little silly. I hadn't clapped in such excitement in years.

"Chee chee!" I heard one of the boys yell, but I couldn't tell whose voice it was. I ran into Mother Jamuna's room, and we saw several large bras hanging from the rafters. I had done her laundry earlier, so the sight of her bras made me angry more than anything.

"Mother Jamuna has huge titties," Puni said. He was salivating.

"Does that turn you on?" Peepa whispered, and Puni wiped his mouth.

"No, I was thinking about the jelabi we might find."

"Right," Peepa said. Ganesh grabbed one and put it over his body.

"This covers my entire torso. She is the fattest lady I've ever seen. Even fatter than my mother, who sometimes had to get more than seven yards of fabric for her sari. Can you believe that?" We all laughed. She must have been huge. The standard Indian sari length was seven yards long, no exception.

"Put that down, it's intimate," Golicchio said. He looked heavy.

"Looking at it isn't like looking at her breasts," I said. I turned him around and forced him to look. "You have seen these before."

"I would never touch them willingly."

"Stop being so saintly," I said. Peepa glared at me.

"Will you leave him alone?" Peepa went over to Golicchio and put his arm around him. I saw Peepa offer Golicchio a tumbler, and he said no.

"What's that?" I asked.

"Want some?"

I took the tumbler and had a drink, thinking it was water. It was alcohol. Peepa was starting to drink this early?

"Where do you get this?" Ganesh then turned around and looked.

"What? The alcohol? From Jamuna's room too. This is the room of pleasures!" He laughed. Hearing Mother Jamuna called just "Jamuna" sounded odd.

"Do you all drink?" Golicchio asked. Puni shook his head no, but Peepa and Ganesh nodded.

"We drink to spite her. The more we drink, the less she has," someone said. I nodded, and I asked to drink some more. Together we toasted to finding more spoils.

"Don't you want some?" I asked Golicchio.

"No. I've already said no to you all many times." He stepped back as if I were offering him chili and lime juice.

"Are you afraid you might do something that you don't want to do?"

"You're drunk," Golicchio said with such hatred, my intoxication began to wear off.

"Don't get angry with me just because you are afraid."

"I'm not afraid. Drinking is bad for you. It kills you."

"Is this another one of your stories?" Ganesh stopped his snooping. He listened.

"No. It's true. Karma enters your body through your blood. When you drink, the alcohol kills your blood. And then you're killing your karma. You're basically telling your body that you don't want to go to Nirvana. Your spirit dies and you are reincarnated into the womb of a jackal."

"Womb of a jackal better than the womb of Mother Jamuna," Peepa said, and we all laughed so hard we had to grab our stomachs to prevent from falling down.

"That's not funny. My father drank. Alcohol is poison. I have seen firsthand the effects of alcohol. You age, you become mean-spirited, you hurt your children."

"Right," I said, and Peepa slapped me. "What was that for?" I asked.

"Alcohol is not the only thing that makes someone mean-spirited. So does the companionship of bad people like Jaga-Nai," Peepa said while looking at me.

"How much can we trust you? You've befriended the enemy. Whatever we say or do might be relayed back to him," Ganesh said.

"What he thinks or does has no bearing on us."

"Yes, it does. He wields a lot of power in this House."

"Then we should try to be his friend instead of hating him so much. Maybe he's lonely," I said.

"Remember the zoo keeper who befriended a lion? The lion ended up eating him alive," Golicchio said.

"What can he do to us that the Mothers already haven't done? Aren't we already at our lowest?"

"Whenever you think you are down, there is always a place lower than that," Ganesh said. His big frame was wobbly with the alcohol, but he kept drinking anyway. "Let's look for ladoo," he said, and the moment was lost. I felt like an outsider, and I knew they looked at me like one.

The others, in particular Ganesh, had driven me away. I had hoped that they would have had a renewed respect for me, thinking that my kinship with Jaga-Nai could neutralize relations. I believed that secretly they were upset that they were not the ones chosen by Headmistress Veli, and as a result, were not the ones in the same camp as Jaga-Nai. Ganesh was right – Jaga-Nai did wield *some* power, and those who were "in" with him had more power than the others. I knew it burned Ganesh's insides to think that a low caste boy like me had more clout in the House than he did. I smiled at the thought.

After leaving Mother Jamuna's room, I found Jaga-Nai roaming about the halls of the House, whistling. His shirt was inside out, but his hair was perfectly smoothed down, perhaps with a fancy cream. He held a tube that said, "Fair and Handsome," which promised "fair skin and lots of marriage proposals."

"Who gave you that?" I asked, but I already knew the answer.

"My lover, eh?" He cocked his head and messed up his hair.

I left it at that and started to walk away when he grabbed my hand. "I need you," he said.

"You can read," I said, when I noticed him take a letter out of his pocket.

"There's a riddle in it. I can't understand it."

I looked at the letter and noticed the writing was more elegant and formal.

"Who is this from?"

"From Veli."

"Why is she writing you notes, as though you were two long-distance lovers?" I would much rather have had her as a pen pal than as a molester.

"What's it to you? Special lovers get special things. Others get her ass to wipe."

I ignored him and read the letter. It said, "He's coming. Please help."

"Why don't you ask her what it means?"

"She refuses to talk about the letter, and when I see her, she pretends as though she never wrote it. But I know she wants me to read it because then she asks if I have read it. I don't understand her." He shook his head, and for a second, it almost felt as though we were friends, gossiping about the women in our lives who tormented us so. This could all be true in another lifetime, with the proper amount of karma and fortune.

"Maybe she is in trouble. She vomited a while back."

"She was sick? I hope she did not give me her illness." He rubbed the skin on his lips and smacked them.

"She vomits a lot," I said, thinking about how often I'd caught her in the bathroom or in her room retching uncontrollably.

"I think you need to ask her."

"No, I think you should ask her. Next time, you know, you're with her. I find that I can ask her anything then." I shuddered.

"I don't think that it's appropriate," I said, waiting for him to accost me.

"Ask her."

"Fine," I said. His stronghold on me was weakening, and he knew that. I had Headmistress Veli's ear as well as other things. I could bend it in other directions, including away from him.

Chapter Fifty-One

SOMETIMES WHEN I am at the bus stop, I think I see him. I have seen all of them in different ways: at the Hindu temple, Ganesh; Puni on the face of a fat child; Jaga-Nai in the space between the rain; Aruna in the flesh of my past lovers; and Golicchio. Golicchio is who I see most often, but perhaps it is because he is the one who I most yearn to see.

Chapter Fifty-Two

I SAW THE girl again, and this time, I was with Peepa. We had gone to get some water from the pump outside. He had contracted a pretty bad cold – he was coughing up phlegm and spitting blood. The Mothers, only after blood started to dry up around his nostrils, let him sit the day out instead of be in class. I was given the privilege of accompanying him because Headmistress Veli had discussed it with Mother Jamuna ahead of time. I tried to tell myself how lucky I was, but the voice inside me sounded sarcastic.

"Water," he said. Golicchio said that karma was being eaten up by the tremendous amounts of alcohol that Peepa was consuming. Lack of karma gave colds. He was frequently getting them.

"I'm getting it, I'm getting it," I said, already impatient. I disliked taking care of sick people and loathed when they needed something they should have been able to get themselves. But I supposed it was better than hearing (and feeling) Mother Kalpana lecture about the role of animals in a Hindu's life.

"Come here," I heard the girl say. The notes of her speech went up and down like the music of a devotional song.

"Amma?" Peepa asked. He was delirious with fever, but the Mothers wouldn't let him sleep it off this time. They felt that if he slept while the sun was shining he would never grow strong. This seemed hypocritical to me because frequently Mother Jamuna would take a "nap" after a meal, too tired to continue without resting her jowls. Then again, they were the weakest of the lot, their fat swaying like meat hung out to dry on a clothesline.

"I have water that is cool, to drink," she said, and I saw her extend her thin arm the size of a bird's beak and offer a tumbler with liquid.

"More," he gurgled. He was roasting; the water instantly evaporated in his mouth.

"I have more," she said. I looked at her. She seemed as though she wanted something. Even she had a bargain to make. No good deed went unpaid.

"What's the price? I thought you were his friend," I said.

Before I realized what was happening, she kissed Peepa on the cheek and then handed him some more water.

"Your face is very hot," she said, and he just nodded. I turned away, disgusted by what I had just seen because their little interlude reminded me – on a small scale – of the sort of things that Headmistress Veli made me do.

"I have to go," I said, and I left Peepa standing there, his body slumped, with the girl kissing his elbow.

I ran inside the House and tripped on something in the middle of the hallway. It was a hair clip. Adorned with beads the size of gulab jamun balls, it was garish. And ridiculous. And something that no person should have been wearing in public. I didn't know very much about fashion, but I was definitely in support of modesty. My mother never wore makeup, and when she would dare smudge kohl under her eyes, we'd call her "komali," the Tamil word for clown. We'd call her names over and over again until virtually in tears, she'd rub her face on her sari end, and my father would clap his hands.

"The komali has retired," he would say. Later, he would whisper in her ear, perhaps apologizing for teasing her. There must have been something that he'd liked about her colors because inevitably after every makeup application, they would be alone on their cot, a red sari laid flat in front, letting us know that we were not allowed near.

I knew that the clip belonged to Headmistress Veli, bright wall. She'd acquired a couple more suitors (her age, she'd said), and as a result, was dressing the part. Yesterday, she'd worn a bright purple sari with orange trim. Her earrings had tinkled everywhere she went, and Jaga-Nai joked that it was her "dog chain." Her arms were filled all the way to her pits with bangles of every color. Although her outfit seemed entirely incongruous, something about it kept all of our eyes on her for a little bit longer than usual.

I was familiar with the Hansel and Gretel nursery rhyme, procured from one of the tattered books I had read from the Mothers' makeshift library. My brain made the connection between her hair clip and the crumbs of bread that the children left to return home. I went to her.

Her door was closed, so I knocked.

"Yes?" she asked. Her eyes were glazed, and she didn't seem to know who I was. "Oh Sid, what do you want?" Her breath smelled of smoke, and her sari blouse was half open. I could see streaks of red down the middle of her chest and divots where fingernails had scoured the skin.

"Is this yours, Headmistress Veli?" I asked in a syrupy voice. I hated to be so cloying with her, but I knew I had to.

"Yes, come in, Sid. How are you?" She ruffled my hair the way a mother would do, but then she grabbed my head and pushed it into her chest. The smell was so strong that I felt instantly aroused. I pushed away.

"Oh that's right, you are not that way, I see. Maybe you like boys then," she said. Her voice was erratic. I wondered if she was drunk or under severe distress. "Jagadesh, now he likes it. He wants me. All I ever want is for you to like me," she said. She sat down and buttoned her blouse. I moved my eyes to the floor where I observed an ant crawling up her foot. She barely noticed.

"I do like you," I said. "But not like that. You are," and I stopped. I couldn't think of what to say that wouldn't hurt her. She and I were connected. If she hurt, I did too. I was afraid that she would explode if I was too honest, and pieces of her breasts would land inside my mouth permanently.

"I am what? Too fat? Too old, what? I have several marriage proposals, you know," she said, and I believed her.

"Why must everything involve touch? Why not talk?" I sat down. I was on her level now. She had made it so.

"Who was the last person you longed to touch? And don't say your mother because I'll scream!" She raised her hand as if to physically imply how her voice would elevate.

"I don't know," I said. I really didn't. I thought I did, but that had changed.

"For me, it is Vareshawaren, the jewelry maker in my village. But he's too low class for me, my parents won't allow it."

"Why can't you decide? You're old enough."

"You are so young," she said and touched the side of my face. "You will realize that just because you're older doesn't mean that you can choose your own destiny, independent of anyone else. That's the myth of age. In some ways, you have more pressure on you as you get older, and you become less carefree. You should enjoy what you have now while you have it."

"Then don't complain," I said, angry with what she had just said about enjoying myself. Our lives weren't carefree. We had our lives taken away from us. I didn't know where choice had much to do with it.

"I am not complaining, I am just telling. There's a difference."

"And Jaga-Nai? Are you going to marry him?"

She laughed. "What does he say?"

"I don't know. I'm not his friend."

"But that's not what he says." She went to a drawer in her desk and pulled out a letter. She handed it to me. I read the top part – it was a letter written from Jaga-Nai to his parents.

"I can't read this," I said.

"Didn't I teach you how to read? Come, read it aloud!" She stamped her foot.

"How come you didn't send this?"

"Because," and her voice became deep. "His parents don't ever write to him. Don't you see? I write to him. His parents don't care enough to. I feel sorry for him. It makes him feel better."

"But it doesn't. He is expecting them to come and you are only building him up!" I raised my voice. "You should tell him."

"No, and why do you care? I thought you and he weren't friends. Read the letter, please. Now!" she shrieked, so I succumbed.

"'Dear Amma,'" I started. "How come this is only to his mother?"

"Because his father alienated him a while ago."

"Is that the real story or the one you made up?"

"Eh, boys don't need their fathers. They only make them abusive. I'm doing him a favor."

"You're playing God," I said, but then again, all of the Mothers here were. They were justified in doing so because they had no one to regulate their actions. What could we do? We were their pet monkeys, our leashes tied too tightly and the bells on our hands worn from all the ringing.

"And? Read the letter, otherwise I will scream." Her hand went up in the air again.

"'Dear Amma, Don't be sad. Things aren't as bad as I said they were last time. I exaggerated because then maybe you'd come get me.'" I stopped. This was too much to read. I was exposing the vulnerabilities of a very hungry cobra.

"What drama. Thththththth, this is better than the cinema," she said. I didn't know how she could be so cruel. I had always imagined her to be kind, generous. Maybe that had been an illusion.

"Did Jaga-Nai do something to make you upset? I thought you were lovers?" It sickened me to think of their limbs wrapped around each other, his uneven teeth making the marks that I had seen on her chest, but if this was what romantic love meant, I didn't want any part of it.

"Yes, but don't you know? Oh little one," she said. "Love is not that far away from hate. You can't really truly love someone unless you can say honestly that you would be able to kill him with your bare hands. That's love." I didn't understand what she meant, but I was afraid to ask for clarification. I started for the door, but she grabbed my hand and put it on her heart. "You are my friend, Sid. Please keep reading."

With tears in my eyes, I read the rest of the letter. "'I lied. Mother Jamuna doesn't really put sticks into my ears. I can still hear fine. Sometimes there is buzzing, but I am okay. And Veli, she's one of the nicer Mothers here. And did I tell you about Yrimal? He's weak, but I like him. He doesn't think I do, but I secretly wish I could have the friends he does. Everybody in the House likes him and takes care of him because he is so pitiful. I wish sometimes that I wasn't so strong. Please come soon. Don't be scared. I will protect you from this place.'"

I cried for a few minutes, forcing myself to stop. I hadn't cried in a long time, at least not publicly, and I felt ashamed to be doing it in front of her. When I was finally able to breathe again, I looked up. Headmistress Veli was at her desk, writing a letter.

"To who?" I asked, barely whispering.

"Who do you think? Wipe your nose and please leave," she said. The glossiness in her eyes was gone.

The next day, I couldn't help but look at Jaga-Nai with sad interest. He had sounded so pathetic, and I studied him as if he were a specimen that I knew felt some affection toward me but that I couldn't really communicate with.

"What are you looking at, eh?" he asked. We were standing in the cafeteria in front of one of the tables, eyeing the wilted, brown pieces of mango and the moth-infested dhal.

"The food." I kept looking at him. I couldn't believe that he, who was so strong, admired the weakness in me. I never thought of weakness as being a trait that was laudable. Golicchio and Peepa certainly didn't think so.

"Then eat it." I laughed. "Why are you laughing? Shut up!" I couldn't stop laughing though. This was all so sad that it had morphed into something funny.

I reached down to grab the mango, and he slapped it out of my hand. "You'll get sick," he said, and although he said it unkindly, there was a hint of tenderness, as if he were protecting a younger brother from stepping into a well of spiders.

"Right," I said, and we both sat down together, in silence. There seemed to be an understanding that was lacking before, but maybe it was all in my imagination. Whatever the case, I felt at ease this time, in a way unlike any other.

"I am going to show you something, and you are going to read it, okay?" He pulled out a stack of letters from his shorts. I didn't want to read them again, and mainly because I knew where they'd come from.

"Something doesn't seem right. I can't read very well, but the letters – they seem too nice. My mother was never that nice. I'm worried that something might be wrong with her." He showed me the latest of the letters he'd received from her. Now I recognized Headmistress Veli's handwriting instantly in a way that I had never before, but the diction and tone were entirely different. That was how she'd disguised herself.

"She is telling me that she loves me and wants me to be happy, and she never wanted that. If anything, she wanted me to leave her alone, so she could be with father. I hate father," he said. I saw the anger in his eyes and was afraid that he would take it out on me. I flinched.

"I need to go see her, and you are going to help. You can distract them with your sickly body."

"You think they care so much that they would take care of me and not see you trying to leave?"

"They like you more than the others."

"They hate all of us equally."

"What if my mother is going crazy?" he yelled. "Then what? This might be the last time I see her!" He pulled out a swatch of his hair that he would've normally smoothed down. I wanted to tell him the truth, but that would've betrayed all of us on so many levels. I couldn't do it. It really wasn't my business. I had to be like my father this time and look the other way.

"Okay," I said. "I'll help you, but I think you should talk to Head-mistress Veli."

He chuckled. "She'll find out after I return with my mother. You'll see. Let's decide when I will leave." We scooted closer to each other and for the first time since I had moved there, we put our heads together and conspired. It seemed that these days were full of firsts. The others were interested, but avoided us. It was better for them to let whatever was un-folding happen without their interference.

Unfortunately, every time Jaga-Nai wanted to leave, he would re-ceive a letter, which would postpone his escape. As the days went by and our plan solidified, more and more letters with frequency and a sense of urgency came.

"I'm trying to protect him from them, that's why I do this," Head-mistress Veli said once when I rebuked her for continuing with this fa-çade. I told her that Jaga-Nai was planning an escape to visit his parents, and she had only responded with a laugh.

"He's not smart enough to leave. He's had the 'address' for quite some time and has he tried to leave? No. And you aren't brave enough to help him." Her letters hadn't changed though. She kept telling him how much she loved him, and how much she hoped that he was doing well in the "House." As much as I hated the lying, she was right. The letters made him less angry, less hurtful. He no longer bullied us to the extent that he did, and he didn't scare me in quite the same way as he had be-fore. She gave him hope, a powerful elixir.

"It seems you being his friend has made matters better," Ganesh said.

"He is happy because his mother loves him," I said, and my voice felt heavy. It wasn't true. Headmistress Veli said that his mother had fallen prey to HIV, and that his father had left her to become a beggar on the street. Even the temples didn't want her. I didn't know how much of that I believed.

"Better his mother than us," Peepa said and laughed. He was feeling much better, and his fever was long gone. I didn't know if he'd remem-bered the kisses from the girl.

"I still don't like him. He reminds me of the skulls around Cha-munda's neck," Golicchio said. We all laughed – Golicchio knew just the right colorful descriptions to use.

"When are his parents coming for him?" I noticed Puni gnawing at his hand. Had he not had enough food to eat today?

"I don't know if they ever are, that's the sad thing."

"Why do you care?" Peepa asked. I chose to ignore that comment.

We were bored, which happened more often than not. Golicchio and I had finished cleaning the cafeteria, and the Mothers had no other use for us. Books didn't seem appealing; after *Revelations*, I hadn't found another book that captured my interest in the same way. For Ganesh there was nothing new to listen to on the radio, and Golicchio didn't have any stories to tell. The rest of the boys had scattered about, none of them interested in starting a game of Kabaddi. The Mothers were inside "resting," so that eliminated the chance for any sort of high jinks.

As luck would have it, I didn't find Jaga-Nai. He found me. I had gone back to the room to prepare my homework. Our assignment was a series of math problems, ranging from easy to difficult. If we didn't at least attempt to solve them, we were told punishments – ranging from painless to painful – would be administered.

"Get up," Jaga-Nai said. "It's time." I looked around.

"Time for what?"

"Time for me to leave." He started to clap.

"Now?" I didn't feel ready.

"I can't wait."

"No, I can't do it. The Mothers are asleep. If they hear us, we will be sent to the hole together. Even Headmistress Veli won't be able to stop that." I felt my insides shaking.

He then punched me in the stomach.

"I thought you were going to help me," he said. He left, and I didn't understand what I had done wrong. Didn't we have a plan? Why must he mess with it? Could he not wait?

"What happened?" I heard Golicchio ask me. He was standing in the doorway, and his bony arms flailed alongside his body like that of a bird with faulty wings.

"You and Jaga-Nai are involved in something. What is it? Are you planning a Great Escape?"

"He is full of delusions."

"Delusions can be beneficial, sometimes. They are like blankets – they shield us from the things that really harm our skin. You know bad thoughts can make our skin go bad? That's where wrinkles come from. Some older people are just so consumed with evilness and how they are going to hurt other people, they develop wrinkles. Look at Mother Jamuna. She is the worst of them all." I couldn't help but agree. When I came here as a little boy, I thought she was older than God. Now I thought she was just old.

"Who said delusions are good? What if they are bad?" I tried to remember if Jaga-Nai had developed any wrinkles since Headmistress Veli started corresponding with him.

"Delusions prevent us from getting hurt," someone said. I recognized the voice. It was Peepa.

"You two are starting to sound the same," I said. Envy boiled inside of me like payasum on a hot stove.

Neither said anything and just stared at me. I felt as though I were in the middle, intruding on a special moment, not unlike the times I'd tried talking to my father while he was playing with Smita. I left, but lingered in the hallway.

"Have you thought some more?" Peepa asked.

"Yes. I think I'm ready. To go," Golicchio said.

Golicchio was – had been – the closest friend I'd ever had. Even though things had changed, I thought (and hoped) that they would go back to the way they were. If he left, I wondered if I'd feel empty inside.

"Good, then it's settled."

"What about money, food?"

"Work. We will find something."

"Shelter?"

"We will manage, okay?" I could hear frustration in Peepa's voice. I half expected that he would begin yelling.

"When?"

"I will tell you when. And then you must be ready."

"Okay." No one spoke for a few seconds, and I was ready to leave when I heard Golicchio ask, "What about the girl? She said you were going to propose to her."

"And?" In customary Peepa fashion, he ignored the question. "I'm thirsty," he said, and before they left the room, I ducked out.

This wasn't the only time that I found myself out of place, intruding where I was not welcome.

The next day I noticed that Golicchio and Peepa sat together more closely. And day after day, they continued to sit together, talking, whispering, figuring things out the way that Jaga-Nai and I had. They didn't even include Ganesh half of the time, who had resorted to trying to befriend some of the other kids who were as large as he was. If I were to look at it practically, Golicchio and Peepa's union made complete sense. They were the most intelligent boys in the House and were probably naturally drawn to each other. From what I'd heard of their conversations, they seemed to stimulate each other in ways that I had never been able to.

Chapter Fifty-Three

MY DAUGHTER, ANANDAKANU, is engaged to be married next year. As with my son, I am surprised that both of my children, though only half-Indian, have gravitated toward the traditions of my birth country. Anandakanu's fiancé is Indian, and his family is from the state of Kerala. His father is a police officer, and his mother does not work. Both of his parents still live in India, and she has insisted that they have the wedding there. I have refused to go, and she is now not speaking to me.

"Tell her why, Sid," my wife says. "She's our only daughter."

I have always hated when people state the obvious.

Chapter Fifty-Four

"THE MAN IS back again," Golicchio said. He pointed through the barred windows in the cafeteria. This time, Mother Jamuna greeted him in a pale blue and yellow sari with matching bangles and leaf-shaped earrings. She looked like an oversized child playing dress up. We couldn't contain our laughter, and Peepa even smiled at me.

"Let's look and see why he's here," Ganesh said. No one moved though. The Mothers' punitive response last time stymied our desire for exploration.

"I'd rather steal food from Headmistress Veli's room," Puni said. He licked the tip of his nose. That boy's tongue was long.

We all just stood there, no one moving or saying a word. I could hear a collective sigh, and then breathing. Eventually, one or two of the boys lost interest and scattered. The rest of us followed suit. Golicchio and Peepa, arms linked, meandered off somewhere. Ganesh continued to look, and Puni said he was going to sit down in the cafeteria, probably hoping for miraculous scraps of food to appear.

"No lessons today," Headmistress Veli came and announced. She went through the entire House, making sure we knew that our classes were cancelled.

"I need you," she pointed to me. Ganesh walked by and gave me a strange look. He didn't say anything though and continued on. He completely ignored Headmistress Veli as if she didn't exist. Puni, on the other hand, stared. He wanted to come along, but I shook my head no at him. He looked hurt, and he turned his eyes away from me.

I went to her room, and she shut the door.

"You have to help me," she screeched. She rubbed her belly. Was it my imagination, or did it seem larger?

"What happened?" She grabbed and nearly suffocated me with her head. She laid it down on my chest.

"Hug me and rub my back," she said. "Pretend you care," she spit out.

"I do."

"Shut up!" she screamed. I did what she asked and waited for her to talk. She was unusually animated. I noticed that her teddy bears were askew. She may have been drinking, although I was avoiding her mouth and wasn't able to smell any alcohol on her breath.

"Do you know who that man is? Horrid, horrid Jamuna. She's always doing this to me. Why?" She started crying. I tried to rub harder and faster, but that only spurred on her crying.

"Who is he?"

"He's a doctor. The most terrible kind. He does bad things to my body every time he comes."

"What does he do?" Unpleasant images flooded my head.

"He kills all of my babies, and she lets him!" she cried, and I pushed her head off of me.

"What babies?"

"Mine," she lunged forward and grabbed my shoulders and looked me right in the eyes. "My babies. He comes and gives me medication and takes blades and scrapes them out. One time, I had two at once. Jamuna refuses to let me have them. She makes him come, and he comes so much, and the pain is unbearable." She continued to stare at me, and I looked at one of the pink animals behind her head.

"Who's the father?" I asked.

"I don't know. This one is probably Jaga-Nai's. The next one may be yours. But why won't they let me keep them? I would be a good mother. I really would."

If she would be a good mother, then I would be a good boxer. I noticed her wrinkle-free skin. The woman was full of delusions.

"I don't want a baby." I pushed her away again and stood up.

"He will come and take it away anyway. He always does." She sat on the floor with her head between her legs. For being so fat, she was flexible.

"Veli," I heard Mother Jamuna at the door. The man was with her, and I noticed his tools this time. He carried a briefcase and several jars of medications. On his face, he wore a lopsided smile; he looked as though he were about to enjoy his first night with a woman – a virgin no doubt.

"Come," he said. He rubbed his hands together in excitement. "Take off your clothes." Neither of them seemed to notice me. I tried to leave the room, but Mother Jamuna blocked me. She forced me into a corner, where I tried to cover my eyes. I couldn't stop watching, though. I saw the doctor give her the medication – practically force it down her throat – and then I saw him examine her all over, especially in her private places. He sterilized several sharp-looking tools, and it was then that I turned away. I could feel Mother Jamuna staring at me, as if saying, "This is your fault. Look at what you've done." And I couldn't help but feel partially responsible for causing her so much pain. If we didn't touch her, she wouldn't have to be touched in this way. She wouldn't lose any babies. Were we the bad ones?

The Mothers had a way of spinning the truth to suit their own needs.

"WHAT HAPPENED IN there?" Jaga-Nai asked. Despite his desperation at wanting to leave, he stayed on in the House. Since we had devised his plan to escape, I hadn't exchanged many words with him.

"Eh? What?" He came closer to me, and I cowered. I was still reeling from what I had just seen: an abortion. It was the most gruesome thing my eyes had ever taken in.

"Nothing." I was scared to tell him – or anyone – what I had seen. I didn't even know if I could put it into words, but the image was on fire in my head, permanently.

"I'll punch you if you don't tell me." I put my hand up, but I knew it was no use. The fact was that I wanted to tell someone, especially him. I wanted to get what I had seen, this vision, away from me and to someone else. If I told him, then I was no longer responsible for carrying it around. It became someone else's problem, as it rightfully should have been.

"Headmistress Veli had an abortion. She thinks it was your baby." He laughed.

"That woman has so many lovers, how could she possibly know it was mine? She was probably getting too fat and lied and told you it was an abortion so you wouldn't think that she was a fat pig. Which she is.

A fat pig."

"No, I saw it. With my own eyes. That man that was here. He is the abortion doctor."

"So? Why are you telling me? Like I give a fuck?" He smiled, and his teeth looked like nuggets of cow dung arranged in a neat line.

"Right. I thought you'd want to know. I would if it were my baby."

"How do you know it's not?" He winked.

"I know." The sad thing was, I didn't know. It could've been mine, and she had just killed it. Here we were without parents, and there that doctor was, killing babies and leaving parents without their children.

"No, you don't. She wouldn't have killed my child. Yours probably would've died on its own." He laughed again.

"Why are you so mean in one instant and then in the other you call me your friend?"

He looked surprised. "I never called you my friend. I would never even speak to you if it were not for the House." He looked at me more closely. "I never called you my friend," he said again.

"Yes, you did!" I screamed. "You told me in your letters to your mother!"

He punched me hard. "How did you read those? Did you steal them and read them? Eh?"

I wanted to tell him, so badly. I wanted to unburden myself of this responsibility too. I had too many as of late, but I couldn't. The timing wasn't right, and I had already told him enough. I wasn't entirely convinced that he didn't care that Headmistress Veli had had an abortion, but that wasn't my problem anymore. I needed to go, and possibly grieve for a child that I may have lost. If it wasn't mine, it was still a child. I knew what it felt like to be lost without a mother. I didn't want to think about what that child must have felt like not even being given the chance to have a mother. That probably was the cruelest punishment of all.

I rolled over on my side and pretended to be unconscious. He kicked me a little with his foot and then stomped away. I knew he was heading to Headmistress Veli's room. He was obsessed even though like me he couldn't stand to be around her.

Minutes later, even before I had a chance to get up and leave, Jaga-Nai returned with Headmistress Veli right beside him, holding his hand.

"What did you tell Jagadesh about the letters?" She stared at me. I could tell that she had been crying. The skin around her eyes was a pinkish red.

"I didn't tell him anything."

She grabbed my ear, still holding Jaga-Nai's hand. "Answer me. I can break you, all of you."

"I didn't—"

She pushed Jaga-Nai away and dragged me to her room. I didn't remember what happened next, but I knew it was unpleasant.

Chapter Fifty-Five

Our bags are packed. My daughter and I never had our talk, but I know that I must do this for her. I must return.

Chapter Fifty-Six

I KNEW SOMETHING was about to happen, something big. I knew it had to do with Jaga-Nai. His obsession with his "plan" of finding his mother and escaping was on his mind all of the time. He hardly had a chance to think about anything else, let alone direct his frustrations on anyone besides me.

In the House was where I began to understand the underpinnings of what a real obsession looked like. Puni began to withdraw, and in the same way that Jaga-Nai was focused on escaping, Puni was even more focused on food. Sometimes he even forgot who I was. If I didn't come bearing sweets, he refused to talk to me. Every now and then, the real Puni – the one I remembered – would appear, but it was rare. Most of the time, he existed in his own little world away from the others and from me.

I tried to get through to him. He was one of the only friends I had left now. Even when I stole kesari or other buttery delights from Headmistress Veli, he still wasn't satisfied. He needed more and more, and I couldn't give it to him.

Today, I gave him a packet of murukku and a bowl of spicy fried noodles. Headmistress Veli had been in a liquor-induced coma, and I was able to sneak into her room and steal a few treats. He looked happy, but he didn't say anything. His eyes devoured it first, and then his mouth took seconds. After he was done, he looked up as if to say something – perhaps to thank me – but he shook his head. It was as if he had forgotten how to speak, or worse, he had forgotten what my name was. After giving up trying to communicate, he left me. And I felt empty. Much like the way I had felt on the day of Smita's birth. My mother was in the kitchen, the red sari at the doorway. Even though our hut was overcrowded with people, so much so that we were literally stepping on each other's feet, it felt barren, and I was alone. Knowing the changes that Smita's birth would bring, I should've rejoiced in my solitude. But I didn't know what was to come, and I had begun feeling depressed, lacking any sort of mental clarity.

I felt a tap on my shoulder, and I turned to look. It was Puni again.

"Do you have more food?" he asked. I saw the focus had returned to his eyes, and I knew Puni was back, at least temporarily. I shrugged no, and he gnawed on his hand.

"Why have you gotten so hungry? You aren't even gaining anything. Where does it go?"

"I don't know. But I keep eating, and my stomach never feels full. I told Mother Jamuna and she just laughed. She laughed while she ate a fresh vadai in front of my face. How could she?" He looked like he was on the verge of tears, so I put a hand on his shoulder.

"Don't cry, Puni. You get enough, more than some of the others. Everyone gets enough to live, even if that's not what we really want to do."

"I am so hungry, that's all I think about. All I think about is food."

"Did your Amma make you a lot of food?"

"Yes, to fatten me up. Later, she slowed down right before the tsunami took them."

"You should be used to how little food there is then, Puni," I said. When I looked at him, I noticed that he wasn't very fat anymore. So consumed with my own troubles, I hadn't realized how much weight he had lost. Where did all the food go, and why were we still calling him Puni?

"I'm not fat, not anymore anyway." He wasn't even looking at me.

"What is happening to you, Puni?" I felt silly calling him that again, and the genuine concern in my voice made him lower to his knees.

"I know, something is happening to me, and I don't know what it is. Yesterday, my nose bled. My nose has never bled before."

"Did you tell the Mothers? Did you show them? Sometimes they don't believe it. They think we're making it up because we think our parents will come for us. Right." I stopped speaking for a second and thought. Most of our parents were dead. Some of the luckier (or unluckier, depending on how you looked at it) ones were unable to be found. Many parents saw the tsunami as a lucky break – a chance to start a new life without the burden of children. Some of us would never know.

"What? Do you have food or not?" He looked at me imploringly, but I could not offer him anything.

"You should talk to Headmistress Veli. She might be able to help you."

He shook his head. "No, she's a fat bitch too." His voice became guttural. "I'm hungry, and that bitch probably has murukku hidden underneath the folds of her fat tummy. I hate them all!" He rubbed his hands together. "If I cooked them all together, I could eat for a whole year."

"You would really eat someone else?"

"The way I feel right now, I would even eat you," and he looked at me in a way that made me uncomfortable.

"I have to go now," I said and scurried, the way lizards ran and then dropped into our laps at night.

I found Jaga-Nai in the backyard wrapped around another letter. This one was very short, but urgent.

"Read, this is why I have to leave NOW," he growled, exposing his naked black teeth. He looked like a smaller version of Mother Jamuna's dogs.

"I don't care what it says," I said, but my voice was so quiet, that he just ignored me.

> *Dear Jaga-Nai, please do not try to come visit me. Your father has threatened to kill me if you do. I will come when I am ready, alone. Please, I love you, but your home is the House now. I love you.*

"She's not telling the truth. What kind of mother lies?" I asked him. Headmistress Veli didn't know how to lie very well, and she was digging herself into a hole. She couldn't bear to let Jaga-Nai escape even though both he and I were getting too old for her.

"Does she love you?" I asked.

"Yes, she just said."

"No, Headmistress Veli. Does she love you?"

"What does she have to do with this? Of course she loves me." He winked, and I imagined one hundred flies landing on me as if I were a piece of decayed jackfruit.

"Because." I couldn't do it any longer. "Your mother isn't the one who is writing you these letters. She is."

He laughed. "I thought Golicchio was the one who was good at making up stories. Seems like you have picked up the habit." He put a fist near my ear. "Do you know what it is like to have a worm stuck inside of your ear?"

I started to wriggle. Not surprisingly, like a worm.

"It hurts. Really bad. Worse than the pain of having your eyelid ripped off." He extended his finger, and he started to stick it into my ear. "So what were you saying about Veli?"

"Nothing," I huffed. I felt my lungs lose air, and he then moved his finger and stuck it into my mouth.

"Breathe. It's a pipe!" he laughed. After he saw that I wasn't able to breathe, he left. I was afraid I might pass out, so I tried to kneel on the floor, folding myself into a tight ball. Headmistress Veli must've sensed my distress because I saw her approach with a pipe in hand. She stuck it in my mouth while she pulled me to her room. She liked to play mother and healer, especially to the sickly boys like me. The other Mothers never questioned her motives; after all, she was the one who took care of orphaned boys, nursing them back to health. She deserved a medal for the work that she did.

After we got inside, she rubbed a hot compress over my chest. I felt her pick at my nipples.

"Stop," I said faintly, but I sounded weak. She liked how pathetic I was.

"You told Jagadesh that I was writing the letters, did you?" She pushed the compress harder into my lungs, and whatever air I had just inhaled left my body.

"He needed to know. He's going crazy," I whispered.

"It wasn't your business!" she yelled. She ripped her blouse open and her big breasts hung out like milk teats on a bitch with a huge litter.

"For that, you will pay. I promise. No boy comes in the way of my relationships with men," she said.

"You were writing the letters?" I heard Jaga-Nai. I got up to look, but Headmistress Veli pushed me back down.

"No, I am not. It's a lie. Siddhartha is just jealous of what you and I have. He is trying to come between us." The scene played out like an

Indian soap opera.

"That's not true," I said. I pushed my way up and looked directly at Jaga-Nai. He was mortified. The color was draining from his face, and he looked like he was on the verge of death. His mouth was open, so his fangs hung down the front of his chin. I prayed that he wasn't going to do anything to hurt me, but he wasn't looking at me. He was staring at Headmistress Veli, and I felt that maybe he finally believed me.

"How else would Yrimal know that I had written about our friendship?"

"You call that friendship? You are despicable. You could be friends with anyone in the House, yet you choose the sickliest of them all. What does that say about you? What does that say about your masculinity?" She goaded him on, enjoying herself. She was smiling, the first since the abortion doctor had come to visit.

"How else would he have known?" he screamed at her. I saw Mother Kalpana walk by the open door. She looked, but was disinterested. Jaga-Nai shut the door in her face.

"I killed your baby," she said blankly.

He grabbed his head and closed his eyes. She kept going. "Your parents are both dead. Even if they hadn't been dead, they wouldn't have wanted you. They would've pretended death like the rest of the parents here. Including Siddhartha's." She looked at me. I hated her for creating ambivalence for power. She was a sad, evil woman.

Jaga-Nai didn't say anything, and that didn't seem to satisfy her. She kept at it, describing in detail the ways he wasn't a man to her, and her disappointment over his apparatus. She also said that she was excited when the abortion doctor got rid of his spawn. She said she laughed. I knew this was not true, but I couldn't say anything. I was shocked at the vomit that she was spewing at such a rapid pace. I was not a good judge of character. I could never have predicted this.

He finally opened his eyes and looked at both of us. Then he left the room. Headmistress Veli turned and began to direct her rage at me. She hadn't gotten a rise out of him, and she needed to feel important.

"Siddhartha, did you know that your parents are alive, and they are having a great time? Did you?" I didn't say anything, having learned from Jaga-Nai. "You want proof?" She opened a drawer and took out a small wooden figure of a peacock, the god Kumara's vehicle. "Who do you think gave this to me?"

It could've been anyone's. My parents were dead. I knew that. I had seen them wash away before my eyes. She knew about Smita's fascinations because I had told her early on, when I didn't know she was stockpiling stories for ammunition later. I knew they were dead, all of them. Why would they leave me behind – a boy who could work and provide money? It didn't make sense. She was a liar. Look at how much she had lied about already?

"Siddhartha? Do you believe me? You aren't so bad, sometimes." She winked and started to rub herself. "Come." I stared at her, at the open door, and her open nakedness. I moved to the doorway and looked to see if anyone was watching. I saw no one. She came close to me and began to shut the door.

"No!" I shouted, and she just laughed.

"Fine, but there will always be next time, and more things to be said."

I WAS IN the bedroom, and it was dark. Peepa was next to me – I could tell. He had a peculiar scent about him, a mixture of cumin and roasted anchovy.

I looked for Golicchio's bony body once my eyes became adjusted to the night. They did, but I didn't see him.

"Where's Golicchio?" I asked Peepa.

"He's in the hole," Peepa said with such forced calmness, I could feel his anger ripple through me like an earthquake from down below.

"What? Why?"

"Be quiet!" Ganesh roared. He got up and kicked me forcefully in the butt.

"He did something very bad. Very, very, very, very bad," Karthik said. Karthik was a boy with no nickname. He was too "normal" for this place. We felt that sooner or later, his parents would come and get him, embarrassed that they had made such an unseemly mistake.

"If you weren't playing with the Mothers, you'd know what was happening with your *friends*," Peepa said.

I got up. I felt something wasn't right, and I didn't know what. I wanted to talk to Golicchio.

"Where are you going?" Peepa asked. "You're only going to end up in the hole yourself."

"Then maybe I can join him," I said, remembering how close they'd become after being thrown into the Closet together.

I walked down the hall carefully. All of the lights were out except in Headmistress Veli's room. It didn't surprise me. I was positive she was entertaining a male suitor, if not Jaga-Nai, at this late of an hour. When I walked by, I could hear her moans, and it sickened me. If I could've vomited on command right in front of her door, I would have.

When I got to the Closet, there was a lock on it. I should've known. How else would we have stayed inside knowing we could escape? The door had a small window with bars though, through which to push food and other items.

"Golicchio? Are you in there?"

"No, stop, leave me alone. I said I have no heart. You cannot eat it."

"Golicchio, it's only me, Yrimal."

"I know you're trying to trick me. I will not give you a piece of my toe. Please," and he whimpered, "Eieieieieio, please leave me alone, I didn't do anything to you, please."

"Golicchio," Peepa said. He had followed me, and instantly at the sound of his voice, we heard Golicchio stop crying.

"Peepa, is that you?" I saw him stick out a very thin hand. His hands were so small they were virtually invisible.

Peepa took it. "Yes."

"I don't even know what I did to get thrown in here, but I can't stay in here," he cried. "Please help me get out."

"I will stay with you until the morning," Peepa said.

"You have to keep talking though. The moment that you stop, that is when the goblins come! They travel in pockets of silence!" he shrieked, and Peepa had to stick his hand into the cell, find Golicchio's mouth, and cover it.

"Why did you get put here?" I asked.

"I told you, I don't know. One moment, I was lying in bed, writing a novel in my head. The next moment, I was in here. Mother Jamuna picked me up, my whole body, and threw me in here. I landed on my knee. It hurts. I can barely stand up."

"Mother Jamuna's punishments have become indiscriminate lately," Peepa said.

"Karthik said you did something very bad. What was it?" We were silent for a few seconds, apparently too long for Golicchio to endure.

"Are you still there? Hello?"

"Yes, we are," Peepa said. "Remember the most recent time we all went into Mother Jamuna's room when they were out? I think she found out."

"Then how come the rest of us weren't punished?" I demanded.

"We all know why *you* aren't being punished," Peepa said. He didn't know when to stop with his bickering.

"Finish, please," Golicchio said.

"Golicchio was the only one who didn't want to play with Mother Jamuna's bras. Puni had forgotten to return one. I don't know what's gotten into him lately, but he was obsessed with the pink one – the one with the ghee stain on it. He wanted to eat it. Golicchio, do you know why you're in here now?"

Golicchio was silent. "I hate her," he said.

"What?" I disliked being in the middle.

"He tried to return her bra, but I think she knew. I think she saw him, and rather than risk embarrassing herself, she just decided to throw him in here. Understand, Yrimal? You are so slow sometimes," he said.

"She shouldn't leave her bras out if she doesn't expect us to tamper with them," I said.

"Puni will get his," Peepa said. "You wait, I will make sure he gets the hole three times as long as you."

"Wait," I said. "You aren't even certain that is the reason Golicchio is in here. And don't you think Puni is suffering enough?" I thought back to our earlier exchange. Even at night, I had seen him gnawing at his fingernails, not spitting them out as the rest of us did. He'd even taken to picking his nose and eating what came out.

"He's right. I think he is an alien," Golicchio said. I couldn't help but laugh, and Peepa joined me.

"Why, Golicchio?" I saw Peepa reach in and grab Golicchio's other hand. He held it as Golicchio explained.

"Because he has an insatiable appetite, and yet he eats more than the sum of what the rest of us eat. It makes sense – even aliens can become orphans."

"And where do the alien mothers leave their kids?" I asked.

"I am working out the details. You see, I am writing a novel in my head." He smiled, and even though I couldn't tell if he smiled – it was dark inside the Closet – I knew. I could hear it in his voice.

"You want to be a writer?" I was resentful that I didn't have similar aspirations.

"No, I never said that. I am just working on a novel in my head. I don't have a title yet, but I have the first chapter written."

"Tell us," Peepa said. I was sure he already knew what the first, second, and third chapters were about. He had probably even known about the novel before Golicchio had had the idea; that was how close their bond seemed to be.

"Perhaps the title should be—" Golicchio started.

"Something about being green, like an alien?" Peepa asked.

"Yes!" Golicchio clapped. They were even finishing each other's sentences. It was as if they had a two-way walkie talkie, but the frequency was lost to my ears.

"The alien has a drinking problem in the first chapter. It's established that he drinks to have a good time. But then when he passes out and wakes up, he has become infinitely older."

"How so?" I asked.

"Every time he drinks, he ages by five years. But he has a chance to change. If he stops drinking and is good to his family, he can slow down his aging. But he makes mistakes each and every time."

"There must be a happy ending. Perhaps in the very last chapter, he ends up doing right?" Peepa asked.

"No, I don't know how to write a happy ending because I don't know one myself," he answered. We all stopped talking, and even though Golicchio said the goblins would get him in the quiet, we felt strangely safe in the understanding we'd created.

The Mothers discovered us fast asleep the next morning. Peepa was holding one of Golicchio's hands.

"Siddhartha, Nirmal?" Mother Jamuna asked. She still had sleep in her eyes, and her nightgown had a stain the size of Tamil Nadu on it.

"Is it time for me to be free?" Golicchio asked. I doubted that he had slept a wink.

"Were they trying to help you escape? Hmm?" Mother Jamuna asked. Mother Kalpana stood to her side but for some reason was quiet.

"He was scared and about to go mad. We saved him," Peepa answered. Overnight his beard had grown a thicker layer of fuzz. He looked as if he had jumped out of the screen of a huge Tamil movie.

"He is not a child. He would've survived in the hole. That's what boys get when they do naughty things. If he fears his sanity, he shouldn't misbehave," she said. Mother Kalpana nodded. She looked as if her mind were on other things. She would've nodded had Mother Jamuna pulled out a knife.

"It wasn't him! Don't you fat bitches understand that?" Peepa yelled.

Mother Jamuna looked at him incredulously. Her hand, the size of a bat's wingspan, spread out across the side of her face. She looked ready to slap him, but before she could even begin to contemplate the idea, Peepa slapped her. He slapped her hard. She was fair, by women's standards, and I could see the pink mark where his hand had met her face. Mother Kalpana stepped forward.

"How dare you hit her like that? Don't you know who you are? You are nothing but an orphan," she snickered. She spit on his face. He slapped her also. Golicchio was still locked in the Closet, but through the slats, he could see what was happening. His hand gripped Peepa's other hand, the non-violent one.

"Your mother was a bitch," Mother Jamuna said. I covered my ears. The words themselves weren't offensive to me; it was her tone.

Both of the fat mothers grabbed Peepa and shoved him into the Closet. Before he could wriggle free, they pulled Golicchio between their knees and locked the door. I could hear Peepa yell and scream.

"Shut up."

"He was just trying to help. His hands have a mind of their own. Even his own mother couldn't control them," Golicchio whispered.

"Shut up unless you want back in there."

I stared at Golicchio. I felt sorry for him. I knew that he cared a great deal about Peepa, but he also feared for his life in the hole. It was as if the Mothers were asking him which limb to spare – the arm or the leg? Both were equally important, but which was the greater sacrifice? I knew that he valued his sanity. As he turned his back on Peepa, I could tell the sacrifice was great.

"Golicchio, help me. Tell them to keep you in here too," Peepa said.

"I can't, but don't worry, the goblins don't like you," he whispered and left. I too left. For once, I was glad for who I was and no one else.

Chapter Fifty-Seven

MY CHILDREN WANT to see where I grew up. They want to visit the ocean.
I take them to the beach in Chennai (then Madras), but so much has
changed now. Though I still see destitution, my eyes are hopeful. I pass
a coin to a child, and soon fifty children have surrounded me. My wife
trembles; I unroll note after note until she tells me to stop.

"Why is everyone so poor?" my wife whispers. She has never seen
such poverty. For her, suffering exists only in the crevices of her canvases.

"Because they don't have enough, Mom," my daughter says. She is
logical, like me.

"I know, but why?" she asks again.

The question goes unanswered.

I know sooner or later, my children will want to see the place of my
destruction, and subsequent birth. Though it is now burned, they will
want to see the ashes, feel the walls of my prison. They think it will be
cathartic. I think it will be harrowing.

Chapter Fifty-Eight

THREE DAYS HAD passed, and Peepa was still in the hole. To thwart us from keeping him company, Mother Jamuna brought one of the guard dogs inside to block the doorway to the Closet. There wasn't much room to spare. The dog was chained to the window on the door, which didn't seem as secure as Mother Jamuna thought. We were not certain if the dog was strong enough to rip itself free, so we avoided going to the back of the House unless we had to use the bathroom. Even then, most of us preferred going out the front and then circling around the side. Although the dog was quiet, we knew that it was there; Puni had suffered a terrible bite on his arm from trying to steal the dog's mutton bones.

"I was hungry," he'd said, when we all chastised him for doing such an idiotic thing. We were inside the House, waiting for class to start, which was very late.

"To steal a dog's dinner is like stealing a key from a prisoner who is stuck in jail. There will be anger, and lots of it," Golicchio said. Since Peepa's enclosure, he had taken to uttering statements of advice or proverbs about life.

"Then why don't they just give me more food?" His eyes looked red now, and he had grown pockets of pus along his face. We assumed his skin was entering the stage of acne like Ganesh's. Ganesh's face looked like the back of a sponge.

"We are tired of hearing you complain about food. Go!" Ganesh had smuggled the radio from the bedroom and hidden it underneath his shirt. He was listening to a cricket match and wanted to sit in the back of the classroom, so he wouldn't get caught. I hoped that Mother Kalpana did not teach class today – not only was she a spitter, she was also slightly deaf, which made Ganesh more likely to escape punishment.

"Shut up! I will cut you up and eat you myself," Puni squealed. We looked at him in amazement.

Ganesh stood up. "No one disturbs Ganesh when he is listening to a game. Do you understand?" His fist was raised.

"Go on and punch me. Kill me. Then maybe you can eat me and be happy. And I can die and be reborn as a tiger, with plenty of elephants and other animals to feed on." His eyes looked hungry, and he really wanted Ganesh to hit him. Ganesh lowered his fist.

"I don't want to. Go." Ganesh's lip quivered and although he didn't look scared, he looked put off. Ever since my last conversation with Puni, he also spooked me. The others had taken to avoiding him also. I knew Golicchio purposely walked with extra space between them when they would pass each other in a room, outside, or down the hall.

"Maybe when you are asleep, I will cut your legs off and make drumstick curry." Puni licked his lips and left. We heard a dog growling, and we assumed that Puni was at it again, trying to steal food.

"Maybe we should try to talk to him, help him. Maybe we should try to save him food. He seems very hungry."

"We're all very hungry!" one of the boys shouted.

"Shh!" Ganesh yelled. We all backed away. I went to go find Puni and try to console him. He had done that for me many times in the past, when I had been beaten severely by the Mothers, so I felt an obligation to him. As I circled to the back, I saw Puni with a fresh, bleeding wound on his arm, and he was licking it. When I came up beside him, his face was smeared red, as if he'd stuck his face inside a kum kum pot.

"Bloody," he said. He slurped as if he were drinking from a tall glass of goat milk.

"You're not giving your body anything extra. You're just taking from your body and putting it back," I said. The look on his face made me incredibly nauseous. He appeared half-comatose as if he'd come upon a large feast and didn't know what to do with it. I kneeled down upon the small patch of grass and let the world swing around me.

"I don't care." After his wound dried, he plucked grass and started to eat it. He even threw chunks of dirt into his mouth.

"Are you crazy?" I asked him. I knew he wouldn't give me a good answer. It was like asking a blind person to describe the sky.

"I am hungry. And no one seems to understand. No one seems to care." He sat down on the grass and started to cry. As he cried, he licked his tears. He kept licking and crying, crying and licking.

"I do care, but there's nothing we can do. We're all hungry. Nothing has changed in the House."

"They are serving less food. I know it. I can tell. They are cheating us and feeding their own bellies."

"You are imagining things. The Mothers have always been fat. They were fat when we got here, and when we eventually leave, they will still be fat." He lay down on the grass, supine, and his arm began to bleed again. He seemed satisfied with whatever morsels he had taken from his arm.

"Do you ever dream of a place where there is always enough?" He pointed up. "I want to go to that place."

I had stopped dreaming of that place a long time ago, but I didn't want to tell Puni that. I felt that somehow my prayers weren't being transmitted properly to the divinities above. When I had asked for protection, I received Headmistress Veli's "favors." When I had asked for more food, I received her leftovers – at a steep price. And most importantly, when I had asked for friendship, Golicchio was taken from me and replaced by Jaga-Nai. I was done asking for anything from anyone.

He got up and rubbed his belly. "I think the dog is tired now. Someday I will get her, and then she will be the one who starves." I looked at him leave, feeling sorry for him.

"COME QUICK!" I heard Golicchio scream. I saw his elbow stick out the back door. I rushed inside, wondering if something had happened to Peepa. Instead, I walked into what looked like a bloody massacre. The dog had taken a large chunk out of Puni's stomach, and from what I could see, he had eaten a lot of grass and leaves. Puni was not breathing or talking. He looked unbearably thin. I shuddered.

"Call the Mothers," Ganesh whispered. He was standing near him, his foot very close to his head. He nudged Puni's face, but it didn't move.

"I am busy, two minutes," Mother Jamuna said.

I screamed, "He is dead, he is dead! You…" but I couldn't complete the sentence.

"What is it?" Mother Jamuna's hair was wet. She hadn't had time to braid it, and I laughed inside. Her hair was thinning. My mother's hair had always been thick.

"Can't you see? He is wearing a bloody blanket," Golicchio whispered.

Mother Jamuna looked sick. She didn't even want to touch him. Instead, she took her sari end and dabbed Puni's stomach with it.

"Didn't anyone tell him that the dog is dangerous?"

I looked past her huge form and into the Closet. I couldn't see Peepa, and I wondered if he was dead too. I supposed it would have been easier to handle two deaths at once, than ones that were spaced apart.

Without fail, Headmistress Veli came to revive the dead, and she brought a bucket of water and dirty rags with her.

"The doctor is coming," she said.

"It's too late. He has gone to sleep," Golicchio whispered. His voice was soft. I felt he could wrap Puni's body with it.

Headmistress Veli took the wet rags and soaked up the blood that had pooled around his body. She dabbed at his body and his face, which then turned into a maroon color. The dog? Someone had stuck a knife into her throat. Oddly, her blood and Puni's were mixing, and they looked the same.

I saw Mother Jamuna crying, and I knew that Puni would've been happy to have known that his life did matter. But when I saw Mother Kalpana hug her and say, "You can get another," I knew then that she was only sad about her dog, not about the wasted life that she had helped to kill. I felt cold. Puni had been my first friend, and the first one to die. There was still so much to say, but I had missed my chance.

When the doctor arrived hours later, the only people left standing near Puni's body were Headmistress Veli, Mother Jamuna, and me. Ganesh had thrown up in the hallway and was escorted roughly by Mother Kalpana to the outhouse. Golicchio – I didn't know where he had gone. His whispers had become softer and softer until I couldn't hear him anymore, and I didn't even know when he had left the hallway. I still didn't know where Peepa was. I was afraid for him, but I was more afraid of the dead dog that lay in front of the Closet door.

The doctor stayed for less than a minute, asking questions that seemed irrelevant. I wasn't even certain that he had proper medical training. The abortion doctor, for all of his unprofessionalisms, seemed more able.

"Whose dog?" he asked.

"Mine." Mother Jamuna looked at him, and he looked at her with sympathy.

"Is he dead?" I shrieked. I felt the back of Mother Jamuna's hand on my mouth.

"Yes, and don't shout."

The doctor and the Mothers talked about other things – like what villages they were from and what women were wearing these days. The doctor also talked about how his own dog had been run over by a rickshaw. It had taken him months to get over the pain of the loss, and Mother Jamuna nodded in agreement. As the doctor checked Puni's pulse, he asked the Mothers if they knew where he could buy good quality burfi. His sister's birthday was today.

I stared at Puni's face for the last time. His real name, Prakash, meant "light" in Tamil. His unblinking eyes were forever unblinking then, and the light from his face was gone.

AT NIGHT WE were all on the floor, trying to go to sleep. The news of Puni's death had traveled; everyone was discussing it. The boys who didn't know what had happened were inventing grand stories of his end. I was positive that Puni wouldn't have minded one bit, so I didn't bother to correct them.

"I heard that Mother Jamuna killed him," one of the boys said. Ganesh, Golicchio, and I remained silent.

"How?" someone asked.

"She got so hungry, she cut him open and ate him!" A bunch of the boys laughed, and Ganesh stood up.

"Fuck you all," he said. I shivered and pretended that I had a blanket over my body under which to keep warm.

None of us slept that night. I couldn't stop thinking about what had happened. We all knew what he needed, yet none of us could give it to him. We could've made more sacrifices, spared him more food. What would it have done me to have had even a gram less of food that was no good anyway?

On one of the rare occasions when Headmistress Veli wanted to talk instead of do other things, she had told me about her brief employment at the Tamil Nadu government hospital. She had remained at her post for only a short time because she couldn't face the patients who came there. She told me that lines of helpless parents would wait for hours for life-saving medications for their sick children. Salvation was so close, yet they had to wait for it. Even then, the government only paid for the very basic medications if they were lucky enough to get to the front of the line. Sometimes those medications didn't work, and the parents didn't have enough money to buy something that would. As a result, they sat and watched their children wither away and die. Headmistress Veli told me that she felt as powerless as a cat on its back in water. She knew what they needed, but couldn't do a damn thing. That was the way I felt about Puni.

I didn't believe that blood coursed through our veins. It was money.

Chapter Fifty-Nine

I DON'T KNOW where they buried him. I never saw his body afterward.

I finally tell my children what happened to Puni, and my wife is the one who insists that we must do something to memorialize his death. I disagree, but the children find a shop specializing in trinkets and purchase a pig made out of plastic. They want to bury it back home, far away from the place that had killed him.

I tell my children I will be back. I take the figure with me, and I find an alley empty of foot traffic and street vendors. I sit down on a crate filled with garbage, and I cry.

Chapter Sixty

When Peepa finally emerged from the Closet, I had lost track of how many days he had been inside. Most of us were sensitive to the ordeal he'd gone through and avoided asking him any questions about Puni. Some of us weren't.

"How come you didn't warn him?" Ganesh asked. He had taken Puni's loss severely, but I wasn't sure if it was because he cared or because seeing his dead body had scarred him somehow. Either way, he was the one who seemed most affected, even though I was the one who had lost a good friend.

Peepa just shrugged. He was much quieter since leaving the Closet, and the only person he said more than a few words to was Golicchio. He had stopped drinking water as well, and his nose bled more. He had also developed tiny sores the shapes of rocks along his arms and legs. We didn't know what it was, but I suspected a needle. Headmistress Veli had the same marks along her arms and thighs from when the abortion doctor came and performed his procedures.

The Mothers had succeeded in tearing apart his spirit by taking away his handsomeness. He no longer was star quality – a future MGR. He was simply a side actor who may have resembled a leading actor at one time. I didn't see him pause in front of a reflected piece of glass or the window anymore, or touch his face as if he were surprised by its softness. He no longer bothered to comb his hair. It poked out at all edges, resembling a man with drills sticking out from his head. Sometimes I wondered if his attractiveness only came from the fact that he believed he was. Now that he didn't care, it was gone.

"What are you thinking about?" Peepa asked. He had resorted to asking us these questions lately. It seemed as if all he wanted to do was think, dream, ponder. He and Golicchio were one and the same in that regard, and after his release from the Closet, even more inseparable.

"Why did you let Puni die?" Ganesh asked. Golicchio looked as if he wanted to say something – anything – to defend his friend, but he remained silent.

"We are all responsible," I said.

"Some of us more than others," he said.

"A new boy has come to the House," Golicchio said, trying to change the subject. "He looks a little like Puni, but he's not."

"No one can replace Puni," Peepa said.

"I know, but—"

"No one," Peepa said firmly.

The conversation stopped, and I hoped that Headmistress Veli would call upon me for a favor, but she didn't. Her timing was impeccable.

The new boy's name was Farouk. He was Muslim, which instantly drew heat from many of the boys. We had never had a Muslim child among us before. To me, religion was like money. The people who seemed to have a lot of it were the ones (like the Brahmins) who sat above everyone else. I was better off without it, so his religious inclinations didn't bother me. What did bother me was how everyone resorted to calling him "Puni," even though he didn't really look like Puni. He could've been Puni's half-brother by marriage not by blood, but he didn't have the unblinking eyes. Instead, his eyes were red and filled with tears, and his ears had cuts in them. He had come alone – no parents had given him away. He was also very quiet. Though we tried to get him to answer our questions, sometimes with force, he didn't respond. Ganesh spit on him, and I saw Jaga-Nai kick him with his foot.

"He's probably deaf or mute," Golicchio said.

"They let everything in here, don't they," Karthik said.

"Leave him alone," I said. I didn't like what was happening, but I was even guilty. No one had even really liked Puni, yet every new kid who came along was instantly compared to him. Was he fat? Did he blink? Was he whiny? Did he shove food in his mouth indiscriminately? Would he make intelligent comments once in a purple moon? If he didn't measure comparatively, which was always going to happen, he was ridiculed, beaten even, and tormented. Jaga-Nai was the worst. He went around calling all of the new boys "First Puni" or "Second Puni" even when they bore no resemblance to the original.

"'Leave him alone,'" Ganesh mimicked. Since Puni's death, I no longer felt safe around him. His muscles were bulging, and he had a perception that his manhood was constantly being "attacked" by the rest of us. Unless we knew as much about cricket as he did, we were not his buddies. He only spoke when he felt authority was needed and didn't like to listen to Golicchio's stories anymore.

"Fantasy is for little boys," he'd said. He sounded so grown-up. He was probably right. Puni had died waiting for a tray of candies to appear.

After a few weeks had lapsed since our last class, Mother Jamuna called us inside. We were to resume our lessons, finally. She apologized for the delay and kindly waved us into the room. Ganesh sat in the front, and I sat in the back, alone. I missed Puni. I liked watching him absorb the lessons with his eyes; they were like magic globes through which to see the future. His interest made me pay more attention in class, and as a result, time went by a little faster. Even though Puni had gotten into trouble often for various altercations, he never was disciplined in the classroom. His homework was subpar, his responses were mediocre, but he never misbehaved or skipped his lessons. He was diligent in learning even though he wasn't a star pupil.

Now Farouk, whose eyes were a sandy color and blinking, had taken his place. I was afraid to be associated with him, but Headmistress Veli had already started asking me about him, and I knew that it was only a matter of time before she included him in her love coterie. He was skinny how she liked, and he reminded me of how scared and naïve I was when I first came here. He was young, and his face was pockless. I knew that he and I would become friends as a byproduct of her advances.

"As you all know, some time has passed since Prakash's death. We are all saddened by the loss, but life goes on. Loss is not new to you all." She looked at us with caring eyes, but I knew better. "Please understand that what happened is not your fault."

"I know, because it's yours," Ganesh said.

Mother Jamuna glared at him, but she didn't punish him. She continued. "Today I want us to talk about how we feel, so that we can put this unpleasantness away." Some of us groaned; I heard Jaga-Nai pretend as though he were going to vomit. Even so, there were a handful of us who did want to talk about what happened. This was a rare opportunity to actually heal, and many of us did not want to pass it up.

"He was my friend," Golicchio said. I nodded too.

"He was friends with many of you," Mother Jamuna said.

"Not me," Jaga-Nai said and laughed.

She went to him and said, "Jagadesh, do not joke." She returned to the front of the classroom and called on Peepa. "How do you feel?" She had never asked us these questions, and I wasn't sure Peepa would even know how to answer.

"How do you feel?" Peepa asked her, and she seemed relieved by his answer.

"Sad as you all are."

He wanted to say more, but he didn't have the energy.

"Guilty," I said. Mother Jamuna turned to me.

"What did you say?"

"Some of us feel guilty. Like we let it happen."

She looked nervous and quickly changed the subject. "Goli, why did you like Prakash?"

The rest of class time was devoted to talking about Puni, his legacy (which was short), and why we missed him. The class was divided; half hadn't and would never give a shit about his life, and the other half loved him in the way one loves a deformed rat. I hoped that if Puni was in Nirvana, he was able to see the size of the hole he had left behind.

Later that evening, when I was with Headmistress Veli, I asked her why Mother Jamuna had devoted an entire class to Puni.

"Why now? She didn't care about him. She cared more about her dog."

Headmistress Veli laughed. "You are about as innocent as when you first arrived here. That is why I like you," she said. She was combing her hair in sections. Tonight, she was going to invite Farouk to her room. She'd already wooed him with mangoes and sugar-coated chilis. She felt ready for more.

"Tell me. Why?" I hated the way my voice pleaded.

"She doesn't want to see any more of you die. Or worse, run away."

"So she does care."

She laughed again. "No, silly. She doesn't care. If you run away, so does her meal ticket. She needs you. This is her job, her livelihood. If you all left or died, what would happen to her?"

"What would happen to you?"

"I always find a way. Now, time for you to leave." She scooted me out of her room and shut the door.

I KNEW THAT I had to go. It had been four days since I had gone. I was sitting in the outhouse, but nothing was coming. I felt as though a thirty kilo catfish was flopping around inside my belly, wanting to be released back into the ocean.

"What are you doing, eh?" Jaga-Nai asked. I heard his scraggly voice even before I saw him. He looked as rundown as his voice had been.

"What do you think?" He had seen my privates so many times, it no longer bothered me.

"Trying," he said, "and failing," and he laughed and sat down. I put my shorts on and sat down against the wall that was least slippery.

"About this plan. I feel it will be tonight. With Piggy's death, the Mothers are distracted. I can leave and they will never know. You must help me."

"It's all a hoax. How many times have I tried to tell you? To help?" I stood up. "I don't even want to help you, but I have already – by telling you the truth. Why won't you listen? You heard her. She admitted that she wrote the letters herself."

He screamed back, "I have to get away!"

"Where are you going to go if your parents don't want you?" I whispered. He whispered back.

"I need to get away. From her." His hands shook as he tried to smooth down his hair. He took a rock from his pocket and tried to carve pieces out of the cheap plaster. I grabbed his hands to stop them from shaking. He let me.

"Listen, running away isn't the answer. She'll always be in here." I pointed to my head. When I wasn't with her, she was with me. Everywhere. In my sleep, in the outhouse, when I was eating, drinking, or even bathing. Her smell, her laugh, and her fat neck were all permanent companions. I knew that Jaga-Nai felt the same way.

"Don't say that. She's just too much for me. I need a break, eh? You understand, right?" He didn't look at me, but I could feel that he was waiting for a response.

"Right," I said.

"So help me find my parents."

"I told you!" I screamed. "Are you not listening to me?" I shouted and jumped up and down and even touched his shoulder. He wasn't listening. I knew then that he was a lost cause, and the moment that he truly believed that his parents were dead, he would be dead too.

Later, the clouds were pouring rain on us, but it still felt good to be outside. The sky was orange, and the rain came down like boiling water over rice. The Mothers so far hadn't called us inside for dinner. We didn't think they would. They had had several visitors and were preoccupied with making the House inviting to those who wanted or needed to stay. Headmistress Veli avoided the rain as though it were acid; she stayed inside, and I knew that Farouk was with her.

I loved the rain. I liked the way it pounded my face with tiny fingers as though giving me a mini massage. I also liked how heavy it made me feel once my clothes were thoroughly soaked. It made me feel bigger than I was. Most of all, I never grew tired of the way the rain smelled. Near the sea, it smelled like salt and sand mixed together. Here, my nose detected jasmine intermingled with a touch of salt. No perfume of Headmistress Veli's could ever imitate that.

Most of the other boys had the same love affair with the rain, and as a result, they were outside too. The weather was right for making objects and people out of the grass that grew around the House. I had started out of boredom, but soon found the process engaging. I tied the ends together and with dirt and water, I formed green sculptures that had life-like qualities. I was working on a profile of Mother Jamuna, which I hoped could be used to torment her.

"What are you making?" Golicchio asked. He was sitting next to Peepa, but I didn't answer him.

"What are you thinking about?" Peepa asked.

"About leaving here," I said. I felt as though I were surrounded by hollow faces and handless bodies, and the rain made Peepa look like an eyeless tiger about to seek refuge. I wasn't sure if we were a camp of survivors or a camp of the dead.

"Hello?" I heard a voice ask. It was a woman's voice. Through the rain, I saw a white sheet and a thin arm reach out and touch my face.

"Smita?" I asked.

"Aruna?" Peepa asked.

"Gurpana," she answered. "Ganesh? Is he here?" She was close enough to me that I could see she was crying. Her eyes were light brown, and she had a small leaf stuck to her cheek. Her hair was not braided, and I could see her belly bare and beaded with drops of water. She was extremely fair-skinned, and for a second, I thought she might have been a ghost.

"Gurpana!" I heard Ganesh scream. We all dropped to the ground as though a bomb had gone off – the noise was that loud. We were aware of Ganesh's powerful voice. We had just never heard it used in such a forceful way.

As the rain began to clear, I could see that Ganesh and Gurpana were brother and sister. Both had the same flat nose and the same expressionless eyes. They talked, then hugged, then talked some more, and then kissed each other on the forehead and hair.

"Enough," she said. "We have to leave, right now." I looked over at Golicchio, and his mouth was open.

"I just can't believe you are alive," Ganesh said. Someone had come for one of us, and it wasn't for Jaga-Nai. I would have even welcomed Smita.

"Why didn't you come for me sooner?" Ganesh asked her. She cried. She cried so hard that it sounded like she was hiccupping. I had to refrain from laughing.

"Shut up," Golicchio said. I looked at him, but he had a smile on his face too.

"A man, he tried to," she covered her face with the end of her sari. I noticed red streaks on the fabric.

"What did he do? Tell me," Ganesh said. He wanted to fight, and I expected an arrow and bow to fall down from the sky and land squarely in his hands. I looked around, wondering if his foe would appear out of thin air the way his sister had.

After she stopped crying, we sat down on the grass. Ganesh was holding her, and Golicchio was playing with her sari. Her beauty held us, but not in a perverse way. I could feel the kindness radiate from her body, and though we all wanted pieces of her in non-sexual ways, she trembled at our touch and Ganesh had to flick us off as if we were blood-thirsty ticks. She was good, but not like Headmistress Veli. I knew that if I were to touch her, she would hate it, and that made her instantly better than any woman I'd known.

"I didn't know how to find you. The government records for survivors are virtually nil." She spoke as if reciting a poem. "I was at a camp. They had rations, shelter. I tried to stay with a family, but they didn't want me. They said I was a lone woman and would bring bad luck. Being pretty is a burden." She paused and wet her lips. "Eventually they came. The sex-depraved men. They stole my food and made me work for it. Some offered protection, only to take it back later. Even the government workers who were there to help." She covered her face and couldn't continue.

"Please," she begged. "Do I have to say more?" I could tell it was painful for her to tell us these things, but I believed it was even more painful to tell her brother these things – a brother who probably had no idea what his fellow man was capable of.

"Who were these men?" She shook her head.

"I don't know," she said.

"Yes, you do." I could see his eyes bulge with anger. "What did you do to entice them?"

"Please," she said again.

"Hasn't she had enough?" Peepa said. I had forgotten that his voice could be strong too, if he wanted. He then stood up. I saw that Peepa had finally surpassed Ganesh's height.

"Don't get in the middle. This is not your sister."

"I would not yell at someone who has just been through what she has."

"You would slap your mother though, the woman who gave you birth?"

"Stop, please," I heard Golicchio say. When I looked at him, he was rocking back and forth with his arms underneath his knees.

"You're no better than the men who raped her," Peepa said, and as Ganesh took a swing at Peepa and fell down, someone else yelled.

"She's gone, she's gone," Karthik shouted. We looked back, and the ghost had disappeared.

"Gurpana!" Ganesh screamed. He ran after her.

Peepa shouted a few obscenities after Ganesh, but Golicchio put his arm on his as if to silence him. As though he were in a trance, Golicchio's touch snapped him back to reality. He instantly became quiet, and he returned to his laconic self.

"So life outside of here isn't much better," Golicchio said. All of us were too stunned to respond.

"Where is Ganesh, eh?" Jaga-Nai asked. We were still standing in the rain, which had restarted. We were drenched. The crows, I believed the same crows from that fateful game of Kabaddi many moons ago, had their wings outstretched, forming temporary umbrella-like shelters for our tiny heads.

Jaga-Nai had only recently joined us. I guessed that he'd been inside earlier, "inducting" Farouk into Headmistress Veli's hall of misbehaving. He had taken a special interest in Farouk, perhaps because Headmistress Veli seemed to really like him. Or maybe it was because Farouk did whatever Jaga-Nai asked him to do, such as giving him any and all food and trinkets that Headmistress Veli overwhelmed him with. I had already seen Jaga-Nai wearing a shirt that said "Farouk" on it.

"Where is he?" he asked again. His voice was loud, as if addressed to all, but he was only looking at me.

"He's gone," I said. "He's left us for good."

"Did he run to home?" Jaga-Nai whispered. I could tell that it bothered him, thinking that someone else had won in the game of running away. Deep down though, I felt that Ganesh would never make it. His sister had barely survived. Two young adults, a desirable woman and an anger-driven child-man, had nowhere to go. As far as I knew, all of their extended family had been killed in the tsunami. She would be raped and beaten. She was already close to death. He would be tortured or killed, unless he was willing to work, which I found unlikely since he'd never done a gram's worth of chores in the House.

The Mothers told us that we were helpless without them, and if we ever ran away, we'd be at the mercy of the pedophiles, the sex traders, the rich men who made young children perform the most hardening of tasks. They supported their claims by making examples out of the boys who did come to the House, some of whom had experienced the very tales that they told us about. They even used the women who came as models for the cruelty that existed outside of these walls. These women were sexually abused so badly that their hair had become thin and their mouths were covered in sores; the Mothers did not have to say anything to affirm their point. I will never forget the day a woman old enough to be my grandmother sought refuge in the House. Her wrinkles couldn't hide the bruises on her body. She had blood dripping down her legs and teeth marks on her neck. Her hair was cut short, and she wore bright red lipstick.

"Please, Acca, water," she'd said as she stumbled onto the steps of the House. Mother Jamuna helped her inside with a kindness absent from her dealings with us. Once the old lady had some water in her belly, her voice grew large and blunt.

"I was raped in the village across from this one. Since when do they like old women?"

The Mothers didn't tell her to be quiet, but instead asked her more questions. Who did it? Was it a group or one at a time? Was it men or women?

She spat. "Men. How do women rape each other?"

"They could, there are ways," Mother Kalpana said.

Golicchio whispered. "They rape each other by yelling at each other and calling each other dirty names."

I didn't know why I thought about the old prostitute then, but maybe Ganesh's sister would be lucky. I didn't even think I knew what luck meant anymore.

"I don't know where he went, Jaga-Nai," I said.

"What good are you? Nothing." He stepped on my foot, and the long nail of his toe cut into my skin. I squawked.

"Eh," Jaga-Nai said to me. He held up a letter. How I had come to loathe his letters. "Veli wrote me a letter. She said she's sorry for all of the mean things she said. Does she ever apologize to you?"

"No," because she thinks she's better than me. But I didn't say that last part. Jaga-Nai already knew that.

"I am ready to leave, to escape. They don't care if I go anymore. Ganesh has left. Puni has left." He giggled. "It's my turn now." He looked at me.

"I will return, you know. I will come back to show you that my parents really are alive. None of you believe me, but I will show you."

"And what if they are not there?"

"I am older now. I could live on my own." I looked at him trying to straighten his hair. He was right. When he came, he hadn't known what it meant to die. Now he did, and there was no way that he was going to allow himself to die in the House. I almost envied his fantasy. I wished that I too could allow myself to indulge in the idea that my parents were alive and would get me. If I could possibly believe it, maybe they would really come.

"Tonight, after the Mothers are asleep, I will slip away. You are right. You are not much of a distraction." He sat down.

"Right," I said. We were all practically invisible to the Mothers these days, especially to Mother Jamuna and Mother Kalpana.

"Then the next morning, you will pretend like I am here. I will return after I locate my parents."

"Why even bother? Just stay there. Don't come back." I couldn't understand why someone would want to return to this place, even if it were for the sake of vindication.

"Maybe I won't," he said. He got up and brushed off his legs. He had taken to peeling his toenails and putting the bits on top of his thighs and knees.

"You don't really need my help, do you?" I asked him.

"Yes, I do."

"How is that? What must I do?"

"Someone has to satisfy my woman while I am gone. Farouk is still young. I don't want her to try to find me." He leaned in like he was going to kiss me, and I pushed him off. "Yrimal has developed strong shoulders, eh?" He laughed and fingered his hair. "Keep her happy."

"And who will reinforce that? You won't be here to see to it," I said. Jaga-Nai thought he was so clever.

"She will. She can make your life a living hell too, you know," and he went inside. He didn't need to tell me that. I knew that already.

Chapter Sixty-One

AT THE SITE of the House, we find that a new building has been erected. I feel a loss so profound that I am speechless.

Chapter Sixty-Two

EVEN THOUGH JAGA-NAI had indicated that he would be leaving soon, he didn't. I began to wonder if he had the courage to.

During breakfast the next morning, the Mothers had discovered Ganesh missing, but they didn't say anything. In class, Mother Jamuna called his name as if he were still in the front row as always. Jaga-Nai for fun said "present" when she called his name, and she nodded, even though she knew Jaga-Nai's voice from Ganesh's. I was glad that denial was the path that they had chosen; I wasn't sure if I could tolerate another lesson on losing one of our own.

Days much like these came and went, and I became comfortable in their predictability. Though Farouk annoyed me with his frequent prostrations and his chubby face and skinny body, he made my life easier. Headmistress Veli was so enamored with him that days went by when I wouldn't see her at all. I thanked Brahma, and then realized maybe I should thank Allah, for the blessings that I had received. Classes became less about math and science and more about how to live a better life. I wondered if the Mothers were using class time as a form of therapy for their own issues because we discussed topics that seemed more relevant to them than us. They particularly liked to lecture about growing older. Were we afraid of death? What happened when we aged, and we could no longer do the things that we had done once before? I thought the Mothers feared their own mortality and the judgment they'd receive upon their deaths.

I did too, in a way unlike any other time. Even though my risk of dying had been imminent right after the tsunami, I wasn't afraid the way I was now. My life had gotten easier when I was used to only hardness. I wondered when the gods would finally realize that they had gotten it all wrong, and I would be thrust into a life worse than death. It seemed melodramatic, but I was not used to a comfortable life, and because of that, I was suffering from a deep-seated form of stress. I couldn't blame Headmistress Veli for it either. In that way, it was worse.

I found Peepa alone outside, and I could feel the anxiety burning inside of my throat. Peepa was twirling a piece of hair.

"Are you losing your hair too?" Lately most of mine was ending up on my shirt or in Headmistress Veli's hands. I wasn't even growing facial hair yet, and I was already going bald.

"No," he said. He didn't look at me, but continued touching the hair.

"Where's Golicchio?"

"I don't know. Why are you bothering me? Why don't you find your friends, Jaga-Nai or Headmistress Veli? Hmm?"

I stopped talking.

"Can you just leave?" Peepa looked at my feet, and I covered them with my hands.

"Why should I leave? This grass is not yours." I got on my side and rolled away from him. I tucked my feet underneath me, so that he couldn't see them.

We were quiet for a while, but I had a feeling that Peepa had more things to say. So I waited.

Sure enough, after perhaps a half hour had passed, he began again.

"Do you know where Golicchio is?" he asked. Headmistress Veli had taught me timing was key. Make a move at the wrong time, and all was lost.

"No. Didn't I just ask you that?" I asked. I waited.

"Then get lost," he said.

"What were you doing in the Closet when Puni was mauled to death?"

"Why? Does Golicchio blame me? Did he tell you that?"

"Yes, he did," I lied, and rolled toward him. He stood up.

"His mind was so focused on the mutton, I think he lost his hearing in the end." He started to leave, but I blocked him with my foot.

"Golicchio will forgive you," I said. I couldn't stop the lying.

He almost didn't believe me, but he had nowhere else to turn, so he chose to put his faith in the lies that surrounded him. That was what had happened to Jaga-Nai, and I saw how easily Peepa fell into it. Headmistress Veli was right about that too.

"Whose hair is that?" I asked him.

"Mind your own business." He put the lock of hair away in his shorts pocket.

I saw Golicchio come into the yard, and he hesitated for a moment, as if he wanted to go back inside, but he changed his mind and came out anyway.

"Yrimal, did you see the color of the sky today?" He looked away from Peepa.

"If you're mad, just tell me," Peepa said. He put his face near Golicchio's.

"I'm not mad."

"Yes, you are. What did I do?"

They continued back and forth. Something had happened between them, but I knew that Golicchio would never tell.

To stop their squabbling, I said, "Peepa has hair in his pocket." Peepa pushed me and motioned as if he was going to hit me. Golicchio stopped him.

"What hair?"

"Nothing," he said.

"Look in his shorts pocket," I said.

Golicchio, as though he were about to stick his finger into a lion's cage, carefully grabbed the lock of hair from Peepa's shorts. He didn't resist. It seemed as if he wanted Golicchio to find it.

"Whose hair is this?"

"Mine," Peepa muttered.

"Your hair is not this dark. Or long. It looks like mine."

"It's not yours!" he shouted. "Yrimal is a fucking liar."

Golicchio was speechless. "What does Yrimal have to do with this?"

"It's Aruna's."

Golicchio nodded. "Who's Aruna?" I asked, but Peepa didn't want to answer.

"She's the girl from the greenhouse," Golicchio said. He was sad all of a sudden, and I had a strange desire to punch Peepa, but I didn't.

Instead, Peepa glared at me. "Whatever you do, be careful who you trust. Yrimal is not one to be trusted."

"You're the one who promised to tell me how our fathers are connected," I said.

"Fuck off," he said. Golicchio looked at both of us.

"Did you lie, Yrimal?" Golicchio asked.

"About what? No," I said. I knew that my time with Headmistress Veli was showing in my personality. Her ways were all that I knew. It was becoming second nature to replicate them.

"Yrimal is the one who is sleeping with the Mothers. All of them!"

I laughed, the way Headmistress Veli laughed at inappropriate times. I learned it made people uncomfortable. "No, just Veli."

Golicchio stared at me. "I thought you said she forced you?"

I sounded like Jaga-Nai. "She makes me feel like a man." I started crying then and tried to override it by laughing again. "I like it," I said over and over, trying to convince myself, the way Jaga-Nai had that time long ago, but it wasn't working. Every time I said it, I started crying.

"Poor Yrimal," Golicchio said, and he reached over to pat me, but I pushed him away.

"Stop! Leave me alone! None of you care. Maybe if you did, you'd offer yourselves to her instead," I said, even though I knew that if the situation had been reversed, I'd have done nothing.

"You always have a choice. You're just trying to make us feel sorry for you," Peepa said.

"Sometimes choices are plenty, but all of them are bad. Then what do you decide?" Golicchio asked. I nodded.

"I don't care what the alternative is. I would never let that fat bitch touch me. Never."

They didn't know. Only Jaga-Nai knew the psychological power that she had over us. Or was I all wrong? Did I have a choice?

"Enough," Golicchio said.

Was it my fault that I was in the predicament that I was in? Did Headmistress Veli only attract boys with evil inside of their hearts? I thought about what it meant to be evil, and the thoughts flowed more easily than I could have imagined. I could feel the stress lifting from my body. There was something inside of me that was growing, and I couldn't do anything about it.

"Go," I SAID to the girl, Aruna. I was inside cleaning the classroom. The Mothers had finished their knitting, and in the process, had left pieces of colored yarn everywhere. The fabric kept getting stuck in the little broom I used, which made the task even more difficult. Aruna's presence didn't help. She had come inside to speak to Mother Jamuna, but had stopped in the classroom to speak to me.

"Peepa is not here." She looked up at his name, and then looked down.

"You have lost weight," she said. Headmistress Veli had said the same thing to me earlier.

"What do you want?"

"I don't know," she said. I looked at her face, and I could tell that she didn't. She seemed lost. "I am sad about Prakash. Puni. I know you were good friends."

"Yes, we were." I filled my shorts pockets with the yarn.

"He told me once that you were the only one who listened to him," she said, and I could feel the tears welling up in my eyes. I swallowed and tried to hold them back.

"Stop talking about him. He's dead."

"That's exactly why we should talk about him."

"Go. I don't need trouble."

She stood, and again I looked at her face. She appeared to search for words – the right words to say.

"I'm sorry," she said.

"For what?"

"For Headmistress Veli. I know." She looked down.

"You don't know anything!" I screamed. She shrank back in fear.

"I wonder if Puni really knew the person you truly are," she whispered.

I saw a shadow, and one of the Mothers had come into the classroom.

"You are not supposed to be here. Get out, now!" Mother Jamuna shouted at the girl. She looked down and ran as fast as she could without bumping into anything. "Why are you taking so long?"

I shrugged my shoulders.

She kicked me in the legs, where I wouldn't show marks.

"Do not speak to Aruna, do you hear me? I don't want her to emulate your filthy ways." She went back outside. As she left, I saw that millions of little crumbs had populated the back of her sari like small ants. I wanted to punch her so badly that I kicked the ground instead.

"Do you need help?" Golicchio had come inside, and he held a longer broom in his hands.

"No."

"Are you mad?"

"No."

"Then what?" I could tell that something was on his mind.

"Why don't you just come outright and say what you want to say?" I shouted. "You don't care a fuck about all of the things with Veli or my father or any of it. All you care about is your own fucking self!"

"That's not true."

"Right. How come then when you knew something was happening to me, you kept quiet? How come you didn't go to the Mothers?"

"Because you told me it wouldn't do any good! You were the one who said!"

"I told you that if I went, it would do no good. But I never said if you went, it wouldn't."

"You are angry about something else. What is it? People hide their real feelings in anger."

"Stop speaking in silly riddles. I'm pissed off at you, not just angry. Does that mean that I have a barrel full of feelings inside?"

"You're not mad at me. You're mad at someone else, Headmistress Veli maybe."

"Don't fucking call her that."

"Stop cussing," Golicchio said. He covered his ears. "You know that I can't stand it. My father used to cuss, and—"

"Right. Your poor drunk father and your beaten up mother. It's the story of every boy here."

Golicchio took a step back and dropped the broom. His happiness at finding me was gone. "You're so mean. I didn't tell you those things so that you could repeat them in anger."

I wanted to tell him that I was sorry. That I didn't mean the things that I had said. That he was my only true friend now. That I loved him more than I had loved my own father. But the words were stuck, and I couldn't. I knew if I spoke them, my anger would dissipate, and I couldn't let that happen. For my own survival, I needed to stay angry.

I just stared at him. "You know things about my father, don't you? If you were my friend, wouldn't you have told me by now?"

"He doesn't know anything more than what he's already told you," Golicchio said quietly.

"You're lying."

Golicchio sighed. "His father was a bad man, Yrimal. He did bad things to others and kept souvenirs of his carnage. That's all I know and he knows."

"You say that I am frail, but who is the one who hides? Without Peepa, who are you? You hide behind Peepa and your stupid stories. To think that I thought you and I were alike in some way. You have no idea what I feel like inside." I could feel my voice breaking, so I stopped talking.

Golicchio was done. He always knew when to end things. "Good bye, Yrimal," he said.

Chapter Sixty-Three

IN MY HEART, I believe that my father had sold himself for his family, which was how he had met Peepa's father. Though we were poor, we weren't as poor as the others. Our stomachs never reached the point of fullness, but we were content, and my mother always seemed to acquire gifts randomly (such as toothpaste or shampoo), which she claimed she'd gotten from cleaning upper class houses. I suppose I will never know for sure.

All those years in the House, it had been so easy to hate him for cherishing Smita and not loving me. But he had been a good father in the only way he knew how; he had surrendered more of himself than even I have been able to do for my own children.

Chapter Sixty-Four

"It's true. We steal the rations that the government provides to us for you all. Otherwise, none of us would see the benefit of working here. Jamuna's parents own a small business. She could do better, but she stays because black market goods bring in a handsome price." Headmistress Veli finally admitted to me what I had already known for a long time.

"Where do you think that I get the money for all of these saris?" She was showing me her wardrobe again. I was to help her decide which one to wear tonight. She was going to the cinema with one of the Mothers.

"I wish there was a way we could get more of you to stay with us. The more boys, the more rations. But the Mothers have found a way to work around that one too." She winked. "Do you know who Pradesh and Mukesh are?" she asked.

"No."

"They are the twins who recently lost their parents in a swimming accident. They have no extended family to watch over them. They are here now, in the House." I thought about the new arrivals. There hadn't been any for a while.

She laughed. "You aren't so smart, are you? They aren't real. But in our books, and in our minds, they are." She laughed again. "Poor, poor Pradesh and Mukesh."

"How do you live with yourselves, knowing that we are starving so that you can make extra money?"

"If you knew what the government was paying us, you would do the same thing. You think they send the rations on time? The true culprit is the government. If they cared about you, why don't they come and visit you? Make sure you are treated well? They send money and food, and that's how they ease their conscience. The politicians gain votes by telling their constituents that they are taking care of the orphans, and then they get voted back time and time again. And, you aren't starving. You are more than well taken care of." She smiled. "Now, which one?"

I pointed to the orange flowered sari because I knew it made her look fat. She clapped her hands. "Perfect! You must love orange because you always choose that color for me. I will remember the next time I use your ration money to buy a new sari."

I sat in the corner of the room, holding one of her liquor bottles. She'd recently begun letting me drink from them because she said they made me more pliant. I took a sip of a clear-looking one. It tasted like sewage, but it calmed my nerves, made things seem less impossible. I knew it would be easy to become addicted, but I was about getting by day-to-day. I didn't allow myself to think too far ahead.

"Drink up, my little honey. Remember how I used to care for you when you first came to the House? You trusted me with your life back then. How come you don't trust me now?" I took another sip. "When I told you that your family was alive, I was telling the truth. Why won't you believe me?" I took another sip. She grabbed the bottle from me. "I don't want you to become too sloppy. That's not how I like my boys."

I saw Farouk pause near the outside of her room. She told me that he had a rash, so he was spared for a few weeks until it cleared up. I was back in her rotation again. She waved him away.

"Where are my parents then? If they are alive? Tell me where."

"Maybe you should write to them, and see if they write you back?"

"I'm not stupid like Jaga-Nai. Don't mistake me for a fool."

"Okay, but if you don't write, you'll never know."

"I don't believe you." I wanted her to drop the subject, but she kept at it, the way a nagging mother-in-law argued with her son's wife about every little thing that was wrong (but wasn't really).

"I showed you Smita's figurine. Do you know how I got it? Smita visited one day. She's beautiful. She is looking like a woman."

"What does she look like?"

"She looks like you, but a more feminine version, and a little bigger, and taller."

"What did she say?"

"Not much. Just wanted to talk to you, say she was sorry."

"For?"

"For all of the things that she did to you when you were growing up."

"Like what?"

She paused. "She didn't say specifically."

"Right."

"Don't talk back to me, boy. Here, drink." She passed me the bottle, and I took more sips to make up for lost time.

"She said something about a razor?" I took more sips. "And your father beat you up about it?"

"Stop lying. She was too young then to remember." I clamped my mouth shut. I needed to be careful of what I said to her. I couldn't keep track of what stories I had told her, and now she was using them.

"Kids remember more than what you think."

"What else did she say?"

"Not much. She said she'd come back another time, when you were free."

"How was I not free?"

"You were in the hole."

"Liar."

"I speak the truth."

"Why are you just now telling me this?"

"Enough questions. I've already told you more than what I should have. She will come again, and then you will see."

"None of what you say makes any sense."

"What purpose would I have to lie to you, Yrimal?"

I took more sips and felt my arms. They were getting bigger. "Maybe you just enjoy torment, and you don't know how to stop." I thought about my earlier exchange with Golicchio.

"That's silly," she laughed. "Remember when you first met me, you thought I was a caring person. Our first instincts are rarely ever wrong."

She began to undress and unfold the orange sari. "I have to go now. We will talk more later. I might come get you at night," she giggled. "Just to talk," she added. "You need to know the truth, and I promise I will tell you."

I took a big gulp before she shooed me out. Whatever she wanted to tell me, I wasn't sure I wanted any of it.

SHE NEVER CAME at night. In fact, I had listened for her footsteps, but they never materialized. I was angry that she had made me endure a night of no sleep.

In the morning, classes were cancelled. It had been at least two weeks since we last had a regular class. Most of the day, the Mothers convened in Mother Jamuna's office, talking and whispering about something. They were too preoccupied to pay mind to us. Unlike before when even a smidge of dirt would render us a beating, now they hardly cared if our faces were clean or our toes clipped. I was worried that it had to do with me and Headmistress Veli.

I also saw Aruna more frequently too. Mother Jamuna didn't do a good job of keeping her away. She was always in the shed, and sometimes she came into the cafeteria and ate with us.

"This is our food not yours. Get your own," one of the chubbier boys said. A small circle had formed around the girl. Today they were serving chicken briyani for dinner, a rare treat even though the chicken was mostly fatty, and the rice was mushy. We were very careful with our leaves, not wanting to waste even a morsel; yet this girl was trying to take our own food away from us, food that the government had sent us. She was just like the Mothers.

"Mother Jamuna said I could eat here if I wanted."

The circle grew tighter, and one of the boys pulled her hair. She screamed, but the Mothers didn't come. Whatever they were doing must have been very important.

"Give me the leaf," one of them said.

"Leave her alone, she eats like a bird anyhow," Peepa said.

"Doesn't matter, food is food," I said.

"Evil," Aruna said. "You are all evil!"

"You are evil for taking our food away from us," I said.

Peepa shoved me. "Where are your protections now?"

"If you touch me again you'll be sent to the Closet for a whole week." Golicchio stayed quiet.

Peepa pushed me again. "I don't care," he said. The girl slipped away in the commotion. He pushed me again. "Try something, I dare you." He wanted to hurt me. I could see it, but since when did he need an excuse?

Jaga-Nai said, "Punch him," and I laughed. Peepa came closer as if to punch me, but decided against it. Instead, he went running after Aruna. Golicchio looked on, unsure of what to do or where to go. I felt a little sad for him, but then I grew angry at how pathetic he was. I was learning how to coat everything with anger.

"My darling," Headmistress Veli called. I went to her room. She was getting bold in her demands.

"What?" I sat on her bed, but it smelled like her, so I moved to the floor. That also smelled like her, but what could I do? I couldn't sit on the ceiling.

"Aren't you going to ask me how the movie was?" She sat at her desk and began composing a letter.

"Who are you writing to?"

"Who do you think? Jaga-Nai is due another letter."

"Why do you both keep this up when both know the other is lying?"

"So much to learn."

"What are you writing?"

"Just that he is a good boy for being patient. That his time will come someday. I'm also asking about what his preferences are for a bride. You see, his parents want to arrange his marriage for him. They want to know if he prefers a wheat complexion or a fair-and-lovely complexion." She giggled.

"Veli," Mother Jamuna stopped at her door. She looked at me, but didn't say anything about me being in her room. I was a permanent fixture.

"Whatever you want to say, you can say in front of him too." She winked at me.

"You want to ruin this poor boy's life too the way you did with the other? He could've been somebody."

"Why must we talk about him? He killed himself because he was stupid. They're all stupid. You are lucky to have me, yes?" I didn't say anything.

"Veli, I think you should go to the hospital."

"If you make me, I will expose your scheme. I will."

"I no longer can live with this madness." Mother Jamuna raised her voice. "I have let you get away with far too much. This has to stop."

"No, it doesn't. If you don't leave me, I will expose you."

"Why do you have so much hatred in your heart?"

"I don't. Why do you?" She pointed to Mother Jamuna. "How is what you do any different than what I do? We are both taking what we feel we deserve. Who is to say which is worse?"

Mother Jamuna sighed. She dragged her feet as she left the room and closed the door.

"These Mothers. They are always trying to judge. But I refuse to be judged by the fat clan."

"But you are fat too."

"Shut up. Shut up, shut up, shut up!" she screamed and slapped me. "Oh, Sid, you made me. I'm so sorry, come here." She grabbed me and forced my head between her breasts. The doughy smell made me sleepy.

"You can nap if you want," she cooed. I wanted to sleep so badly, but I didn't trust her with my body. I needed to be alert, so I stayed awake, forcing my eyelids to blink against her clammy skin.

Chapter Sixty-Five

NO ONE KNOWS what to say. My wife takes the children and tells me that they will be back. She believes I need to be alone, but that is the last thing I need.

I sit at the base of the site and feel the sand with my fingers. I try to remember where the House had sat, where the dogs had been chained, where my room had been. The area looks smaller than I remember, but I suppose everything looks larger to a child. I want to cry – to feel some sort of release – but I don't. I am angry that they have decided to build upon a site dirty with death and deceit. How will the new place have a chance?

The foundation feels warm, and I take my shoes off and walk around. The same coil wires are there from before, though no crows are present. I lean against the eucalyptus tree, grown larger, and see the marks we had made on the bark as children. I close my eyes and try to recall the spirits that I had loved so much: the ones that I had disappointed and abused.

I feel some time has passed when I open my eyes. I look around for my wife and children, but they have not yet returned. I see a figure though, standing in front of the new building, looking at me. He is thin and bespectacled. He walks with a cane.

Chapter Sixty-Six

"ANOTHER LETTER HAS come," Jaga-Nai said. He was wearing the same shorts and shirt he had worn yesterday. "This one says that my parents are coming for me. Soon. My mother has convinced my father to come. That the time is right now, and they need me. My brother has vanished – the no-good bum – with a girl it says."

"Headmistress Veli has some imagination." He slapped me.

"These letters are not from Veli."

I was tired of playing these games with him. He was as stupid as he was ugly.

"Did you hear me, eh?"

"Yes."

"I will just wait for them to appear, and then you will see for yourself. How shameful you will feel when you see them taking me home, and you are stuck here with them." His eyes moved to point out the nameless and faceless boys that now lived here.

"Right."

He stood, waiting for me to say something. The moment was awkward.

"Yrimal, good luck then, eh?" He grinned. He was happy. I wasn't.

"Right." He patted me on the back, the way he had done many times before beating the crap out of me.

He then motioned toward Headmistress Veli's room, and I knew he was going there next to tell her the news. He waved his arms as if he wanted me to come along too, and I did. I wanted to listen – to see her fall. I wanted her to feel the control slipping, her power insignificant.

As I reached the door, I was a few seconds late and stumbled into the conversation already half-begun and halfway heated.

"Your mom is a drug addict and diseased," I heard Headmistress Veli say. She sounded as if she were talking to Mother Jamuna – very professional and distant.

"This letter says that they are coming for me. I don't care what you say about them, but I am just letting you know. You won't be having me anymore, eh?"

Headmistress Veli laughed. "I've had plenty like you before, and I will have plenty like you after. But don't worry. You won't be leaving, and I will have you all that I like. Let me show you something."

I heard the rustling of papers, but I didn't dare turn to look. Several of the boys saw me eavesdropping, but many were afraid and avoided the hallway.

"Compare the handwriting." I could almost hear Jaga-Nai smooth down his hair.

"Yes, your writing is similar to my mother's, but that doesn't mean that you are the same person."

Headmistress Veli then recited every single thing she had written in the letters, down to certain sentences. She recounted stories he had divulged in his letters as well. She was brutal, spelling out a few of the tender things that she had written as his mother, such as wanting to rub his calloused feet or making his favorite dessert, coconut burfi.

"You are lying. All lies." But I could hear his voice faltering. He was starting to believe.

"Am I the liar, or are you for believing what is told to you without question?" She laughed again, and I heard the sound of fabric shifting. "You believe what I want you to believe. You don't exist outside of this House or me. That's been the arrangement, and will always be the arrangement, do you understand?"

"She said she loved me more than my brother."

She laughed again. "How easy the pen makes lies that the heart believes. The pen is really the culprit, eh?" She mocked his tone.

I left the hallway, afraid that the conversation was going to end and that they would see me. Even though her lies had been exposed, I knew she wouldn't stop. She would devise another world in which Jaga-Nai would live. She was good at that.

For dinner, we were served fried okra and tamarind rice. The food was getting better, or maybe since I was eating less, it seemed tastier. I noticed that there were few of us to enjoy it though. Puni's face flashed in front of my eyes, and I wished that he could have been here now, eating what he had longed to have.

"Have you seen him?" Headmistress Veli was at my back. She looked hideous in a new persimmon-colored sari. It made her look as though she had swallowed five orangutans.

"Who?"

"Don't play dumb, dummy. Jagadesh. I need to talk to him." She looked down. "Tell him I'm sorry."

"I haven't seen him."

"Stop looking at me and help me find him." We split up, and I took the outside, while she took the inside. Wherever he was, he probably wanted to be left alone, I concluded.

"Jaga-Nai," I called. Some of the other boys had finished eating and were playing Kabaddi. They looked up from their game just for a second. "Where are you?" I asked. I laughed. Maybe he was taking a shit. I went into the outhouse, and the door was closed. "Jaga-Nai, are you in there?" I didn't hear an answer. I knocked, and then pushed the door open. Inside was Golicchio. He looked up, but didn't say anything. I stepped back and closed the door. Then I heard a scream from inside the House. My face grew hot; I remembered the day Puni had died.

"Boys, stay outside, do not come inside, you understand!" Mother Jamuna yelled at us. I saw Headmistress Veli – she looked tiny all of a sudden – behind her. She motioned with her hand as if she wanted me to come inside. I obeyed.

"Jagadesh, I found him," she said.

"Where is he?"

Mother Jamuna grabbed my ear. She dragged me to her room. "Do you want to see what happens to little boys who are involved with Veli? Do you?" Mother Jamuna shouted, and I wanted to cover my ears, but she had such a tight hold on my left one. She pushed me into her room. I looked up at the beams on her ceiling, the same beams that she used to hold her oversized bras and undergarments. Now they held Jaga-Nai's dangling body. It twisted back and forth, his head tilted in an unnatural way. He held a letter in his hand.

"What is that?" I asked.

"It's a letter from his mother," Mother Jamuna said. I could smell

Headmistress Veli behind me. She sobbed.

"You did this," Mother Jamuna said. "Just like you did to Aruna's father." No one answered. We all knew whose fault it was. I ran into the room, grabbed his legs and held them. In the end, I had become just like him. Now that he was dead, a part of me had died too. I no longer had an ally – someone who was a victim of the House like me.

"Jaga-Nai," I said. He didn't say a word. Mother Jamuna tried to pull me off of his body, but I didn't want to let go. I held on until someone came and removed his body. When they cut him down, the letter he was holding fell to the ground. I picked it up and put it in my pocket.

News of Jaga-Nai's death didn't create much of a stir in the House in the same way Puni's did. Most of the boys were happy, but were too ashamed to show it. Peepa and Golicchio seemed smug. Even though I knew it burned Golicchio to not know what happened, he was stubborn. He wouldn't ask me.

When I got to the outhouse, there was still enough light to read. I opened his letter.

Dear Jagadesh, I am coming. I need you and love you. Be patient and don't be scared.

So Headmistress Veli had kept his hope alive to the very end.

A few days after his death, his mother did return for him. She came in an auto the way he had said she would. She was old, with white hair, and she walked with a slight limp. In her hand, she carried a plate of burfi. After Mother Jamuna told her that her son was dead, she flung herself onto the steps of the House. At the sight, many of the smaller boys started to cry. Through her tears and choppy sentences, I understood that it had never been her idea to leave him. That it was his father's idea. And that she would have come sooner if she could have. That she wasn't a bad mother. Although I wasn't entirely sure, I believed that Headmistress Veli hadn't known his mother was really alive. She had kept him in bondage the only way she knew how – by creating the hope that someday his mother would return to the House. In the end, Headmistress Veli had invented a fantasy world that had turned real, with deadly consequences. She had rivaled Jaga-Nai's psychological control, and in that way, both had been well-suited for each other.

When the woman finally stopped her crying, she left the way she had come – quickly and without warning. Only minutes after she was certain that the woman would not return, Mother Jamuna turned to come back inside, and I saw a look of relief on her face. I knew she would leave Jaga-Nai's name on the list. She needed his share of rations.

"THE WHOLE TIME you were lying to Jaga-Nai about his parents. You killed him, and he could've gone home, and been happy," I said. Headmistress Veli was smoking. I'd never seen her smoke, but I suspected it was more than just tobacco. Her eyes looked glassy, like the eyes of her infamous teddy bear collection. She had the lamp in her room switched on even though the sunlight coming through the window was bright enough. She squinted.

"He would never have been happy without me."

"Does this mean that my parents are alive too?"

"If you think I lied to Jaga-Nai, then why do you think your parents are alive? Please come here. Let's kiss. I am tired of talking." She tried to grab me, but she was so lethargic, that she flopped around like a fat fish. She could barely reach down to the floor to touch me. I inched away.

"I don't know what to believe. You have completely altered my perception of reality. You are a bad version of Golicchio." She kept trying to grope, but eventually gave up out of tiredness.

"Shut up, already. I don't have to tell you anything. The fact is that he is gone, and you are all I have left now."

"Farouk?"

"His rash is permanent."

"Aruna?"

Headmistress Veli shook her head.

"I am special."

"You are," Headmistress Veli said. She didn't detect my sarcasm. "You are so special. You are not like the others. You are sensitive, thinking." She was buttering me up.

"I am not going to do anything with you right now. Please." I stood up.

"I will tell you more about your family if you do," she pleaded.

"How do I know that you are telling me the truth?"

"You will know. You can look at me and know." She smiled, and for once seemed sincere.

"Okay." I did what she asked. Now I was the one who felt like the slimy fish, winded and exhausted. I lay down on her bed while she sat at her desk, continuing to smoke.

"Now, what do you want to know?"

"Did Smita really come to visit me here?"

"I don't know."

"You said she did. You showed me the figurine of hers."

"I got that at the temple."

"Did she visit here?"

"She may have. Many girls have come and gone. Some looking for shelter, others related to you all. How can I remember?"

I stared at the back of her neck. The smoke was rising around the sides of her engorged frame. She looked like she was on fire. I wanted to see that for real.

"Are they alive?"

"I don't know," she said again.

"You promised me answers."

"I did. I didn't tell you when I'd give them to you." She laughed and sucked in some air.

"Fuck you," I said.

"Don't talk back to me."

I unzipped my shorts. I had an unbearable desire to masturbate, right there, in front of her. I had never touched myself before; I had never allowed myself that luxury. I was worried that if I did, it would lead to other things that I wouldn't be able to control. Now, I wanted to see what would happen, and I felt incredibly turned on by the power I felt. I watched her the entire time, and as shaken as she looked, she pretended she was also aroused.

"You are getting so big," she said.

"Right," I said. I zipped up my shorts.

"Perhaps I do need another," she said.

I grabbed her hair and pulled hard.

"No!" She stopped talking. I put my entire fist in her mouth and pushed down as hard as I could. She gagged. Then as big as she was, I pushed her to the ground and raped her with her pen, feeling that I owed Jaga-Nai that much. After I was done, I spit on her and told her I was done with her for good.

I walked out of her room.

Chapter Sixty-Seven

No one, not even my doctors, knows that I have raped a woman. It is not me. It was never me. But I know no one would understand.

I think about it everyday though. The look on her face, the way I felt inside. Sometimes, when I try to reconcile that person with who I am now, I cannot. The two pieces are so fragmented; it is like trying to put together a jigsaw puzzle where the shapes are malformed.

Chapter Sixty-Eight

I WAS CONFLICTED about what I had done. On the one hand, I was happy that I had finally vindicated myself and given Veli what she deserved. On the other, I felt as though she didn't deserve what I had done to her. In a way, she had saved me. She had given me something to hate, and that was as good as hope.

In the end, none of it mattered. The anger was changing my personality, making me less empathic and more selfish. I no longer cared about anyone else in the House. I trusted no one and wanted to talk to no one. The anger made everyone else invisible.

Golicchio seemed amused by my subtle transformation. It's as if he knew that I would end up this way, like a mini Jaga-Nai. All those times I hated Jaga-Nai for who he was made me sick. If I had known then what I knew now, maybe we all could have been a little bit more sympathetic. Maybe he wouldn't have perished.

"Golicchio," I called. Unfortunately, both of us had been assigned to wipe down the bars on the windows. Mother Jamuna forced us to stay together because she assumed we were less likely to snoop if one was with the other. She didn't know that we weren't friends anymore.

"Golicchio?" I asked. He pretended like he couldn't hear me.

"Golicchio? Peepa told me a secret. Do you want to hear?" He turned his head in the direction of my voice, but he didn't say anything.

"He told me that he does not want to run away with you." I wasn't sure if that was true, but I wanted to see if I could provoke a response out of him anyway. He remained silent. "Golicchio, don't you care?" I saw him hurry and clean the bars. After he finished, he sat in the corner with his eyes down, probably hoping that I would finish quickly. I completed my task as slowly as I could.

After we were both done, and we had deposited our dirty rags outside for later cleaning, Peepa came and tried to talk to Golicchio. He put his arm around Golicchio, but he shrugged it off.

"What?" Peepa asked. Golicchio didn't respond and left to use the outhouse. I remembered how back when Golicchio and I were friends, how easily I could hurt his feelings. He needed such reassurance, and now Peepa was the one who had to provide it. I smiled with fondness. Peepa turned to look at me.

"What?" I didn't speak. He bared his teeth and hissed. I smiled, and he punched me. As I fell down, I could feel the blood running down my face. The warmth was reassuring. I wanted to beg him to stop, the way a faint memory tugs at the brain. But that was the old me. The new me didn't care all that much.

"You are filth, like I always said." He kicked me in the nose, and I heard a crunch – the sound of bone breaking.

"What is going on here?" Mother Kalpana was holding a bucket of bones ready to deposit them into the dogs' eating bowls. I noticed that the bucket said "Jagadesh," which was fitting.

Unfortunately, I was immobile, and all I could do was look up her skirt, which I loathed to do. Peepa just stared at her. He hated her so badly that he couldn't even answer her. She grabbed him by the ear, and he pushed her away.

"Jamuna, Veli," she screamed. It took three Mothers to subdue him. They tied his hands with rope and gagged his mouth with the meaty bones. Mother Jamuna slapped him on the face, and they dragged him to the Closet.

"You are going to be in there until we forget about you!" Mother Jamuna shouted. Mother Kalpana went to make a poultice that would stop the burning on my nose. I feared it was broken.

"Here you are," Mother Kalpana said. She put a wet cloth on my nose, and it stung. The pain was searing, but I didn't want to cry. I was done with crying. "Your nose looks broken."

"Can I see?" I asked her.

She brought me a mirror. I looked deformed. My nose bent to one direction.

"It looks like it will set that way. Unless you want to go to the hospital. I could ask Veli—"

"No," I said, pushing her away. "I want to leave it like this."

"Why? You look hideous," she said.

"I know." I smiled.

Mother Kalpana shuddered and went back to her room.

I RARELY SAW Veli anymore, and if I happened to catch a glimpse of her, she would disappear into her room. I once tried the door, and it was locked. I knew she was drinking heavily though. The bottles of liquor piled outside of her door, and as often as the Mothers tried to clean it up, we still saw the mounds. Some of the boys stole the bottles because she was a sloppy drinker and left drivels at the bottom. Getting caught with a bottle meant two weeks in the Closet, so most stopped trying.

Three weeks had gone by, and Peepa was still in the Closet. The Mothers kept their promise; there were days I had even forgotten about him. I wondered how much longer they would keep him in there, and once let out, would he continue his attacks against me, or would he retreat inward? The questions were there, but no answers.

Golicchio looked happy most of the time. The look didn't become him. He smiled randomly or laughed every so often at nothing in particular. Sometimes I'd catch his mouth moving or his eyes darting around the room, searching for something. He never told his stories anymore. Like he had once said, his stories were only captivating if an audience was there to listen. No one cared for Golicchio or believed his stories anymore.

"Yrimal," Golicchio said. I hadn't heard his voice in such a long time. I had forgotten how melodic it was.

"What do you want?" I moved toward him and clenched my fists.

"When do you think Peepa will be let out, eh?" he asked.

"Are you mocking me?" I grabbed him by the shoulders, but when I looked into his eyes, I saw that amused look again. It unnerved me.

"What is so fucking funny?"

"Fuck fuck fuck," he said. I had never heard him cuss before. He jumped up and down and laughed.

"What is your problem?"

"Nothing. Nothing at all. Just thought I would say ey. Now I must go. You see, my friends are coming, and they are bringing a big meal. I need to get ready." I saw him turn back and smile. "I forgive you," he said. He gave me the thumbs up.

I ran to the outhouse and vomited. Then I cried for a long time, even though I hated every minute of it.

While Peepa was locked in the Closet, I was not kind to Golicchio. Sometimes I felt remorse, but most of the time I felt liberated. I lost track of the number of days.

"Tell me a story, Golicchio," I asked him. We were eating together, and it seemed like old times, but it wasn't.

"What story?" Golicchio asked. "I am empty of stories."

"What about the one with the sisterfucker who gets pushed over?" I laughed and shoved him. He dragged his leaf, and rice bits scattered all over his shirt. He laughed too.

"That was fun – like a ride. Can you do it again?"

"Yes," I said. I played along. I kept pushing him down, and he kept getting back up. Finally one of the boys with a conscience asked me to stop.

"If I don't, what will you do?" I asked him. I continued to push Golicchio down until he stopped getting up.

"Are you going to get up?"

He didn't say anything, but his eyes were open.

"What's wrong? Did I hurt you?" For a second I felt panic, but then he smiled. I balled my fists.

"You are ugly," he said. "Down here, things are much clearer. I don't know why I never saw things the way they were. I always saw things as I thought they should be."

"Get up, already. I'm getting bored."

"I've been bored and have already exited." He flailed his arms. "You can do what you want with my body. That's not what I care about," he said.

"Tell that to Veli."

He continued to lie there. I wanted to lift him and beat him down, but I decided to leave before I did something even Jaga-Nai wouldn't have done.

"Where are you going?" he asked. "Don't leave me," he pleaded. I rolled my eyes at him.

THE DAY THEY discovered Aruna missing was the day they realized that Peepa was still locked in the Closet. Bad events always seemed to happen in twos, and Mother Jamuna was no fool. I believed she knew even before she opened the door that Peepa would not be inside. He had run away, with Aruna I hoped. After I had discovered that Veli was indeed her mother, I felt sorry for her. She was an orphan just like us, with a mother who could never love her. Her father may have, but he was dead. He had died also waiting for a world that Veli had promised him.

"Where did he go? Did he leave? He LEFT me?" Golicchio shrieked. I tried to gently tell him what I knew, for I felt that I owed him at least that much kindness, but he did not take the information well. I told him during meal time, when most of us were at the peak of serenity. After the news saturated his brain, Golicchio stood up, and his entire body shook. He had fully lived up to his namesake – his arms and legs dangled like the limbs of a string puppet and his mouth twitched as if saying words, but the wrong words.

Mother Jamuna seemed confused, and she didn't respond to Golicchio's screams. Instead, she closed herself in her office, as she had taken to doing lately. I decided to leave and be alone with my thoughts as well; I felt I had done what any "friend" would have given the situation. As I was about to walk away, Golicchio grabbed my arm.

"Don't leave. Who do I have left now? Peepa is gone… who is left? Who?" He kept saying "who" over and over and over again. He sounded like a crazy owl. I yelled at him to stop, but he wouldn't.

When the sun set and the Mothers were corralling us to bed, Golicchio was still in the cafeteria, saying "who, who, who" again and again. The Mothers tried to gag him into silence, but they couldn't, and when his mouth went blue and his eyes were red from tears, he stopped, but he continued mouthing it, over and over and over, and I could see in the moonlight in our room at night that his little fists were clenched so tightly that his palms bled.

I DIDN'T HEAR a word from Golicchio after that. He stayed quiet. He had become a tragic figure, and even I was sad for him. His friend, Peepa, was gone now, and he had no one. His mind had left him as well. He was truly alone.

As was I. Even though I was respected, the boys avoided me. I was bigger, and I didn't care what my fate was. In that way, I grew fearless.

Most of these kids were afraid of me now – my nose mostly – and I heard rumors circulating that my mother was human and my father a monster. Even Veli, who avoided looking at my face, was scared of me too. I noticed that she had taken a new lover – a small, bird-like boy I called Vaanampaadi because he always looked to the heavens.

During our regular afternoon play, I rounded up the boys for a game of Kabaddi. I was captain, and I chose some of the bigger boys to be on my team. Golicchio was chosen for the opposite team – even though he didn't want to play, the others forced him to because we were short on players.

Before we began, I had a vision. When I looked up, I thought I saw a dog in the sky. It had long yellow teeth and springy hair. I remembered that day, years ago, when I had tagged Jaga-Nai and forced him to carry my feces. Golicchio and I had talked about Jaga-Nai returning as a ghost dog then. We said that the role of captain would not be lost on him even after death. He would return to play, and would always return to play.

"What are you looking at?" one of the boys on my team asked. I looked at Golicchio.

"Jaga-Nai," I said.

"Who?" None of the newer boys knew who he was, but some of the older ones remembered. I saw Golicchio nod at me.

Chapter Sixty-Nine

I AM AFRAID.

Chapter Seventy

IT HAD BEEN a brutal few days; several of the boys had been sent to the Closet for various offenses, such as itching one's self in public or not washing behind the ears. I wondered how many of them they could fit into that tiny space, and the Mothers seemed to want to find out.

Around the time the Mothers should have been serving us lunch, I saw Mother Kalpana leave the House with a suitcase. Mother Jamuna followed her to the door and looked worried – more so than usual, and Veli had been with Vaanampaadi all day.

"Do you know what's happening?" I asked Karthik. He nodded no and backed away. I knocked on Veli's door. I would've gone in, but it was locked. She had taken to locking her door lately.

Vaanampaadi answered in just his shorts. He had the tiniest nipples I'd ever seen. They looked like little brown lentils.

"What does he want? Ask him, and tell him I'm busy," I heard Veli say.

"What is happening? Where are all of the Mothers going?" I knew she'd tell me the truth. She came to the door, a mango piece in her mouth.

"Why should I tell you?" She sucked the juice out of the mango. Vaanampaadi took a chance and slipped away. "Come back!" Veli screamed. I pushed her back inside, shut the door, and locked it.

"Tell me," I said.

"Why? Or you'll molest me again? What if I liked it?" She winked, but I could tell that she was lying. Her hands were shaking, and the juice from the fruit was dripping down the front of her blouse. She didn't bother to wipe herself. I just stared at her.

"Will you leave then?" I nodded. "The government is sending officials to inspect this orphanage. They are coming today, so most of the mothers are leaving. They don't want to get caught. The books – they're doctored. There are only a handful of you now, but we're collecting for twenty or thirty kids. I don't know. Jamuna is the one with the evidence. She's shitting her pants, if you ask me. I don't care. I've done nothing wrong, let them come."

"What will happen?"

"What do you think? They will shut down the House, and you all will be sent elsewhere. I will be sent to work with boys at another home – preferably a younger boys' home."

I left her room and ran to Mother Jamuna's. Her entire office had been cleaned out; she was nowhere to be found. She'd even taken her dogs with her.

"They're coming, they're coming!" someone screamed. A few minutes later, several young men in tan-colored suits entered the House. They were followed by a couple of old nurses – not unlike the old women medics we were used to. They gathered us into a group, counted us, took our names, and examined our bodies. The ones who were healthy were thrown into the back of a van and driven away like goats. I looked out the window and saw the nurses take Farouk in a separate van. His rash had spread, and he now had it all over his face and hands. I wondered if they would take him to the hospital.

Before I knew what was happening, the House was fading. It was dying in the way my family had – instantly, without a chance to mourn. I knew for sure that if my parents or Smita were alive, they'd have no chance of finding me now.

I was placed into another foster home, kilometers away from the House. This home was different – there were male as well as female caretakers. The men were grandfatherly and the women were young and thin. We were given uniforms and forced to take baths every day. Classes were much stricter, but the food was better. We were not divided by caste, but seated in alphabetical order by our names. I was destined to always remain in the back.

"What's your name?" a rather large, thuggish boy asked me.

"Siddhartha," I said.

"That's a strong name for an ugly boy, eh?" he said and laughed. I hadn't lost my breath in a long time, but I began to feel it leave me now.

"What a pansy," I heard someone say. I heard another say, "Perhaps he is going to visit the heavens and will tell us what it is like!" He sounded like Golicchio, but I knew it wasn't. He had been taken in the other van – the one for the boys who were unhealthy.

I closed my eyes, and I knew when I opened them, this place would be like the House all over again. I would be given another chance to do things better this time. I would start at the bottom – that was certain – but maybe there was a reason for it. If there was a pretty girl with long black hair here, maybe she wouldn't call me evil. Maybe I wouldn't abuse the only boy that had ever loved me, and I wouldn't let anyone die.

I hoped things would be different, but sometimes we had a difficult time escaping the fate that was meant for us.

Chapter Seventy-One

I RECOGNIZE THE puppet-like movements, the sketchy dance of his arms.

"Golicchio?"

He looks at me, dazed. It's as if he's been walking for miles, without water and without a belief in God.

I move closer to him. "Golicchio?" I ask again.

"You are home now," he says.

"Yes," I say, weeping. "I am."

Acknowledgments

This book would not be possible without the compassion of so many people.

Firstly, I'd like to thank Stephen F. Austin State University Press, in particular Kimberly Verhines and Laura McKinney. Without their belief in this manuscript and their hard work and dedication, *After the Tsunami* would not be here.

I'd also like to thank Mel Freilicher, who had faith in my talent from the very beginning and encouraged me to commit to writing. Also many thanks to Diane Smith, whose guidance and mentorship have helped me and this novel immensely.

My deepest gratitude goes to Hugh Fox, Indira Chandrasekhar, Sita Bhaskar, and Sonal Aggarwal for their kind words.

Special recognition goes to two very dear friends, Doreen and Mandi. Their thoughtful criticism was crucial to the completion of the book.

I would also like to thank my family and close friends, who have been generous with their time in helping me find my voice: Vanni and Kathiravan, my sister and brother, Carmen, my most loyal and ardent supporter, as well as Jennifer, Merimee, Anna, Cindy, Janet, and Sonal P.

I'd like to thank my parents, Pushpam and Chockalingam, whose rich culture and work ethic shaped me, and Jean and George, my in-laws who amaze me with their overwhelming care and support.

The novel is primarily dedicated to Nirmala and Vimala, my sisters, whose childhood will forever be an inspiration to me. I thank them for trusting me with their stories.

And last, but certainly not least, I am indebted to Sathya, my little boy whose wonderment at life and the world of books is my muse, and Alex, my wonderful husband.

Never once did Alex doubt my ability to see this manuscript to the end, and eventually, to publication. Thank you, Alex. I love you. You are an amazing and beautiful man.

ANNAM MANTHIRAM is the author of the novel *After the Tsunami* (Stephen F. Austin State University Press, 2011) and a short story collection (*Dysfunction: Stories*), which was a Finalist in the 2010 Elixir Press Fiction Award and received Honorable Mention in Leapfrog Press' 2010 Fiction Contest.

Annam's prize winning work has been published in over twenty literary journals, and she serves as Associate Editor for *Grey Sparrow Journal*, the recipient of the 2011 Council of Editors of Learned Journals' (CELJ) Best New Journal Award. A graduate of the M.A. Writing program at the University of Southern California, Annam resides in New Mexico with her husband, Alex, and son, Sathya.

You can visit her online at AnnamManthiram.com.

Annam Manthiram
P.O. Box 44051
Rio Rancho, New Mexico 87174
www.annammanthiram.com
annam@annammanthiram.com

3081003

CPSIA information can be obtained at www.ICGtesting.com
Printed in the USA
LVOW100111031011

248750LV00005B/1/P

9 781936 205431